HELSINKI HOMICIDE:

VENGEANCE

JARKKO SIPILA

Translated by
Peter Ylitalo Leppa

Ice Cold Crime LLC

Originally published in Finnish as *Prikaatin kosto* by Gummerus, Helsinki, Finland. 2009.

Translated by Peter Ylitalo Leppa

Published by
Ice Cold Crime LLC
5780 Providence Curve
Independence, MN 55359

Printed in the United States of America

Cover by Ella Tontti

Ice Cold Crime LLC gratefully acknowledges the financial assistance of:

FINNISH LITERATURE EXCHANGE

Library of Congress Control Number: 2010920755

ISBN-13: 978-0-9824449-1-7
ISBN-10: 0-9824449-1-5

Also by Jarkko Sipila

In English:

Helsinki Homicide: Against the Wall (Ice Cold
   Crime, 2009)

In Finnish:

Koukku (Book Studio, 1996)
Kulmapubin koktaili (Book Studio, 1998)
Kosketuslaukaus (Book Studio, 2001)
Tappokäsky (Book Studio, 2002)
Karu keikka (Book Studio, 2003)
Todennäköisin syin (Gummerus, 2004)
Likainen kaupunki (Gummerus, 2005)
Mitään salaamatta (Gummerus, 2006)
Kylmä jälki (Gummerus, 2007)
Seinää vasten (Gummerus, 2008)
Prikaatin kosto (Gummerus, 2009)

In German:

Die weiße Nacht des Todes (Rohowolt Verlag, 2007)
Im Dämmer des Zweifels (Rohowolt Verlag, 2007)

HELSINKI HOMICIDE: VENGEANCE

CAST OF CHARACTERS

Kari Takamäki...................Detective Lieutenant, Helsinki PD Violent Crimes Unit

Suhonen...................Undercover Detective, VCU

Anna Joutsamo...........................VCU Sergeant

Eero Salmela.........Suhonen's old friend and ex-con

Ear-Nurminen...............Salmela's drinking buddy

"Macho" Mertala............Salmela's drinking buddy

Juha Saarnikangas....Ex-junkie, Suhonen's informant

Tapani Larsson........................VP of the Skulls

Niko Andersson........Skull member, "The Elephant"

Osku........................Skull prospect, "The Goat"

Roge........................Skull prospect, "The Bull"

Steiner.....................................Skull veteran

Sami Aronen...................Skulls' weapons expert

Mike Gonzales.......aka Mika Konttinen, black market operator

Toukola...............Narcotics Detective, Helsinki PD

Jaakko Nykänen.........Head of Intelligence, National Bureau of Investigation

Aalto.....................................NBI Lieutenant

Lind..NBI Agent

Honkala......................................NBI Captain

Marju Mägi.................................Estonian mule

Sergei Zubrov...................Estonian-Russian gangster

Sanna Römpötti..........................Crime reporter

TUESDAY, OCTOBER 20

CHAPTER 1
TUESDAY, 2:53 P.M.
HELSINKI AVENUE, HELSINKI

Suhonen glanced in the passenger side rear-view mirror of his unmarked Peugeot before making a quick shoulder check. Sitting in the left-turn lane near the Helsinki Botanical Gardens, the undercover detective had been waiting to turn toward police headquarters in Pasila, but had abruptly decided to continue along Helsinki Avenue.

The light for ongoing traffic was green and Suhonen scanned the tight line of cars behind him, waiting for a suitable slot. A red Volvo zoomed past and Suhonen judged the space behind it to be enough. He punched the gas and cut in front of a black Mercedes taxi. The gleaming sedan honked and Suhonen gave a friendly wave.

He passed Töölö Bay on the right, its waters suffused with cool autumn sunlight. Behind the bay, about a mile off, the granite façade and copper apron of the Helsinki Central Railway Station stood out against downtown's low-lying skyline. September had been unusually warm for Helsinki, and scores of people had been about with shorts and mini-skirts on. Only recently had the frosty nights finished off the vivid display of fiery leaves.

The impetus for the sudden lane change was a baby-blue two-seater sports car, now heading under the railroad bridge a couple hundred yards up the road. Suhonen had noticed the Beamer back by the Opera House, but had initially ignored it. At the intersection, he had changed his mind.

About half a dozen cars stood between Suhonen's gray Peugeot 205 and the BMW Z3 Roadster. Now there was one more, as the ruffled cabbie pulled ahead on the right and cut him off to make a statement. Good—more cover, Suhonen thought, though the driver of the Beamer probably hadn't even noticed him.

A red and white commuter train rumbled across the bridge over the road.

The BMW climbed the hill in the center lane. Suhonen guessed the car would hang left onto Sture Street at the Y-intersection up ahead. Only the right lane continued along Helsinki Avenue.

Suhonen dug his phone out of his worn and abraded leather jacket. His jeans were faded. A holster containing a small Glock 26 was strapped to his left side. His black hair was gathered into a ponytail and his face was shadowed with stubble, making him look older than his forty-odd years.

He called dispatch at Pasila and checked the registration for the BMW. The car had not been reported as stolen and a local leasing firm was listed as the owner.

No surprise, he thought. Not that he had assumed the car was hot—the driver, on the other hand, was another issue.

The Beamer continued along Sture Street past the Kulttuuritalo Concert Hall. The Peugeot's radio was playing classic Finnish rock—Hassisen Kone's '80s hit "Walking Fever." Suhonen's mind wandered back to his teenage years when he had gone with his best friend Salmela to see them play at the Concert Hall. Was that 1980? Maybe. A long time ago, anyway. For a couple of small town guys, it had been a lot of fun. Maybe a little too much.

He should call Salmela to see how he was getting along, Suhonen thought. Judging by the latest news, probably not so well.

The Beamer stopped at the lights at the intersection of Sture Street and Aleksis Kivi. A streetcar clattered by. Only the Mercedes taxi separated the two cars now, but its rear window was tinted enough that the target couldn't possibly make out Suhonen. He cozied right up to the back bumper of the taxi so he couldn't be seen in the side mirrors either, though the cabby probably took it as an affront.

Suhonen wondered where Mike Gonzales was headed in the Beamer. A few miles up, Sture Street led to the Lahti Highway.

A hunch had spurred Suhonen to trail this Gonzales, who had changed his legal name from Mika Konttinen, but Suhonen didn't plan to shadow him for long. All he wanted was to link Gonzales to some residence, office or other address.

Suhonen neared the bridge over Teollisuus Street, and the aroma of coffee poured out of the vents. As the coffee mill receded into the distance, Sture Street rose steeply to a bridge. The bridge connected the stone buildings of Kallio to the Vallila district. Up until the 1970s, Vallila had been a mixture of industrial buildings and old wooden dwellings. Most of the factories were either converted into lofts or demolished and replaced by apartment and office buildings. Its wooden houses, though, had been spared, and formed an idyllic enclave surrounded by modern construction.

The taxi changed lanes, leaving Suhonen directly behind the Beamer. He lagged back a little.

This Konttinen-Gonzales was an interesting character. The man owned a small temp agency. On a few occasions, the Financial Crimes Division had suspected him of money laundering and supplying illegal aliens for construction jobs. Though the firm's books were turned inside out, Gonzales hadn't been indicted.

The baby-blue Beamer stopped at the lights on Mäkelä Avenue and its left-hand blinker went on. Suhonen thought for a second before deciding to stay on his tail. So far, they had stuck to major thoroughfares, where the traffic was heavy in the afternoon rush. On smaller roads, he would have never dared stay this close, but perhaps Gonzales wouldn't suspect the cops of following him in such an archaic way.

As an undercover officer in the Helsinki Violent Crimes Unit, Suhonen wasn't interested in petty financial crimes. A couple months prior, this Gonzales had attended the Skulls' annual party. The Skulls were an outlaw biker gang, which had held its sixth annual bash in the summer, and this time the police had put it under photo surveillance. All fifty-plus attendees had been secretly photographed.

The big league hockey players and the B-list actors had been easy to pick out, but identifying the others had taken a lot of work. In the end, the cops had a comprehensive picture of the Skulls' inner circle.

Gonzales was somewhat of a familiar character on the Helsinki party circuit, but that wouldn't have earned him an invite from the Skulls.

The lights changed and the Beamer turned left onto Mäkelä Avenue. It shot ahead, but Suhonen was in no hurry. The next light would be red anyway.

He figured he'd follow the car a few more miles at most, then swing back toward Pasila headquarters. Maybe Gonzales wasn't up to anything—actually that was the most likely possibility.

The BMW continued northward along Mäkelä Avenue past an indoor swimming pool and the renowned Mäkelänrinne Sports High School, which had graduated many top Finnish athletes.

Suhonen had fallen back a hundred yards or so, and three cars had filled in the space. The street curved gently to the right and the Beamer's brake lights came on. Gonzales was set to turn left into the parking lot of the Velodrome cycling stadium, unless he was whipping a U-turn.

During his years in Narcotics, Suhonen had seen dealers try all kinds of surprise loops to shake off a tail. A proper surveillance operation had demanded at least ten officers, all of whom patrolled the area in zigzag patterns. Nowadays, technology made the job considerably easier. The police had only to fix a GPS tracking device to the target vehicle, or know the cell number of one of the car's occupants to know its exact location.

The BMW roadster waited at the tree-lined median for a break in the oncoming traffic. Suhonen continued onward and shifted into the right-turn lane at the intersection about a hundred yards up. There was no sign, but Suhonen knew the street led to the rear parking lot of the Katilöopisto Hospital. He swung right, passed a line of parked cars for about fifty yards, and squeezed the Peugeot into the first available spot. Over his shoulder, he saw the Beamer continuing into the parking lot of the cycling stadium.

The white Velodrome had been built in the late thirties for Helsinki's 1940 Olympics, which were cancelled due to World War II. The stadium eventually fulfilled its purpose when Helsinki hosted the games in '52. The Velodrome had fallen into considerable disrepair, but a million-dollar remodel at the end of the '90s had returned the modernist design to a relatively functional condition.

Suhonen got out of his Peugeot, grabbed a backpack out of the trunk and hurried back to the intersection. The traffic was dense enough that he didn't dare jaywalk, so he waited for the light. The Velodrome parking lot was visible from the intersection, but the Beamer was no longer in sight. The parking lot had no other outlets.

A woman dressed in a red coat and a black knit hat was pushing a baby carriage toward the intersection. She shot a wary glance at the stubbly, street-worn Suhonen in his biker jacket. He smiled, but the woman quickly looked away.

He crossed Mäkelä Avenue and approached the rear of the stadium. From this vantage point, the trees and the curvature of the cycling track obscured the parking lot. That was both good and bad. Maybe more good, since he'd be able to use it for cover to get closer.

Suhonen skirted the edge of the stadium past three tall lindens toward the parking lot. The rear wall of the cycling track formed a massive lean-to shelter. He considered circling around to the hill on the opposite side of the parking lot for a better view, but decided that this spot would suffice. After all, this was no official surveillance operation, just a hunch. He didn't have the slightest clue what might be amiss.

Still, he unzipped his backpack, flipped on his Nikon SLR and checked that the settings were correct. A 300mm zoom lens was attached to the camera body. He had performed rapid photography numerous times before. It produced better shots and attracted less attention than scrunching down behind a tree.

His gait had to be ordinary and carefree. A leather jacket wasn't the best garb—a parka and knit cap would have given a more relaxed impression. Suhonen was about twenty yards from the asphalt parking lot when he spotted Gonzales standing next to the Beamer on the other side of the parking lot.

The man's clothes recalled the 1980s TV series *Miami Vice*. Despite the cool weather, Gonzales wore a blue blazer and a white T-shirt. His black hair was combed to the side and it reached over the tops of his ears. Gonzales' features were nonetheless softer than those of the taller man standing next to him, whose brown leather jacket, buzzed haircut and gaunt cheeks signaled the toughness of the streets.

Gonzales had been alone in his car, so "buzz cut" must have come in his own ride. With dozens of cars in the parking lot, Suhonen couldn't determine which one belonged to him.

The men stood side by side, in full view, a good fifty yards away, speaking fervently to one another.

This was the moment. With his backpack hanging over his left shoulder, Suhonen held the camera in his right hand and raised it into position. He didn't stop walking, since his targets might have noticed the sudden change in movement. The camera's motor whined and the picture came into focus. Suhonen pressed the shutter button and the camera took a series of four photographs.

Within four seconds, the Nikon was stashed back in the bag. The targets hadn't noticed him and continued talking. Suhonen reached the edge of the parking lot and headed back toward Mäkelä Avenue, about thirty yards away. The lot was used by people working in the nearby office buildings of East-Pasila, so Suhonen's presence didn't attract attention.

Once Gonzales and his mysterious friend were well in the distance, Suhonen casually swung the backpack to his front and peeked into the bag to check the quality of the pictures. They were sharp—both men were recognizable. No need to clamber on the hill for more shots.

He smiled and decided to circle the high school and swimming pool before returning to the car. For a moment, he considered staying longer to observe the pair, but then decided against it. A more extensive surveillance operation would have demanded more units anyway, and there was no need.

Suhonen didn't know if the photos would be useful, but they couldn't hurt either. Gonzales was a player of some stature, and a meeting in the parking lot of the Velodrome was probably not connected to legitimate staffing negotiations. Suhonen had a vague notion that this "buzz cut" was Estonian, Russian or a mixture of the two. The man's tough presence gave that impression. His stern facial expression, too, hinted at more eastern origins.

That vague notion might come into focus if someone could identify the man from the photo.

* * *

It took a few seconds for the computer to upload the photos from the camera. Suhonen was sitting at his own workstation in the back corner of the VCU's shared office at Pasila Police Headquarters. Time had left this building behind as well. A massive remodel was in store.

He had taken off his leather jacket and draped it over the back of his chair, leaving only a black T-shirt. His pistol and holster were in the bottom drawer. Unlike in American TV shows, exposed weapons were not carried in the hallways of the Violent Crimes Unit. That would have called for a referral to a police psychologist for an excessive show of force.

Suhonen's computer sat on a small, otherwise empty desk. The other officers in the room had more space, but they had more paper to fill it, too.

Mikko Kulta, a tall man with a shock of blond hair, sat nearest the door with headphones in his ears, poring over an interrogation transcript. Sergeant Anna Joutsamo was talking on the phone, and Kirsi Kohonen's spot was empty. Suhonen seemed to recall that she was on vacation.

A teammate on vacation had no effect on Suhonen's workload. Of the four officers on Detective Lieutenant Kari Takamäki's team, Suhonen was the only one who didn't deal with the daily grind: domestic abuse, missing persons, cause-of-death investigations and other routine cases. He carried out his work on the streets of the city, collecting intelligence at the behest of others or on his own hunches. Captain Karila, the head of the VCU, had often suggested that Suhonen should be transferred to the surveillance group, which fell under Narcotics, but Takamäki, Suhonen's direct supervisor, was strongly opposed.

"They found him," said Sergeant Anna Joutsamo,

somewhat in disbelief. Joutsamo was in her thirties and wore blue jeans and a black wool cardigan. Her dark hair was swept into a loose ponytail.

"Who?" Suhonen asked. He didn't know what case she was on, but finding someone or something was usually a positive development in police investigations.

"Mauri Laukka."

"Should I know who that is?" Suhonen asked.

Kulta had interrupted his work and taken the headphones off. "Suhonen, I thought you knew it all."

Suhonen ignored the ribbing. "Who is he?"

"You haven't heard about this case yet, but last week we received an inquiry from Norway about an unidentified corpse. A month ago, the Oslo police found a dead man at a local beach. No papers, nothing. Supposedly about twenty years old and fairly clean. Nothing seemed to indicate homicide. Well, the fingerprints didn't match anyone in their database, so they were at a loss. Sharp as they are, a week later they realized that a rented Mitsubishi with Finnish plates was still sitting in the parking lot."

"Promising," Suhonen noted.

"Yes, it was," Joutsamo went on. "The case was being handled by Magnus, someone I know in Oslo, who called to ask if I could find out who rented the Mitsubishi. That's when this Mauri Laukka stepped into the picture."

"The guy who rented the car?"

"Correct. His age matched the body, and on top of that, he had been reported missing about a month ago. His father couldn't get a hold of him and contacted the police. So I chatted with the investigator at the Vantaa PD, who told me that

Laukka was a troubled kid suffering from depression. Booze and pills, et cetera, but nothing criminal, which is why he wasn't in our database."

"And…"

"And with the depression and all, I was absolutely convinced that the body was this Laukka. Anyway, I was only a middle-man between Oslo and Vantaa—between the two, they were taking care of the DNA and the other formalities. So I was chatting with a friend at the National Bureau of Investigation records department last Friday and I asked about him. Well, she just called me back to say that they've received a communiqué through the Foreign Ministry about this guy. Sometime between Friday night and Saturday morning, Mr. Laukka got into a drug-induced brawl in Nice, punched a cop in the face, and is sitting in a jail in Southern France."

"So the corpse in Oslo…"

"Is not him."

Suhonen snickered. "No way. Who is it, then?"

Joutsamo shrugged. "No clue, but yet another example of why you should *never assume*." The foursome had made a hobby of repeating their Lieutenant's favorite phrase.

"Laukka sounds like a good candidate for the police academy," Suhonen chuckled. "Hey, come take a look at this photo."

She walked over to Suhonen's desk and he stepped aside.

"You know these guys?"

Joutsamo sat down in his chair. He stood behind her and detected the sweet scent of her perfume, which conjured visions of spring.

"That one's been running with the Skulls. Thinks his dad is some Argentinean. Was it Gomez?"

"Gonzales. He's the darker one. What about buzz cut here?"

Joutsamo turned and looked up from the chair. "Should I know who he is?"

Kulta came up from behind to look over their shoulders.

"No. I don't know either," said Suhonen.

Kulta smirked. "That's twice already today."

Joutsamo ignored the comment. "Doesn't look like a local. Based on his features and clothing, I'd bet he's Estonian or Russian. Toomas might know."

"Not familiar to me either," Kulta said, though nobody had asked. "I'd also suggest you get in touch with Toomas."

"Alright, I'll do that."

Toomas Indres was an Estonian policeman who had been with the Helsinki VCU on an exchange program. He had returned to Tallinn six months ago.

Joutsamo stood up and Suhonen stepped back. Kulta returned to his desk.

"When was that photo taken?" Joutsamo asked.

"Half an hour ago in the Velodrome parking lot."

"Of course," Joutsamo smiled. By the way, did you hear about today's sentencing in the Skulls' extortion case?"

"Not yet. Do tell."

"Alanen got three years and two months and Lintula two years and ten months. Captain Karila himself came to congratulate us on a job well done."

Suhonen scratched his head at the captain's visit. "Oh really? I wonder which leadership program taught him to do that."

"He even brought coffee and cookies. There's probably some left in the conference room."

"That's okay," said Suhonen. "We worked hard on

that case—glad they were convicted."

Alanen and Lintula were Skull prospects who had extorted protection money from a north Helsinki pizzeria owner. Key evidence had been obtained by planting a hidden camera in the restaurant. Obtaining the terrified proprietor's consent for the camera had been the most difficult part of the case.

"Yep, they'll be off the streets for a while," Joutsamo remarked.

"True. But what doesn't kill you makes you stronger."

Joutsamo grinned. "I think I'll make myself stronger with a jog tonight."

Suhonen felt a pang of guilt. He, too, should take better care of himself, but jogging was not his thing. At least he managed to play hockey with some other cops a couple of times a week.

"You going alone?"

"Yeah. You live alone, you jog alone."

Both of them were single. Though they had had many relationships, most had broken down due to the demands of their work. Or it could be that both just preferred the single life. That way, they answered to nobody.

"Why don't you come along?"

"You asking me on a date?"

"No, a jog."

Suhonen paused. "Aaah, maybe not; I probably couldn't keep up."

Joutsamo shrugged. "You got that right."

WEDNESDAY,
OCTOBER 21

CHAPTER 2
WEDNESDAY, 11:20 A.M.
PUOTINHARJU SHOPPING CENTER, EAST HELSINKI

A white Fiat Ducato van sat in the parking lot of the Puotinharju Shopping Center. The van, which was caked with dirt and rust, was pointed toward downtown Helsinki. Outside the driver's side window were the streets of Itäkeskus, and on the passenger's side lay the crumbling mall.

Juha Saarnikangas tapped out the rhythm to "L.A. Woman" on the steering wheel. The old Ducato's radio was defunct, but he had an iPod and a couple of tiny speakers on the passenger seat. He gazed out the windows, looking for familiar faces, but saw none. Many passersby carried umbrellas. Saarnikangas hadn't followed the weather reports, but apparently showers were in the forecast. Though the windshield of the van was dirty, it was still dry.

"Drivin' down your freeways, midnight alleys roam..." sang Morrison. Saarnikangas didn't know that the mall he was parked next to was built in the same year that The Doors were founded. Then, Puotinharju had been Finland's largest shopping center, and the pride of a burgeoning East Helsinki.

Saarnikangas was wearing a green military coat. His dark, greasy hair reached his shoulders. The man's face was thin, his skin pale and pock-marked.

But having kicked a heroin addiction, he was in better shape now than he had been for years.

His gaze was fixed on a group of about a half-dozen black men, who were slowly climbing the stairs to the second floor of the mall, where a mosque was located.

He pulled out his cell phone and glanced at the time: 11:22. He'd give the guy three more minutes before leaving, and wouldn't take his calls anymore.

The man had promised Saarnikangas twenty euros just to listen to a proposal. Free money was enough of a reason, but it wasn't the only one. Was this guy in as bad of shape as word on the street would have it? The fact that he was willing to pay for a meeting wasn't a good sign.

A knock on the passenger side window startled Saarnikangas. He hadn't noticed the man approaching—he must have snuck up from the rear.

The Ducato didn't have power locks, but if it did, they would have been broken. Saarnikangas leaned over, lifted the passenger side lock, and snatched his music system off the seat. He shut off the music.

"Hey," said the forty-something man. His hair was short, his cheeks sunken. The lambswool collar of his brown leather jacket was dirty.

The rugged-faced Eero Salmela seemed initially like his former self, but then Saarnikangas looked in his eyes: blurry and full of fear.

"They let you out of the hospital?" said Saarnikangas, smiling with his mouth carefully closed. Heroin had ruined his teeth. He also wanted to be cautious. He knew that a year ago, while in prison, Salmela had taken an iron pipe to the head, and had done a long stretch in the medical ward before returning to his cellblock to serve out the final months of his sentence. A blow to the head can make a man unpredictable. Saarnikangas might be sharper, but Salmela was still the stronger man.

"Yeah. Back in the summer."

"Cool. You alright?" Saarnikangas said, more as a statement.

Salmela said nothing, just settled into the passenger seat and stared over Saarnikangas' shoulder at the mall.

"That place is so big, I'd get lost in it."

"Yeah, same here."

Salmela shot a cold look at Saarnikangas, but then fluttered his eyelids so long that it gave the impression of stupidity. "I lost a few brain cells back in prison, but don't mock me. You know how ex-cons deal with people who give them shit."

"I didn't say anything. Wasn't laughing," Saarnikangas apologized. No doubt Salmela had a knife on him.

"You know where I just was?"

"Nope."

"Playing bingo."

"Huh?"

"Fucking bingo."

Best be quiet, Saarnikangas thought, and said nothing.

Salmela calmed down. "The doc said it might help. The lady says 'B-6' and I match it on the sheet. I got thirty euros of bingo money from the welfare office. They call it therapy."

How come I don't get that kind of assistance, Saarnikangas wondered.

Salmela continued, "Kids' crossword puzzles supposedly help too, but they make my head hurt like hell."

Saarnikangas didn't know what to say, so he just turned and nodded. Kids' crosswords? He felt like laughing, but the threat of a knife kept his mouth shut.

A few years back, Salmela had run a stolen goods business and bought some hot cell phones and laptops from Saarnikangas. Salmela had paid a shitty price, but at least he had paid. Some buyers had just walked off with the stuff Saarnikangas brought, ignoring his pleas for money.

Salmela had been tough, but fair. A couple of years ago, Salmela's son had been killed in a turf battle between rival drug gangs. In his sorrow, the devastated father was driven to more serious crimes. Saarnikangas didn't quite know for what, but Salmela had spent a few years in the pen. There he had apparently mixed with the wrong crowd and had been found in a stairwell, beaten unconscious.

"So what happened in the slammer?"

Salmela sneered. "You know. Those…the stairs there are damn steep. Easy to trip. Don't remember much else."

"That so?"

"Yeah. That's what happened." Salmela averted his eyes.

Saarnikangas was quiet for a moment. "You had something you wanted to talk about?"

"Yeah. Listen…" Salmela began hesitantly. "I need some help with something I'm working on."

"What's that?" Saarnikangas asked, though he was already certain he'd say no. It was still good to know about any deals out there.

Salmela glanced about, though there was nobody else in the cab. "I got a little deal going on and I need some assistance."

Saarnikangas understood immediately. "How much you need?"

"Say, about three grand."

Saarnikangas didn't have that kind of money, but went on with the game. "What kind of deal?"

"You'd be able to help me then?" Salmela brightened.

"I asked what kind of deal. Didn't promise anything."

Salmela lowered his voice to a whisper. "Four pounds of speed from Tallinn. You get a piece of the action. Your three Gs will be six within the month."

Yeah, right, Saarnikangas thought. A drug smuggling operation run by a bingo whiz that can't figure out kids' crossword puzzles. Count me in for sure. "I'm not so sure," Saarnikangas mumbled.

"My partner has good contacts there. The job is a piece of cake, really. A-all I need is a little financing and it'll take care of itself."

Saarnikangas made eye contact with Salmela. "Eero. Why you doing this? I thought drugs weren't your thing."

Salmela was quiet for a moment. "They're not."

"Then why?"

"I owe some money. This is the only chance I have to w-wiggle out of it."

"Is that really it?"

"Yeah. That's it."

"Four pounds of dope costs ten grand wholesale. What about the rest of it? The other seven? You have them yet?"

Salmela smirked. "Almost."

"Who's your mule?"

"That's one thing I have to figure out. The dope costs ten grand wholesale in Tallinn, but twelve

21

shipped here. I can save two grand if I bring it myself."

"You got a buyer?"

"Yup."

"Who?" Saarnikangas demanded.

"I'll tell you when I get the three grand."

Saarnikangas shook his head. "Sorry, no loose cash right now."

"Huh?"

"None."

"Alright. No problem."

Disappointed, Salmela turned abruptly away. "I'll get the financing, you know. You'll miss out, but that's your loss."

Saarnikangas was sure he could live with the loss.

"Hey Eero. Maybe I can help with the other part."

"What other part?"

"Well, getting the dope across the gulf."

"H-how? You'd bring it yourself?"

"I've got some old drug convictions so I can't do it myself. Too risky."

Saarnikangas pulled his phone out of his jacket pocket and looked up a number in the directory. Next to the van's hand brake lay an old receipt, and Saarnikangas jotted a name and number on the back.

Salmela extended his hand, but Saarnikangas didn't offer the number.

"I'll give it to you for a hundred."

"What is it?"

"An Estonian girl's number. She's ferried a few shipments before. Charges maybe three, four-hundred euros for a four pound job."

Salmela stared at Saarnikangas' hand.

"Can't promise she'll do it, but she knows the drill."

Salmela fished a hundred euros out of his pocket and handed it over. "Okay."

Saarnikangas noticed some more bills in Salmela's hand. "And the twenty for the meeting, too."

The ex-con dealt out another twenty and Saarnikangas shoved the money into his jacket pocket.

"Anything else?" he asked.

"Nah," said Salmela. As he swung out of the van, he reminded Saarnikangas not to say anything about this job to anyone. Saarnikangas agreed.

He watched Salmela's departure with a heavy mind. The number he had sold was indeed for Tallinn, but that second-rate whore certainly wouldn't agree to be anybody's mule.

This would not end well. Narcotics and Customs ate these kinds of operations for breakfast, at least if Salmela could actually get his hands on the dope. Especially with rookies like Salmela, Estonian suppliers had a reputation for taking payment but delivering nothing. In any case, Salmela would probably be better off in prison.

CHAPTER 3
WEDNESDAY, 2:30 P.M.
TALLINN HARBOR, ESTONIA

The effect of the sea was usually amazing. If it was raining in Helsinki, a few hours on a southbound ferry brought passengers to sunny Tallinn, with temperatures 15 degrees warmer. Usually, that is, but not this time.

A hard rain beat against the windows of Terminal Four at the Tallinn harbor. Suhonen was squinting out the window to see if any taxis were waiting; he didn't want to step out into the torrent for no reason. Not one in sight.

A small group of travelers was waiting in the concourse, everyone with the same thought. The rain was driving sideways, rendering umbrellas useless, so they were lined up inside the terminal. In a hurry, the undercover officer decided to defy the elements. No big deal—his leather jacket could take a little sprinkling. A few of them snuffled at him as he stepped out. Apparently they thought the taxi line was inside, and Suhonen was jumping to the front. Several of the passengers still looked a bit pasty, as the gales had made for a rocky boat ride.

Suhonen stood alone in the rain and wind for about a minute before he spotted a white car pulling up to the curb. Any ride was fine with him; his destination guaranteed nobody would try to rip him off.

The driver didn't step out to open the door, not that Suhonen expected it. Not in Helsinki, Tallinn or anywhere else. The gesture would be friendly, of course, but also awkward. Worse was if a cabbie hustled over to open the door at one's destination.

His tanned leather jacket had gathered some rain and Suhonen shook it off before stepping into the white Nissan.

"Hi," chirped the smiling cabby, a cap perched on his head. The driver wasn't sure if his passenger was a local or a northern neighbor, so he dispensed with the small talk. Or maybe he had enough sense to know that this hard-nosed customer in a leather jacket wasn't looking for conversation, just a ride.

"Tööstuse 52," Suhonen snapped and the driver stepped on the gas.

The windshield wipers were going at full tilt. The sky was dark gray and the flags on the ships were fully unfurled, snapping in the wind.

* * *

Detective Lieutenant Kari Takamäki was sitting at his computer at Pasila Police Headquarters when Sergeant Joutsamo stepped into his office. Heavy raindrops battered at the windows.

"Well?" Takamäki said in a friendly tone, looking up from his monitor. He was wearing a white shirt and navy tie. A gray blazer hung behind the desk from a screw in a bookshelf that had been deliberately loosened. Forty-five-year-old Takamäki had short brown hair, sharp features and taut cheeks, highlighted by a muscular jaw. His piercing blue eyes straddled a handsome nose.

"That welder's suicide case is ready for your sign-off. The case is closed. I'll file the paperwork." Joutsamo offered Takamäki a stack of papers.

All deaths that occurred outside of hospitals or similar institutions became police investigations. The starting point was simple: the death was a homicide until proven otherwise. That's what the police had done here.

The lieutenant remembered the case. Twenty-four-year-old Pekka Kyllönen had been fired at the end of his workday, but had wanted to work late to finish a job. The boss had told him he wouldn't be paid overtime, but that hadn't bothered Kyllönen. In the morning, the young welder had been found hanging from a rope in the shop. Nothing indicated a homicide and a handwriting analysis proved the suicide note was written by Kyllönen.

"No home, no job, no woman, no life," read the note stuffed into the breast pocket of his overalls.

Not a master of literature, but he had known how to summarize. Joutsamo had combed through his background, albeit briefly. Kyllönen had dropped out of high school first, then vocational school to pursue professional hockey. But at seventeen years old, his promising career had ended with a knee injury, and he wound up in a series of dead-end jobs. He had lived with his alcoholic father, who disclosed that Kyllönen's girlfriend had dumped him a month earlier. The job loss was the final blow.

Takamäki took the papers and scribbled his signature on them. The cause of death had been established. From this point onward, Pekka Kyllönen was just another number in the dismal suicide statistics. Autumn brought plenty of stories like this one to Helsinki.

The case was closed. Takamäki felt no sorrow, but wondered why Kyllönen had wanted to finish the job he'd been working on. Maybe the guy just wanted to accomplish something.

Earlier in his career, suicides had bothered him more, and the lieutenant had tried to think of ways of preventing them. Now, however, they were just numbers to him. Annually, about a thousand people took their own lives in Helsinki. Society seemed to have no interest in determining why and journalists were unable to cover the stories since the files for suicides were sealed.

Suicide brought shame to family members, often because they hadn't done much—if anything at all— to prevent it. Secrecy helped cover up the shame.

Joutsamo took back the papers. "I'll file these."

Takamäki nodded. He could've said something, but there was no need. Every case that went through the Helsinki VCU was tragic. Clichés had no place among professionals. What was said to family members and the public was a different matter.

"Listen," Joutsamo began.

"What now?"

"Suhonen went to Tallinn."

"What about it?" Takamäki had signed off on the trip after seeing Suhonen's photo of Gonzales and "buzz cut". A day trip cost only twenty euros.

"Well…"

"Do you have a problem with it?"

"Right, well… Routine cases are piling up here and Suhonen is off chasing ghosts. Far as I'm concerned that's the surveillance group's job."

Takamäki looked sharply at the sergeant. "Really."

"I think we need another detective in lieu of Suhonen."

"We need about twenty more detectives for all of the VCU. But we'll get none. If I transferred him to the surveillance group, we wouldn't get anyone to replace him."

Joutsamo shifted her weight to the other foot. "There are just too many cases. We need help."

"Listen, Anna," Takamäki said. "It makes no sense to squander Suhonen on paperwork. He's much more useful when something bigger is brewing."

"Yes, I know that. But this so-called paperwork is burying us. We really need help."

"Well, we won't get any. Keep prioritizing. Focus on the major cases—same process. In other words: in, over and out on the stack. Forget craft, just nail the bad guys."

"Right, of course. Wouldn't have it any other way."

"Shitty job…" Takamäki began.

Joutsamo finished his sentence, "…but why did you go to the Police Academy?"

* * *

Suhonen was in the back seat of a taxi, watching out the rain-streaked window as Tallinn's Old Town hurtled past. Though Estonia's capital was a hot tourist destination in the summer, on a day like today, its charming buildings, restaurants and shops were devoid of tourist crowds. Only a few locals were about. After about ten minutes, the Nissan slowed to a stop in front of a white limestone building. The sign read: Estonian Central Police.

Suhonen paid and sprinted to the entrance to avoid

the rain. Somebody had been monitoring his arrival through a surveillance camera, as the lock was buzzed open immediately upon pressing the doorbell.

The hallway was cramped. Though the building was the former home of a local insurance company, it seemed to have been designed for the Estonian Central Police. At the beginning of the millennium, the ECP had still operated out of the old KGB building in Old Town.

Suhonen was quickly cleared through the security checkpoint, since his Glock was in the bottom drawer of his desk back in Pasila—the Helsinki police didn't allow weapons to be carried abroad.

A dark-haired woman in her thirties checked Suhonen's badge from behind the bulletproof glass and nodded. Suhonen tried to make small talk in his elementary Estonian, but she didn't respond, just picked up the phone and gestured for Suhonen to wait in the small foyer. The phone call was brief and soon a second young woman—blonde this time—came through the doors and gestured for Suhonen to follow. No Finnish officer would come to work in a skirt above the knee, Suhonen thought.

White walls lined the narrow staircase. The blonde led the way and Suhonen followed her legs to the third floor.

The matter could certainly have been handled over the phone or by email, but Suhonen preferred face-to-face meetings. Tallinn was only a short boat ride away, and besides, he'd get to see Marju. Suhonen had met the brunette the previous spring. He had been in Tallinn, shopping for parts for his motorcycle. Thirty-year-old Marju had been in the same store at the same time looking for a clutch plate for her Enfield. The possibility that her bike was the

British classic had caught his attention, but it turned out to be an Indian knock-off. They had continued the conversation, and ended up at an outdoor cafe for coffee. Since then, they had met two or three times a month in either Tallinn or Helsinki.

The meeting with Toomas Indres would take an hour at the most, and then he'd have time for dinner with Marju. He had a ticket for the nine o'clock ship back to Helsinki.

The skirt directed Suhonen into a huge, modern conference room. "Have some coffee. Toomas will be in shortly," she said in Finnish with a slight accent.

The long conference table could seat twenty people. The walls were aquamarine and the carpet a dark tone. The tall windows were dressed with floor-to-ceiling vertical blinds. Police crests from various countries, which had been given as gifts, decorated the walls. Among them was a plaque from the Helsinki VCU.

Before Suhonen could pour his coffee, Toomas Indres glided into the room.

"Hi," Indres said in Finnish, hurrying over to shake Suhonen's hand.

"Hello," Suhonen answered in Estonian. The man's handshake was intense.

Indres, the head of intelligence for the Estonian Central Police, was ten years Suhonen's junior. Young leaders were not unusual in Estonia. The head of the entire ECP was only thirty-two years old. In post-Soviet times, the ECP was known for quickly promoting young, able agents in order to sever ties with the old Soviet system. Indres wore a pair of black jeans, a white T-shirt and a light blue blazer. His hair was blond and closely cropped.

"How are you? Still swimming?" Suhonen asked. He recalled that Toomas was an open-water swimming enthusiast, and had logged some long distances.

"Heh, yeah. Next summer about ten friends and I plan to swim from Tallinn to Helsinki. It'll be good practice, just in case the Ruskies take their tanks across the border someday."

Suhonen chuckled, though he suspected Indres was only half-joking, at least in his hatred toward the Russians. The Soviet occupation from 1940 to 1988 had carved deep wounds into the Estonian psyche. Rather than watching Soviet propaganda, many Estonians had watched Finnish TV, which easily carried over the Gulf of Finland. As a result, and because Finnish and Estonian were closely related languages, most Estonians were nearly fluent in Finnish.

"What about you guys?" Indres asked, gesturing for Suhonen to sit across the table. He poured the coffees.

"What about us... The big-wigs have grand plans and even grander visions. But despite them, we still solve our cases."

"Hear you there. You had some photograph?"

Suhonen dug two folded letter-size printouts out of the breast pocket of his leather jacket. It was his best photo from the Velodrome; one of the images was the original, the other a close-up of Gonzales and the unknown man.

Suhonen set the printouts in front of Indres and pointed to Gonzales. "This one I know, but who's this other guy?"

Indres looked at the photos for a moment. "What's this about?"

Suhonen chuckled to himself, but not aloud. This is how it always went with these intelligence types. Nothing was free. Everyone wanted to know more about the case.

"This is Mike Gonzales…"

"A foreigner?" Indres cut in.

"Nope," Suhonen shook his head. "A homeboy. Formerly Mika Konttinen."

"OK. Go ahead," Indres said, tasting his coffee.

Suhonen did the same before continuing. "So, this Gonzales-Konttinen is a pretty well-known black market operator. Construction fraud and such. That in itself doesn't interest us, but lately he's been hanging around with the Skulls. And the day before yesterday I snapped these photos of him with buzz cut here."

"Gonzales is under surveillance then."

"Nope. Just a coincidence."

Indres laughed. "Good police work calls for coincidences. Do you have an open investigation on this Gonzales?"

"No. Just gathering intel."

"But there's something interesting about him?"

Suhonen thought for a second. "Isn't it enough that the guy is a con-man, hangs out with real bad guys and drives a BMW sports car?"

"Sure. That's plenty. Especially the Beamer. Nobody with that car could be a good person."

Indres, Suhonen knew, rode a Harley in the summer months.

"So you know him?" Suhonen asked. He was beginning to tire of the prying.

"A Russian is a Russian, even if he's fried in butter," Indres said dryly.

"Though in this case it's one of our own homegrown Estonian-Russians. The man's name is

Sergei Zubrov. Lives in Tallinn. A good year ago, Zubrov was involved in a big cocaine trafficking operation, but never ended up in court."

"What's he doing now?"

"We haven't been tracking him," Indres said, shrugging.

"So he hasn't been involved?"

"You think he's doing some business with this Gonzales?"

"It's a possibility, at least."

Indres nodded. "I can look into it a little further. It's easier to track the Russians than our own outlaws. The Russians still have traditional hierarchical organizations where each man has his own role. Our local hoodlums have shifted to more of a project-based model where the group comes together for one specific gig, and when it's completed, the team breaks up. We really don't have any pure drug or theft gangs anymore. Each gang member works and gets paid on a job-by-job basis. It's pretty damn difficult to keep up on who's dancing with who."

Suhonen poured himself another cup of coffee.

The men chatted for nearly an hour before Suhonen announced that he had to leave.

THURSDAY, OCTOBER 22

CHAPTER 4
THURSDAY, 8:30 A.M.
VANTAA PRISON, VANTAA

Tapani Larsson was marching along a concrete walk through the prison yard, headed toward the perimeter wall and the main gate. His pace was brisk and the pot-bellied guard struggled to keep up. Last night's rain had dwindled into a light drizzle.

Larsson's tattoos rose from beneath the collar of his leather jacket, reaching toward his bald head. Winding around his neck were a snake, a naked woman and an eagle. His cheeks were sunken and his eyes hard and piercing.

Larsson was fuming, but less so today than over the last year and a half. The man's hand continually closed into a fist and reopened again. Hand, fist. Hand, fist. Larsson, the Skulls' second-in-command, had served most of his sentence in Turku's new prison in Saramäki. In accordance with standard procedure, he was to be released from the prison nearest his home. The Helsinki Prison was full, so the pen in suburban Vantaa got the job. Larsson couldn't care less which institution's door slammed shut behind his back, as long as he was on the outside.

The prison guards at Vantaa would have rather kept the violently unpredictable man longer, but the Court of Appeals had shortened his extortion sentence from three-and-a-half years to sixteen months. Today marked the end of Larsson's term.

Larsson's last three months in the Turku Prison had been spent in the maximum security ward. He had wondered about the decision, but somehow the warden had been convinced that Larsson had been orchestrating criminal activity from within the prison walls.

The maximum security ward was no *Papillon*, but it wasn't far off. An hour a day outdoors, a miserable weight room and all visits conducted behind thick plexiglass. The purpose of maximum security was to try to soften up the inmate. Try harder, Larsson had thought. Captivity had only made him more defiant.

Government oversight of the maximum security ward essentially consisted of an assistant parliamentary ombudsman visiting once a year to make sure the flowers were watered.

Larsson spit on the wet prison lawn. Not to protest, just to spit.

The previous day, he had been transported from Turku on the prisoner train and had slept the night in a Vantaa cell. Wake-up call was at 6:30, breakfast 7:00 sharp. At 8:00, he turned in his prison duds and signed for his civilian clothes: boxers, a dark green T-shirt, white sport socks, combat boots, camouflage pants and a black leather jacket. His other belongings—a radio, books, shaver and toothbrush—were in his duffel bag. He had given his tube of toothpaste to a friend in the Turku pen.

After receiving his civilian clothes, Larsson was given a Certificate of Release verifying that he had served his time. The guard had cautioned him not to lose it—the police database wasn't updated immediately, so in the interim, Larsson would be considered a fugitive without the certificate.

Next stop was the teller. Some inmates had earned thousands of euros by working, but Larsson hadn't been interested in that. He signed for eight euros, all that was left in his prison account. Prisoners weren't allowed to carry cash, so all transactions in the cafeteria were paid electronically.

Larsson reached the checkpoint in the perimeter wall. Beside it was a large metal gate for cars and trucks. The guard in the booth pressed a button and the lock on the interior door buzzed.

Larsson yanked the door open. Freedom was less than five yards away. On the left was a plexiglass booth and directly in front of him, a metal detector. The guard almost made a crack, but then bit his tongue. "Papers," he said dryly.

Larsson said nothing, just dug the certificate out of his pocket and handed it to the guard. His escort had stepped aside to wait by the door.

The guard examined the document and pushed a second button. The exterior door was now open. Larsson took his certificate, folded it back into his pocket and left without a word.

Once he was outside the walls, the guard in the booth looked at Larsson's escort. "So... You think he's been reformed?"

* * *

Suhonen lay on the bed of his Kallio apartment. Two minutes ago, his clock radio had kicked off the day. For some reason, he had tuned it to Radio Suomipop, and at 8:30 sharp, the morning DJ had played a classic Finnish hit "Adult Woman." Before that, he had joked about condoms that were tough enough to be passed from father to son.

Suhonen listened to the tired Finnish pop song, unable to summon the energy to get up and change the station.

"All that we share, together we bear," the singer crooned over the airwaves.

His trip to Tallinn had been worthwhile. Toomas had revealed an important name, even if Suhonen didn't know why Sergei Zubrov was in Finland yet. Today he would dig. Maybe the Narcotics guys would know something about the man.

Dinner with Marju had been enjoyable. Just for fun, they had decided to dine at one of the tourist restaurants in Old Town. After strolling hand in hand down the cobblestone streets, Suhonen and Marju had settled on the Olde Hansa Restaurant, where the wait staff was dressed in medieval garb and served beer in ceramic steins. Ordinarily, Suhonen wasn't fond of the tourist traps, but then it had felt good. If he only could've stayed the night. Rocky seas had made the return trip less than pleasant, but Suhonen had napped in his chair the entire trip.

His thoughts were cut short by the ringer on his phone, which lay next to the radio. Suhonen flicked off the music as he picked it up. The caller was displayed as "private."

" Ye-eah," Suhonen answered.

"Ainola here," a man said. Suhonen recognized the voice of the Helsinki Prison warden. "Bad time?"

"Not too bad. I'm at home in bed."

"At home? In bed? Aren't real civil servants supposed to be out there fighting the evils of the world?"

"What evil is transpiring now?" Suhonen said, stretching his toes. He hoped he could make it to the station gym today.

Ainola's voice became serious. "I don't know if you've heard yet, but you should know."

"What's that?"

"Tapani Larsson is getting out today. Vantaa Prison is releasing him this morning. Actually, he's probably already out, since it's half past eight."

"That I didn't know."

"You do now," Ainola said. "I thought I'd call, just in case."

Suhonen wasn't really afraid of Larsson, but it was always good to know when gangsters were released. Especially since the Skull had put a bounty on Suhonen's head a year ago.

The summer before last, Suhonen had been shadowing Larsson's girlfriend and had wound up in the pair's shared apartment. Larsson had managed to surprise Suhonen, and had mistaken him for a small-time criminal. He had demanded a ten-grand ransom, but got the S.W.A.T. team instead. The District Court had convicted him of extortion, but according to the Court of Appeals, Suhonen should've shown his badge in the apartment, thereby defusing the situation.

Larsson's lawyer had stressed that the situation had escalated only because Larsson mistook Suhonen for a member of a rival gang, and felt threatened. Were Suhonen to have identified himself as a police officer, the matter could have been settled with words. As a result, the Court of Appeals had shortened Larsson's sentence.

Suhonen had laughed aloud when he read the decision. Had he shown his badge to Larsson, the only thing discharging would've been Larsson's CZ pistol.

"How'd his time go? You hear anything

interesting?" Suhonen asked.

"He served most of it in Turku, so I haven't heard much. He's a pretty sullen bastard, or so I'm told, so be careful. Never worked, just loafed around in his cell, lifted weights and read books."

"Read books? Well, I guess he's not dumb," Suhonen said.

Larsson's background differed from most other criminals. He wasn't raised in a reform school or by alcoholic parents—nor was he known to have been abused. A child of a "good" family, he had graduated high school with top honors, but had drifted into the Skulls during his college years. His ruthlessness lifted him quickly through the gang's ranks.

"Smart, but dangerous," Suhonen muttered. "That's true of many women too, adult women," he added.

"Yeah, yeah. You go back to bed—I've got a pile of parole requests to go through," the warden said.

"Deny them all. With Larsson on the loose, we don't need any more criminals on the streets."

"Okay," Ainola said. "Watch your back."

"Thanks for the call," replied Suhonen. He hung up the phone, slid out of bed, did twenty push-ups and stepped into the shower.

* * *

Larsson stopped briefly in front of the prison's brick perimeter wall. He listened as the gate clanged shut behind him. The sound caressed the gangster's ears. A fucking year and a half. Well, at least the time hadn't been a total loss.

He looked up at the gray skies and a light drizzle wet his face. Couldn't he at least get a proper rain?

It'd wash the stink of the pen right off of him.

He was standing at the end of the road. On the right was a parking lot about the size of a football field. On the left and to his rear was a graveyard for German soldiers from the first and second World Wars. A good four hundred bodies had been moved there in the 1950s. He could clearly hear the hum of the nearby Lahti Highway.

Larsson spotted a light-blue BMW sports car standing about fifty yards up the road. It started to move toward him.

The Beamer accelerated quickly and Larsson stopped.

When it was about twenty yards off, Larsson recognized the driver. The coupe pulled up and Larsson opened the passenger door.

"Hey. Nice to see you," said Sara Lehto. She was pretty: tall and thin, with a nice figure. Her bleached hair was gathered into a ponytail. She had appeared in various domestic adult videos and magazines.

Larsson circled to the rear of the Z3 and tossed his bag in the trunk.

No sooner had he slid into the car than they began to passionately kiss. Larsson's hand pawed at Sara's heaving breasts.

"Sure is," Larsson said.

Sara Lehto had been convicted as an accessory to the same extortion charge as Larsson, but had received a suspended sentence as a first-time offender.

She swung the car around and punched the gas. Even on a short stump of road, the Z3 gained impressive speed.

"Who's wheels?"

"Mike's," she answered, braking at the

intersection. "He thought you'd want a proper ride."

She turned onto the old Lahti Highway heading south.

"From you, sure… Where we going?"

Sara smiled at her bald-headed man. "Kalastajatorppa. Mike got us a suite there."

Kalastajatorppa was one of the finest hotels in Helsinki, located on a sprawling campus overlooking the sea. Its beauty and remote location had made it a favorite for visiting statesmen.

Sara's right hand slipped from the stick shift to his thigh.

* * *

Suhonen strode down the bleak, fluorescent hallway of the Violent Crimes Unit. The undercover officer glanced into Takamäki's office, but the detective lieutenant was away.

The floor was quiet. He wondered if something serious had happened—where was everybody?

He walked into the detectives' shared office and saw Sergeant Joutsamo staring at her monitor, presumably typing out some case notes.

"Hey," Suhonen said as he proceeded to his desk in the corner.

"Take a look at this," Joutsamo said before Suhonen could take off his coat.

Suhonen circled behind Joutsamo and shrugged off his jacket.

Joutsamo pointed at the screen. "This is last night's security footage from a downtown restaurant."

The video was dark but clear, though jumpy, as it only recorded one frame per second. The time appeared in the lower right corner: 2:45 A.M. The seconds ticked by one by one.

The video began with a view of a street and a group of four young men staggering down the sidewalk—obviously drunk. Suhonen fully expected one of them to throw a punch and for the victim to fall over and crack his head on the asphalt.

But that didn't happen. Instead, one of the guys ran across the street and climbed onto a metal bridge railing. A set of train tracks ran fifty feet below. The other three came closer and cheered him on.

Joutsamo slowed down the tape. Nonetheless, things happened quickly. In the lower corner, the restaurant's burly bouncer took a couple of steps toward the group and apparently said something, since one of the men turned his head to look. The man on the railing was still standing upright, but in the next frame he was pitched backwards at a peculiar angle with his arms spread wide, and in the following frame, he had disappeared. In the next three frames, the trio and the bouncer dashed to the railing.

Joutsamo stopped the video. "He died immediately."

"How old?"

"Twenty-two. The night-shift guys interviewed his friends at the scene. They were university students celebrating their friend's birthday, and this twenty-two year-old got the drunken notion that he should jump onto the railing for a balancing act. No mental health problems, suicide threats or anything like that."

"Finnish machismo," Suhonen yawned.

Every year, about six hundred young men died of violent causes or of accidents, so there was nothing extraordinary about the incident…except to his family and friends.

"I guess. Risky behavior in a blur of booze," she went on. "This morning I went to deliver the bad news and the parents took it pretty hard."

"Not many laugh in that situation. Crime scenes are a piece of cake compared to that."

Suhonen laid his hand on her shoulder.

"The mom cried the whole time and the dad went mute from shock. I listened to her cry for an hour, but then I had to leave. Apparently, he was a good kid. The police pastor stayed with them for support."

"Accidents happen," Suhonen said. He returned to his desk, tossed his jacket over the chair and booted up the computer. He took his keys out of his pocket and checked to see that his gun was still in the bottom drawer. Check.

"How was Estonia?"

Instead of answering, Suhonen tossed out a question. "Did you know that Estonia's Supreme Court ruled that if a defendant changes his testimony in court, then the court can only take the new testimony into account. So all police interviews have to be scrapped. And if the defendant doesn't testify, then none of the police interviews are admissible."

She nodded. "I heard about that, but I meant your case."

"Oh, some progress. Face-to-face meetings are always better than phone conversations," he said evasively. He hadn't told Joutsamo about his dinner in Tallinn. "Toomas recognized the guy in the photo as an Estonian-Russian named Sergei Zubrov."

"Means nothing to me."

"Same here, so far."

Dressed only in boxers, Larsson gazed out the bedroom window of their suite at the Kalastajatorppa resort. The gangster's body was almost entirely etched in ink, from just below his knees to the nape of his neck. The sea looked just as gray as the sky. It was almost dark outside, though it was just past noon.

At least the view here was better than staring at the fields surrounding the Turku brig.

Sara had gotten the key from the lobby and Larsson had come straight to the suite from the garage. He knew his appearance attracted attention, and that cops paid the porters for information on interesting guests.

The suite had two rooms: a bedroom with a large bed, and a living room with a sofa and wet bar. A bottle of champagne on ice had been waiting for them in the living room and they had popped the cork before decamping to the bedroom.

Now Sara was lying on the bed, watching pay-per-view.

Gonzales had arranged this nicely. The room had been ready right away in the morning, not at two in the afternoon, which was the usual check-in time. Maybe he had slipped the porters a little extra. The 350-euro check had been pre-paid. Larsson wondered why Mike seemed so eager to please. What was behind all this? He'd have time to reflect on that later.

"What movie's this?"

"It's not a movie. It's a TV series called *Rome*. First season."

Larsson glanced at the enormous screen. Legionnaires were smacking at each other with swords. It couldn't have interested Larsson less. "Uh-huh. Looks good."

"It is. Sex and violence. Just like our life." Sara reached for the half-empty glass on the nightstand. "We were born at the wrong time. Should've lived with these guys."

Wrong time, wrong place, thought Larsson. An airplane cleaved through the sky.

He needed to get the Skulls out of their slump and back on their feet. The simultaneous sentences of the kingpin and second-in-command had weakened the gang. Their president was doing life for shooting a businessman six years ago. He had carried out a contract and taken the life sentence rather than rat on the customer. That was the right attitude.

The cops had lucked out too often. Sara had told him that Alanen and Lintula had been locked up for the pizzeria extortion case. Out of a good two dozen gang members, about ten were sitting in cells now.

The president, who had been with Larsson in the Turku pen, agreed. The gang's scope needed to be broadened and strengthened.

The champagne bottle was in an ice pail next to the TV. Larsson filled his glass with the last few drops.

"We need more of this."

"There's more in the fridge," she said without looking away from the screen.

"You warm up the sauna?" Larsson asked, slamming the champagne.

"No need. It's one of those rapid-ready ones. Just lift the cover off the stove and it'll warm up."

"OK."

His plans weren't so urgent that they couldn't take a sauna. But at some point, he should call Aronen and summon the gang for tomorrow. For now, he could borrow Sara's phone, but he'd have to get his own soon.

* * *

The jukebox at the Corner Pub was playing something new for a change. Happoradio's lead singer belted out their recent hit "Che Guevara," *"In clouds of smoke, we rebel. Against the machine, we raise hell,"* The words were inaudible in the back corner, but not the pounding rhythm.

Eero Salmela, "Ear" Nurminen and "Macho" Mertala were pounding cut-rate beers. Each of them had been coming and going all day, stopping in and out of their corner table. Of course, spending time here called for money—either your own or borrowed. Stolen money was fine, too.

The conversation dealt mostly with recent activities. If things were actually going well, they told their friends that everything was going to hell. And vice versa. Anything and everything was a joke.

Weakness had to be concealed. They had all learned that in prison. Two criminals at a table could talk about real misfortunes, but three was one too many.

Ear-Nurminen, sporting a thick beard and dated eyeglasses, piped up. "So, you guys know what my social security check and a woman's period have in common?"

Salmela and Macho shrugged their shoulders.

"Both arrive once a month and last about a week."

All three laughed.

Ear-Nurminen had to sit further away from the table so his tremendous belly had room. According to the official story, he had received the "Ear" nickname because of his cauliflower ears, but the unofficial story had it that when he was younger, he had crept around apartment buildings and eavesdropped on people's lives through the mail slots.

Macho-Mertala was around thirty, narrow-faced and wore a jean jacket. He had burglarized dozens of grocery stores and kiosks, but when he told the stories, they changed to department stores and electronics shops.

"Fuck," Macho began and the others raised their mugs.

"To memory," Salmela said, his mug in the air.

"To memory," Macho wheezed.

The men drank. Their toast was to the memory of "Fuck" Jore, who had died just last summer. The bushy-browed Jore, a long-time member of their group, had received his nickname for his rather liberal use of the F-word. In his usual way, he had made the mistake of mocking a violent and mentally insane outpatient who was bumming a cigarette a few blocks from the Corner Pub, and took a knife in the gut for it. The ambulance had come quickly, but the eighteen stab wounds were too much for the doctors.

The killer had been found not guilty by reason of insanity and was committed to a mental hospital. Every now and then, rumors circulated in the Corner Pub that the guy had been spotted nearby.

"Jore was a good man. His heart was in the right place, but his tongue was twisted all wrong," Ear-Nurminen grumbled. At a minimum, every third word that Jore uttered had been "fuck."

Salmela remembered a time when he had disdained the drunks—Jore, Ear-Nurminen, and Macho—at the corner table. Big talk about the past and no hope for the future. But he didn't care anymore. He felt he belonged with them.

Actually, crime didn't interest him anymore. He wanted out. He'd rather sit in the pub with friends, shoot the breeze and marvel at the youth of today. That was enough for him, but his old debts were a problem. To be precise, the problem was the party to whom he was indebted. Before he could ever withdraw into retirement to hoodwink the welfare office and tell tall tales to the rookies, he'd have to pay the Skulls.

Now he had the opportunity. The money for the speed was all there, even if he had had to borrow all of it. It had demanded focus and tireless work, but he had succeeded against all odds. The middle-man had been paid, and the shipment was due to arrive any day.

The girl Saarnikangas had recommended hadn't even wanted to talk about smuggling, but with the middle man's help, he had found a mule.

Salmela was a man with a plan. Once he sold the dope to the buyer, he'd pay back the Skulls, plus keep a few grand for himself.

The scheme seemed a little complicated now, but if he could only concentrate for a couple of days, it would be over and all would be well. His head pounded every so often, but not so much that he didn't know to keep quiet about certain things, even among his buddies at the Corner Pub. These certain things were two: the scheme underway and the wad of cash in his billfold.

"Life is life," Salmela said, quoting Matti Nykänen, Finland's greatest ski jumper. Famously flawed, Nykänen had battled alcoholism, launched an unsuccessful singing career, fallen on hard times, and even done a stint in jail for the drunken stabbing of his girlfriend.

The mugs rose once more for Jore.

"Wonder if we could get Matti Nykänen to play a show here?" Macho thought aloud. "I know a few guys who've hung out with his crowd."

"Fuck," Ear-Nurminen went on, raising his mug again. "Sure wouldn't find me here if he did."

Macho gave his buddy a scornful look.

Ear-Nurminen hacked loudly, clearing his throat, "Gotta give him credit for the gold medals, and he's an old felon too, but he damned sure doesn't know how to sing."

"That's why he'd fit right in," Macho cackled. "An ex-con whose best years are behind him, but can barely manage a hum nowadays. That's why he's one of us."

"Okay, you organize it, I'll come."

Salmela glanced at his phone. No missed calls. It would come…for sure. Probably tomorrow. He'd find out where the shipment was stashed, and just forward the location to the buyer. Hell, no. He'd have to meet the mule at the harbor, of course. That's how it went. Then he'd have to hide it somewhere, but not at home. Maybe bury it somewhere. Then he could sell the location of the stash. That's how it'd be. He reminded himself to focus.

Then he'd pay his debts and focus on retirement without any threats or obligations.

The pain at the juncture of his skull and spine began to throb again. Best not to think too much. He tried to empty his head of thoughts.

Hey, he was among friends at the Corner Pub. Things would work out. No worries, no woes.

He emptied his pint. "Hurry up, you old fools. The next round is on me."

"Wow," Macho grunted and tossed back his mug. Ear-Nurminen finished last by three seconds—his glass had been the fullest.

CHAPTER 5
THURSDAY, 5:20 P.M.
PASILA POLICE HEADQUARTERS, HELSINKI

This Zubrov was still one strange bird. There was a Sergei Zubov who played in the NHL, but that was definitely a different guy. Over the course of the day, Suhonen had drunk half a dozen cups of coffee, made about fifteen phone calls and sifted through as many police databases as possible.

Now he was even more pleased he had gone to Tallinn, even if only for a small morsel of data. He had found nothing in the Finnish databases.

Of course, there were other possibilities. Perhaps Zubrov had changed his name or had several identities. Suhonen had searched using the names "Sergey, Serghey, Zhubrov," as well as many other alternatives and combinations. He didn't buy the notion that Zubrov was just a law-abiding citizen, meeting Gonzales at the Velodrome to chat about the weather.

Something was up, and it drove Suhonen nuts that he didn't know what.

Joutsamo returned. He had no idea where she had been, nor did he care.

"You find anything on that Sergei?" the Sergeant asked.

"Nope."

"Well, we at least know what he looks like if he ever actually commits a crime."

"Yup."

Joutsamo's attitude irritated Suhonen. Organized crime investigations should focus on these "Zubrovs" earlier and nail them for crimes in the making. Once the murder, robbery, assault or drug deal had taken place, it was too late.

Suhonen believed that the police lacked preventative tools and needed more capable undercover officers. He had spent a lot of time thinking about it, and inevitably, the United States and September 11, 2001 came to mind. Intelligence organizations had several indications of a possible terrorist attack, but they were unable to connect the dots. On top of that, the U.S. intelligence community had forgotten the importance of human assets in the field. Because they had relied too heavily on technology, which the enemy had learned to circumvent, the connections between the terrorists and their plot remained undetected until it was too late. Effective prevention required field work.

To Suhonen, the emphasis of criminal investigations was misplaced. Organized crimes should be prevented, not pursued after the fact. Even if the perpetrators were never charged, at least a crime would have been stopped.

Typically, the police had to wait until a crime was committed to get started. But by then, the damage was already done. Detectives would prioritize the cases based on the severity of the crime and available evidence, then go after the most dangerous suspects. Even with the Finnish police solving 95 percent of homicide cases, there were still many dead victims and many criminals left on the streets. For Suhonen, undercover work was an essential part of police work.

Zubrov's case gnawed at Suhonen because he didn't know what it was about. Or was he paranoid? Who could tell him more about this character without word of his interest drifting back to Zubrov himself? Somewhere, someone knew more about the man. At least Toomas Indres had promised to dig up more. At some point, he'd have to put in a follow-up call to Estonia.

Suhonen had also considered a possible connection from Zubrov—through Gonzales—to the Skulls. The Skulls carried out their own hits, so they didn't need a hit-man. Recently, the sphere of the Skulls had only included drugs, extortion and debt collection contracts anyway. This was primarily because the gang's brains, Tapani Larsson, had been behind bars. Now, however, he was back on the streets.

"Wanna go to the gym?" Joutsamo asked. She had a black coat in her hand and a gym bag over her shoulder. She had noticed Suhonen's duffel bag on the floor. "Thought I'd do some bench presses and I need a spotter."

"Just pumping iron? No stationary bikes?"

Joutsamo shook her head and smiled. "Not even a treadmill."

"Yeah. Alright, I'll come. Not getting anywhere here," he said and started to shut down his computer.

Still, that didn't shake off his nagging uneasiness. Suhonen kept thinking that somebody had to know this Zubrov, but who? He couldn't escape the thought that he should have tailed the man after the meeting at the Velodrome.

Suhonen was lying on his back on the leg press in a white T-shirt and black shorts, his ponytail hanging off the bench. He was at the end of a set and his face was flushed. With every press, the forty-something cop exhaled hard and as he lowered the weight, he inhaled.

Joutsamo sat at the foot of the bench press in gray sweatpants and a red top, drinking water from a plastic bottle.

It was quiet in the station's dated gym. The smell of sweat had permeated the space, much the same as a men's locker room.

Besides the two VCU officers, an immense, bald-headed traffic cop with whiskers was hitting the heavy bag. Suhonen knew his name was Strand and that he had a K-9 named "Esko." Occasionally, they had worked together on raids. The men had exchanged nods.

Suhonen finished his set and lowered the weights. He got up, slid the plates off and walked over to Joutsamo.

"Well, your turn."

She laughed. They had been hard at it for nearly an hour.

"Maybe one more set."

Suhonen's phone rang next to the leg press, about six feet off. "Of course," he grumbled and snatched his phone.

Again, the caller was unidentified. No surprise. The majority of cops and criminals alike had set their phones to block caller ID.

"Yeah," Suhonen snapped into the receiver.

"Hey. Toomas here," said a man with an Estonian

accent. "Bad time?"

Suhonen glanced at Joutsamo, who was waiting under the bar for him to spot her. "No. Go ahead."

"About Zubrov," he began. "We're still digging for more, but I did hear that a woman from his circle is arriving in Helsinki tonight with a smallish batch of speed."

Suhonen wanted to ask where he had gotten the info, but Toomas wouldn't have told him anyway. "Smallish?"

"A few pounds. We don't have the resources to go after it, nor would we want to risk exposing our informant for a small-time deal like this."

"I understand."

"Just thought I'd call you. Hopefully, this will open up some new leads for you."

"Hopefully," said Suhonen, his gears already turning. "Who's the woman?"

"I'll send you an email with a photo and some other info on this Marju."

A shock ran through Suhonen's body—he tried to calm himself. Marju was a relatively common name in Estonia. It couldn't be his Marju. No way.

"OK. When is she due in?"

Joutsamo was looking inquiringly at Suhonen. The traffic cop was still beating the bag.

"This evening. The Tallink Star leaves here at eight and should be in Helsinki by ten P.M."

"Good. I'll talk to Takamäki about what to do."

"What's that noise in the background?"

Suhonen chuckled. "I'm at the gym."

"Hmm. You guys have time for that?"

"One more question. What exactly is this woman's connection to Zubrov?"

"We don't know for sure. This Marju has been

going to his parties and our surveillance has spotted Zubrov and her eating together. She's not his girlfriend, but not a prostitute either. Probably somewhere in between."

"The tip is good, though?"

"I wouldn't have called otherwise. I'll send someone to the harbor to check out what kind of clothes she's wearing and call you later."

"Good. Thanks."

The conversation ended and Suhonen hung up.

"Who was that?" Joutsamo asked.

"Toomas. A small shipment of speed is coming over this evening. Somehow it's connected to Zubrov."

"You should probably call Takamäki."

"Yeah."

"Well, come over and spot me. I'll do a set of ten and then let's go."

Suhonen wanted to march straight to his computer and check his email for the woman's picture. He hoped this had nothing to do with his lovely Marju. What would he do if it were the same woman?

* * *

The hallways of the Narcotics department were as gloomy as the VCU's, one floor up: gray laminate floors, dirty walls and cold fluorescent lighting.

Suhonen had spoken with his boss and his orders were clear. Drug smuggling was Narcotics' business, not the VCU's. Suhonen agreed with Takamäki, but that didn't prevent them from cooperating. To the contrary, inter-departmental cooperation had always been encouraged.

Immediately upon arriving at his desk, he had

checked his email for the photo of the mule, and though this woman was also beautiful, dark and fit, she was luckily another Marju. Suhonen had taken a deep breath, and tried to calm his nerves.

Narcotics Lieutenant Rauno Ristola's office was halfway down the hall. Suhonen knew the veteran narcotics cop well, as they had worked together on a number of cases over the years.

The door was open but Suhonen knocked anyway and the rugged, bald-headed lieutenant invited him inside. His office was just as small as Takamäki's. On the desk sat a computer and a pile of papers. His bookcases held fewer binders than Takamäki's.

A half-empty cup of coffee was parked next to a small travel radio, which was playing hard rock. The sound quality was so shoddy that Suhonen couldn't recognize the song.

"So this dope deal," Ristola muttered. He was dressed in a black sweater.

Suhonen had already explained the key points over the phone. He had suggested that the mule should be followed to determine who would receive the shipment. He walked over to the window and sat on the sill.

"The ship comes in at ten," Suhonen answered. "Three hours from now."

"Time isn't the problem."

"What is then?"

"Men. Two of our teams are tied up on a coke case. I don't have the manpower to take this on," Ristola explained.

"I could certainly…"

Ristola laughed. "One Suhonen equals ten narcotics officers. Of course. But a real surveillance op in downtown Helsinki would call for a few more

Suhonens. Tech can't help either, since we don't know what she'll do once she's off the boat..."

"You know a Sergei Zubrov?" asked Suhonen as he slid a copy of the Velodrome photograph to the lieutenant.

He looked at the photo. "This one here looks familiar. Gutierrez or something like that."

"Gonzales."

"Yeah, that's it, but this Russian-looking guy I don't know. Sergei Zubrov, huh?" Ristola said, handing the picture back. "What's this about?"

"I snapped these a couple days ago. Gonzales and Zubrov were meeting in the parking lot of the Velodrome."

"Do you have an open case on these guys?"

"No. Just curiosity. Gonzales is interesting because he's connected to the Skulls. I chatted with an Estonian colleague about Zubrov. He's some kind of a drug boss in Tallinn, and somehow linked to tonight's dope shipment."

"Can't be that big if I've never heard of him."

"Apparently not. Though his association with the Skulls makes him an interesting customer."

"Of course, I get it. But I can't pull guys off this cocaine case. They've been working on this for months. Surveillance eats up a hell of a lot of time," Ristola explained. "Of course, we can't let the dope into the country either."

"I suppose not," said Suhonen.

"Let's take her out at the harbor and interrogate her. You can have one of our men. That should be enough."

Suhonen was disappointed. "Okay..."

"One is enough?"

"It'll have to be."

Ristola stared at the wall opposite his desk, where several framed diplomas from the Scotland Yard and German Central Police drug trafficking courses hung. He was silent for a moment. "You know what, Suhonen?"

"What?"

Ristola turned to face him. "Our best times are behind us. Resources are constantly being cut and the cases are getting harder. Trivial protocol directives get tighter by the day, and on top of that, our undercover teams are stretched way too thin. The only thing missing is an American-style law that makes evidence inadmissible if some minor procedure is violated. It's all going to hell."

Suhonen said nothing. *Just wait until we adopt a law like Estonia's, where a change in testimony expunges all previous statements. Then Narcotics will be in real trouble,* he thought.

"Take Toukola with you to the harbor. Technically, he leads your little troop and this is my case. You can sit in on the interrogations with the woman. I assume Takamäki knows about this."

"Yeah," said Suhonen. "Let's just hope we find her."

CHAPTER 6
THURSDAY, 9:45 P.M.
HOTEL KALASTAJATORPPA, HELSINKI

The room was dark. Tapani Larsson lay on his back on the hotel bed, watching the flicker of the television on the white plastered ceiling. Sara was still staring at the blaring TV, but Larsson didn't hear a sound.

In prison, he had had to learn to block out the noise from his ears and mind.

He had lain the same way on the bunk in his cell. This one was just softer.

The thick walls of the pen had smelled of pain. *That* he hadn't been able to shut out. Now he smelled the sweet scent of champagne in a half-empty glass on the nightstand.

Larsson recalled a line from the film *Deer Hunter* where a Frenchman named Julien remarked, "When a man says no to champagne, he says no to life." In the film, Julien recruited players for Russian roulette.

He had had plenty of time in prison to watch movies.

The prison psychologist had wanted to meet with him. Larsson wondered why he had consented. Maybe just for something new. The shrink had asked about his childhood and adolescence. She had been especially interested in his relationship with his parents. Larsson had fed her a lot of crap, but he really hadn't known what to say about his parents. He remembered them as cold and distant, though he recalled that his dad had slapped him on the ear when he was ten. Some years later, he hit back. But that episode was minor compared to the stories of other inmates.

If he was wronged, he always took vengeance—maybe sooner, maybe later, but without question. He saw no alternatives, though he didn't tell the shrink that.

The psychologist had done her homework. She knew Larsson had gone to the Helsinki School of Economics and wondered why he had become a career criminal when he had the opportunity for honorable work.

Larsson had ended the conversation then and there, and had asked the guard to escort him back to his cell. Honorable work. What was honorable about raking in five grand a month as the VP of some company? He didn't want to be like his father. Damned middle-class dreams of a house and car. Larsson was interested in money and power, both of which he obtained through violence.

Of course, her next question would have been what it feels like to commit a crime. That was just a stupid question. It didn't feel like anything. Was it supposed to feel like something? It just happened—nothing special about it. He could have proved it with a few left hooks, but that would just have lengthened his sentence.

Larsson had never regretted the choices he had made. His fellow business students had been good customers of his small-time marijuana operation. At its peak, he had earned about twenty grand a month. Larsson had hunted down the guy who had ratted him out to Narcotics. His first stretch in prison lasted a year. After that, Tomi had paid for his betrayal in cash, and received two broken arms as a bonus. Say you fell on your rollerblades, Larsson had barked as he left Tomi groaning on the floor of his apartment.

The rat hadn't dared to go to the cops again.

Maybe he should pay another visit to Tomi, just out of principle. Maybe the guy would have a wife, two kids, a house and a nice car. He could repo the car as additional compensation for the old offense. Interest was always accruing. At least it would be fun to see the look on Tomi's face when he rang the doorbell.

Tomi was sound evidence that nobody could be trusted. The guy had bought some weed and got busted soon after. Of course, the chump squealed on the spot. The Skulls were different, though. Trust was sacred within the brotherhood.

Larsson laughed. Just look at Niko Andersson. The guy was fat, ugly and stupid. Years ago, when he was standing trial for a bank robbery, the prosecutor had asked him why he had robbed the bank. Niko said simply, "Because that's where the money was." The prosecutor had no further questions.

Niko would never betray him, nor would any of the Skulls' men. They wouldn't dare. Tomorrow he'd see his brothers again.

* * *

The ship's hull was neon green, with a giant ribbon pattern woven through the middle. It reminded Suhonen of the flames that biker gangs used to decorate their leathers. As it neared the wharf, the dull yellow floodlights of the West Harbor softened the bright paintwork on the ship.

The undercover cop had heard from Estonia that the woman had boarded the ship alone. She had been wearing a dark red coat, a skirt and black leather boots.

Suhonen and Toukola ducked out of the walkway into a small control room, which was equipped with numerous CCTV monitors that displayed security footage from the passenger gangway. The room was also fitted with tinted glass, through which they could observe the passengers leaving the ship. The control room was situated so that travelers approached straight toward the window, and then curved left to the Customs checkpoint.

Toukola was a small forty-year-old man whose quick movements evoked those of a weasel. Suhonen had heard that Toukola played bass in the Narcotics department's band. The man's brown hair just touched his shoulders and he was wearing a black track jacket and jeans.

Suhonen and Toukola were sitting on two office chairs, observing the monitors. Nothing moved on the screens.

The Tallink Star could accommodate 1,900 people, and 450 vehicles on the car deck, but according to the shipping line, only 600 people were on board. That was good news, since it would be easier to pick out the mule in the exit rush. Of course, she might disembark in a car, but that was a risk they had to take.

There was a time when finding this woman would've been easy. The police would have simply instructed border officials to stop the woman at the passport checkpoint. But the EU's Schengen Agreement, which removed passport checks when traveling within the EU countries, had wiped out the practice.

"We've been here in the same room once before," Toukola began. "Looking for a heroin mule, wasn't it? That one was an easy case. Remember we nabbed a guy about five-foot-seven, wearing size 15 shoes? Found almost two pounds of smack in them."

Suhonen didn't respond—he was focused on the monitors. Toomas hadn't known where the woman had stashed the dope. Four pounds was enough that she wouldn't be able to swallow the bags. They would probably be hidden in her clothing or taped to her body. That would rule out skinny types in skin-tight clothing, then. Of course, at this time of year everyone wore a coat.

"Well, here we go," Toukola muttered as the first passengers came into view. The ship was moored at the port's southern end, so the walk to the terminal amounted to several hundred yards. The security cameras showed footage of the entire walk.

The first passenger was a man in a suit who nearly ran down the gangway. Suhonen wondered why he was in such a hurry. Maybe to catch a taxi, but where to then?

Next was a group of women in their sixties, each of whom had a pull cart filled with ten cases of beer and cider. A few were also carrying six-packs of one-liter vodka bottles. Many Finns happily paid the twenty-euro roundtrip fare in order to buy as much cheap Estonian booze as they could carry.

Both Toukola and Suhonen followed the footage with intense focus. People trickled off the boat in sporadic clumps. Several women in red coats appeared, but their ages didn't match.

A man in his thirties wearing an old army jacket

caught Toukola's attention. "You know him?"

"Yeah. Karjalainen."

"We should stop him. I busted him once for a couple pounds of hash. Apparently he's out of jail again."

The man's gait was a little wobbly. "Too smashed to be a mule," Suhonen remarked.

"You never know—this is just a small-time job. The big loads are trucked in along with legal cargo, unpacked quickly and then stashed somewhere in the sticks. It's an old trick already, but it still works."

"There," Suhonen cut in. The woman walking past the camera was wearing a dark red coat, and Suhonen recognized her attractive face from the photo. She walked off the screen shortly.

"You sure?" Toukola asked.

Suhonen nodded.

Toukola picked up his phone and sent word that the target had been located. "Let's be ready," he said.

Half a minute later, the woman in boots appeared on a second monitor. Her pace was casual, and her appearance didn't show any stress, worry, furtive glances or the like. Not once did she look at the security cameras.

The woman had made it to the third monitor when Suhonen and Toukola slipped out of the control room and drifted along with the crowd past Customs to the terminal's concourse. They pulled to the side but kept their eyes on the doorway where the passengers were exiting. Some stayed and waited on the concourse. The numerous beer carts made a mess of traffic.

The woman in red came in following two men closely. Nothing indicated that they knew each other.

Neither Suhonen nor Toukola wanted to make an arrest on the crowded concourse, so they let her exit.

Once outside, she veered right and the officers did the same. The covered ramp descended toward the taxi line and the Helsinki city bus stop. Up ahead was a parking lot packed with cars and inter-city buses. The signs advertised their destinations: Forssa, Hämeenlinna, Kouvola.

Maybe her ride was already waiting, Suhonen thought.

About fifteen yards up was a police van, which Toukola had arranged. A large male uniformed officer stepped out of the passenger's side and a female officer got out of the driver's side.

The red-coated woman spotted the cops and glanced both ways, looking for an escape route, but there was none.

They approached the woman, who stopped.

"Good evening," the big cop said. "We have an issue we'd like to clear up with you."

The woman didn't respond.

"We've received a complaint from the ship about a shoplifter and you match the description," he continued.

Suhonen followed the events at a distance. With dozens of passengers around, it wasn't the most discreet arrest, but at least they could tell Toomas that some attempt at a cover-up had been made. Had she been arrested in the terminal, it would've revealed that the cops had been tipped off. This way, at least, they wouldn't directly jeopardize Toomas' informant in Tallinn. Their other alternative would have been to station a drug-sniffing dog at the Customs checkpoint, but on short notice they hadn't been able to find an available dog.

"I no thief," the woman muttered in a broken accent.

"We'll just clear that up."

"No, I have to…"

"This won't take long," the cop continued. "We can check out your bag and clothes in the back of the police van there."

The female officer opened the doors and hopped inside. "This way," she said firmly. The big cop steered her in through the back doors, then stayed outside to stand guard.

Suhonen and Toukola headed for their car, which they had left in the terminal parking lot. The orders for the uniformed officers had been simple: If the woman was packing dope, bring her to Pasila. If she was clean, let her go.

FRIDAY,
OCTOBER 23

CHAPTER 7
FRIDAY, 8:30 A.M.
PASILA POLICE HEADQUARTERS, HELSINKI

Suhonen descended the stairs to the Narcotics department. Toukola had called to ask if he'd like to observe Marju Mägi's interrogation. Of course he would.

The previous evening, Toukola had dropped Suhonen off at his apartment in Kallio on the way back from the harbor. Then he had continued on to the station to take care of some paperwork connected to the case. The uniformed officers had found two ten-ounce packets of amphetamines taped to her ribs.

Once the amount of amphetamines surpassed four ounces, it became felony drug possession. Lieutenant Ristola had arrested Marju Mägi the same night. Toomas Indres had talked about four pounds, but they hadn't found nearly that much. Perhaps Toomas' intel was inaccurate, or maybe his informant had exaggerated to make the scoop seem more important.

Except in extraordinary situations, interrogations had to be conducted before 10 P.M., so the police had waited till morning. Twenty ounces of amphetamines didn't qualify as extraordinary.

Suhonen strode down the hallway to Toukola's office, the same type of smallish open office the VCU used.

He had showered before work and left his long black hair over his shoulders to dry. A few gray hairs had already taken root.

"Morning. Go late last night?" Suhonen asked.

"I got outta here about midnight," Toukola said, a baggy white T-shirt hanging off his shoulders.

"She say anything?"

"I tried to soften her up, but she's clammed up pretty tight. We'll see what happens today. You want to be in the room or watch behind the glass?"

"Behind the glass is fine."

The preparations took another ten minutes. Toukola directed Suhonen into a room off a long hallway, and continued to the next door.

Through the mirrored glass, Suhonen watched Marju Mägi adjust her green coveralls. Her dark hair was tousled and her delicate face seemed paler. Her first night in the brig didn't look like it had gone well.

Behind her, the jailer kept watch.

Toukola stepped in and took a seat opposite her at a gray table with a computer.

Suhonen heard the voice through the microphone. "Good morning," said Toukola.

She glanced up, but said nothing.

The guard left.

"How are you?" He went on.

She shrugged. Good, Suhonen thought. At least it was a reaction. In recent years, so-called "mummy-interviews" had become more common. In these, the suspect would not even agree to leave the cell, so the guards had to roll them out in a wheelchair. During the questioning, the mummy wouldn't respond to anything, not one word. Sometimes, they wouldn't even open their eyes.

"Just want to confirm your identification. Marju Mägi?"

"Yeah."

Toukola went on with her date of birth, address and other information needed for the record, and was also sure to remind her that the interview would be recorded. Then he informed her of what crime she was suspected and asked if she would need a lawyer present. She didn't—in Northern Europe, requesting a lawyer for the first interview was rare, and some thought of it as an admission of guilt. The woman had suddenly learned to speak fluent Finnish.

"Tell me about the incident," Toukola began.

To Suhonen, Toukola's tone of voice seemed tired, almost bored. Was it fatigue or strategy, he wondered.

Marju kept her eyes on the table. "Not much to say. I came from Tallinn by ship. The police claimed I was a thief, took me into the van, and found the packets."

Good, Suhonen thought.

"The amphetamines were in your possession?"

"What, you stupid? If the stuff was taped to my side, doesn't that mean it was in my possession?"

Toukola was quiet for a moment. "Yes, you're right. It was a stupid question."

Suhonen didn't think it was stupid, and of course, neither did Toukola. She had just confessed to possessing twenty ounces of amphetamines. That would earn her two-and-a-half years behind bars.

"Where did you get the drugs?"

The woman stiffened.

"Can you tell me where you got the drugs?"

Mägi thought for a moment. "No."

"Why not?"

"I don't want to answer."

"Why not?"

She didn't respond.

Suhonen thought about Toukola's strategy. With this approach, the interviewer was able to determine that she had acquired the drugs from someone.

"Who were you supposed to bring the drugs to?"

The woman remained silent.

"Can you tell me who you were bringing the drugs to?"

Again, a silence preceded her response. "No."

"Why not?"

"I'd rather not answer."

"Why not?"

Silence.

At least it was now clear that she was a mule, Suhonen thought. He guessed correctly what Toukola would do next.

"Interview concluded at 8:53 A.M.," Toukola said into the microphone.

He stopped the recording on the computer. "Marju, the interview is over," he said softly.

The microphones to the observation room were still live and Suhonen heard them continue to talk.

"You were in possession of twenty ounces of amphetamines. If it's the usual 20-40 percent grade, it will mean two-and-a-half years in prison. If it's 80 percent, you'll get four to five years."

Her expression was dour.

"If you tell us where you got it and where it was going, it's possible you could get a suspended sentence. I can't promise anything, but we can speak with the prosecutor on your behalf," Toukola said, pausing to let his words sink in.

"I can't."

"Why not?"

"Don't be stupid again. You're a cop—you know how these things work. "

"Yes, I know," Toukola said. "But you'll have some time to think about it in your cell."

"Can I take a shower?" Mägi asked.

"Don't know. You'll have to ask the guards. They'll put you on the list. Usually you're allowed two to three showers a week."

"I didn't take one yesterday."

"And you might not tomorrow, either. Yard time is one hour a day on the roof of the station."

"Do I get my things back?"

"Nope."

"Not even books?"

"At least not your own," Toukola said. A couple of Estonian books had been among her things. "Ask the guards if they have anything."

"Can't you help?"

"If you help me," he answered, and rose without waiting for a response. She'd have time to think it over in her cell. Here, time was on the cops' side. Toukola pressed a button on the wall, summoning the guard in. "The interview is over. Take her back to her cell."

Marju Mägi stood up and the guard escorted her out. Toukola let them go first, then swung in behind.

She asked the guard about the shower. "The list is full. Maybe day after tomorrow," he said.

The suspect was led to the right and Toukola turned left into the observation room.

"Well, what'd you think?" Toukola asked.

"Doesn't know anything. A clean mule."

"My thoughts exactly. She might be able to tell us

where she got it and where it was going, but nothing more."

Suhonen shrugged. "We should've followed her further, but I get it. No sense getting all hysterical over twenty ounces."

"Well, I'll let her wilt in her cell a couple days and then we'll see what she has to say. Jail is a grim place for a young woman. She'll say something just to get her books back, at least off the record. Hours are a lot longer in jail."

"I spent a night in there once," Suhonen said.

"Really?"

"We were trying to figure out how jail affects suspects and their statements, so I agreed to be the VCU guinea pig and spent twenty-four hours in a cell. It was a few years ago, but the only thing we concluded was that time slows way the hell down. The boredom wears some down, but for others it just toughens them up."

"Well, we'll see which group Marju Mägi fits into."

Suhonen's second cell phone rang. He glanced at the display: Eero Salmela.

* * *

Roge was sitting behind the wheel of a matte black '74 Chevy Nova. He had a broad, flat face with a ponytail and was large, though clearly not the colossus his passenger Niko was. In the back seat sat a third Skull, Osku. All were wearing black leather vests. Niko's patches indicated he was a senior member—the other two were prospects.

"That the right car?" Niko asked.

"Yep. That red Alfa Romeo."

"Good, let's roll then," Niko said. He stepped out of the Nova.

The Alfa Romeo was parked in the driveway of a rickety yellow ranch house encircled by a leaf-bare hedge. Beside it sat a rusty Volkswagen Beetle, which appeared to have once been blue.

The three swaggered down the long dirt driveway. The elephantine Niko lumbered along in the middle. On his right, lagging back a bit was the bull-like Roge, and on the left, little Osku, sporting a goatee that only made him look more like his beard's namesake.

As they reached the Alfa Romeo, a man of about thirty with a blond shag of hair and a jean jacket walked out of the front door of the house. He closed the door behind him before noticing his visitors.

"What the hell?" he blurted, stopping in front of the door. The trio was about ten yards away. They kept coming.

"We want to talk to you," Niko growled.

"About what," the man stammered, his eyes darting about for an escape route. There was none and the door behind him was now locked.

Roge approached from the right and swung his arm back, snapping an eighteen-inch chain from his sleeve to his hand. Without a word, he lashed the back of the man's left knee.

The man cried out and stumbled backwards. Niko caught him and slammed him against the door. "You little shit!"

Osku landed a hard side-kick in the man's ribs. "Fuck!"

The man slumped to a sitting position in front of the door. "What is this?" he sputtered. "What'd I do?"

"The blonde at the bar last Tuesday," Osku snarled. "That was my girl you tried to pick up. I told you to back off, but you didn't."

"I didn't…"

"I told you to back off!"

"I didn't…"

Roge flogged the man's shins with the chain.

"Stop! Fuck!"

Niko squatted down in front of the man.

"Hopefully you learned something today. You hit on one of the Skulls' women, you suffer the consequences," he said, then thundered, "You fucking get it?!"

"Yeah, yeah. I get it," he murmured.

"Good. And if you go to the cops, we'll come back, nail you to the living room wall and burn this house down."

"No, no… I won't," he wailed.

Niko stood, turned and walked away. Roge and Osku followed. As they reached the Alfa Romeo, the bull-like Roge took one last swing with the chain, shattering the passenger side window. "Just a reminder!" he shouted. The man was still lying in a heap at the door.

Their footsteps quickened on the way to the car, and the lumbering Niko was already out of breath. Roge and Osku didn't pass him, however.

Roge swung into the driver's seat and tossed the chain into the passenger footwell before Niko could sit down. Osku slid into the back seat.

Roge stepped on the gas and laughed. The adrenaline was still pumping in their veins.

"Shit, he sure learned his lesson!"

"You got that right," said Niko. "How'd it feel, Osku?"

"Great. Looked like the guy must've bleached his hair, though. It was still brown back at the bar. Ha-haa!"

Niko turned and shot a look at Osku. "It was the same guy, though?"

"Yeah," he answered hesitantly. "Pretty sure it was."

"Pretty sure?"

"Yeah. Yes, it was him."

Niko turned his gaze back to the road. "Alright. Your word is good enough for me."

Osku was satisfied.

"Drive back to the office," Niko commanded. Larsson will be there around noon. You guys haven't even met him yet."

* * *

Detective Lieutenant Takamäki was sifting through a batch of unsolved cases. The list seemed to grow by the day, and though they were mostly routine crimes, that was only the police's view. The victims likely had a different opinion.

If the performance objective of the Helsinki Police Department was a solid 'B', the actual grade usually was somewhere around a 'C-' or a 'D+'. The overall percentage of solved cases had declined sharply in the 1990s, though violent crimes continued to be solved at a satisfactory rate. The reason, of course, was that with violent crimes, most victims were able to identify who had hit, kicked, stabbed or raped them. If the victim was unable to communicate, that usually meant that the crime was more serious, and police allocated plenty of resources for those cases.

Takamäki's cell phone rang. He instinctively

looked at the display: unknown.

"Hello," he answered.

"Hey there," said a woman's voice.

Takamäki recognized the caller before she could identify herself: Sanna Römpötti from Channel 3 News. For the past twenty years, she had worked as a crime reporter for various media outlets.

"How are you today?" Takamäki inquired before Römpötti could ask him anything. That was a first.

"What, have you switched to some specialized intelligence unit investigating the mood of the media?"

Takamäki chuckled. "Nah, just interested. You promised to teach me ballroom dancing. When do we start?"

Now it was Römpötti's turn to laugh. The previous winter, the TV reporter had been selected for the popular television show *Dancing with the Stars*, and had agreed to participate. Römpötti had never really understood herself why she had consented. She did remember that she had drunk two glasses of wine before the call came. Afterwards, it had been too late to enter a plea of temporary insanity. Along with her dance partner, Römpötti had made it to the final four pairs before the dance-ignorant masses dropped her.

"Listen, Kari," she said. "Anytime."

Takamäki was somewhat disconcerted. "Aah, let's look at our calendars. Shall we?"

She got to the point. "About the Skulls."

"What about them?"

"This week the judge levied three-year sentences on our 'dynamic duo' for that pizza shop extortion."

"Right," said Takamäki. "Alanen and Lintula."

"Have you read the court's ruling?"

"No," the detective lieutenant said candidly. "But I'm quite familiar with the details—it was our case, after all. What about it?"

Römpötti paused briefly. Takamäki wondered if she was surprised he hadn't read the court's ruling. He simply hadn't had the time.

She went on, "Well, in court, the prosecutor argued for stiffer sentences because Alanen and Lintula were members of the Skulls, an organized crime ring. But the court rejected the argument because it determined the gang hadn't been founded as a criminal organization. Do you have any comment on that?"

Takamäki paused for a moment. "Is this an interview?"

"No. Just gathering background information."

Her answer made him wonder if she was working on a bigger story about the Skulls.

"Well, I wasn't surprised," he answered. "Generally, these laws pertaining to criminal organizations have become impossible to apply in practice. They're like cake toppers."

"Huh?"

"The cake looks better with the decorations, but nobody eats the plastic."

Römpötti laughed sarcastically. "Right, like freedom of speech in the constitution. There's a cake topper for you."

"No comment."

Römpötti steered back on course. "So what's the status with the Skulls, by the way? Are they under police surveillance?"

"We don't have time for that. Routine cases are coming in at a brisk enough pace that we don't have the manpower to conduct extra surveillance, even if we'd like to."

"Aren't there almost ten of them in prison now?" It was more a remark than a question.

"Somewhere around there. I don't know exactly. Are you working on something bigger about them?" he asked.

"Maybe. We'll see what I can dig up."

Takamäki considered how to put it. "Well, if you intend to get in touch with them, watch out. They're unpredictable."

* * *

Aleksis Kivi Street had once been wide and spacious until the addition of a streetcar line had eaten up half of the road. A few empty bottles of beer lay on the pavement in the yellow glow of the street lights. Suhonen knew it wouldn't be long before someone gathered them up for the deposit.

About five yards away, an older man with a thirties-style cap exited Stairwell F on the ground floor of a seven-story building. The ponytailed cop slipped in before the door could close and the man shot him a cold stare, but Suhonen didn't care. He was happy to have slipped inside without resorting to trickery.

Built in the 1960s, the stairwells of the building had been painted many times over the years, but judging by the flaking paint, yet another coat was in order. Suhonen stepped into the elevator and pressed the button for the fifth floor. The elevator reeked of urine.

There were four apartments on the fifth floor. Next to the stairwell leading upstairs was a brown door with no name tag.

Suhonen couldn't remember if he had ever been here on a bust. The VCU had ransacked quite a few of the flats on Aleksis Kivi Street.

Suhonen rang the doorbell.

His old friend Salmela opened the door, and the nauseating stench of sweat and rotting food mixed with fresh cigarettes wafted into the hallway. "Come in," said Salmela.

Dirty clothes lay all over the entry. Shoes were cluttered about and only two coats remained on the hangers; the rest were in a heap on the floor.

Suhonen didn't say anything, just followed Salmela, who was dressed in jeans and a grubby white shirt, into the living room. Suhonen dodged the beer cans, bottles and laundry littering the floor, glancing briefly into the bedroom on the right. He wouldn't have been surprised at all to see a city rat slink out from behind one of the cardboard boxes.

The living room was on the smaller side, with a TV in the corner, and in front of that, a gray sofa that even the Salvation Army wouldn't have deemed acceptable. Its seat cushions were sagging and the upholstery was torn in many places. Salmela sat down at the table. A full ashtray, glasses, two opened cartons of milk and a few dishes lay on the table. Apparently, Salmela enjoyed liver casserole as well as mac-and-cheese.

Looking fatigued, Salmela dug out a twenty-two caliber pistol and set it on the table. "Take it."

"What's going on?" Suhonen asked, a shade of worry in his voice.

Had his friend shot someone? The apartment stunk, but not of a corpse.

"I was thinking about shooting myself, but then I came to my senses. This .22 is just too small for the job. If you'll give me your Glock, I can take care of it right now."

Suhonen's 9mm Glock 26 was in a shoulder holster beneath his leather jacket, but he had no intention of lending it to his childhood friend. Developed specifically for concealed carry, the "baby" Glock packed power and accuracy into a small package.

Suhonen and Salmela had been friends since childhood. They had both grown up in Lahti, a town of about 100,000, an hour north of Helsinki. The two had belonged to a small youth gang that burglarized attics. When the gang was finally busted in action, Salmela was along, but Suhonen was at home with a raging fever. The best friends had ended up on opposite sides of the law, though their friendship hadn't ended. It had actually blossomed—Suhonen picked up street intel from Salmela, and in return, had helped his friend out of a few legal jams.

But Salmela was now in a steep downhill slide, not unlike many of the other former members of their youth gang. Their alternatives had been violent death, suicide or drinking themselves to death. Some romantic might think that a tough enough woman would be able to set her man straight, but that wasn't really true. Suhonen knew that the women in these circles were every bit the alcoholics the men were. A tough woman would just make the fights more vicious and inflate the risk of a violent end.

"You won't get *my* weapon," said Suhonen.

"Not fair."

In a tough situation, a firm approach was best. "If you shot yourself with my gun, how do you think I'd explain that to the NBI?"

Salmela's eyes met Suhonen's for the first time.

His eyes were bleary, but at least he wasn't terribly drunk.

"Guess you have a good point."

"Right." Suhonen chose not to ask questions, but waited for Salmela to make the first move. The man sure hadn't called him here to win pity with his suicide talk. Or at least Suhonen presumed so.

"Listen, Suhonen."

No response.

"You know my life has been going down the shitter for the last twenty years," Salmela continued.

Suhonen knew. His prison terms had destroyed his marriage. His son—a promising soccer player—had ended up a drug dealer and was shot to death in an apartment a half mile from where they now sat. During his most recent stretch in the brig, Salmela had gotten mixed up with the Skulls and took an iron pipe to the head. Not from the Skulls, but from someone else.

Suhonen thought about what to say. Expressing regret for the past was pointless, but Salmela shouldn't expect much from the future either. "What happened now?"

"How'd you guess?"

"Come on… I know you. What's there to whimper about in the past?"

A tear came to Salmela's eye. "A lot, actually."

"Well, I know," Suhonen eased off. "You're right about that."

"And you're right that there's nothing I can do about it," Salmela brushed the tear out of his eye and lit a cigarette. "Suhonen, our history…"

"Eero, don't bother…" said Suhonen unflinchingly. "Get to the point."

Salmela laughed. "That's what I've always liked

about you. Nip the bullshit in the bud. Good."

"So?"

"I need some money."

"How much?"

"Ten...actually twenty."

Suhonen looked pensively at Salmela. Under other circumstances, he would have fished out a twenty-euro note and handed it to Salmela as a joke. But he knew what the man had meant: ten or twenty grand.

"What happened?"

"You know I wouldn't have called unless I was in real trouble, given you're a cop and all. I'm in pretty deep shit."

"So?"

Salmela took a drag on his cigarette. "Actually, it started with this childish idea that I should get off this damn hamster wheel. I ran up some debt in prison and wanted to take care of it once and for all. So, with some help I managed to order a few pounds of speed from Tallinn."

Suhonen stared at Salmela, whose eyes were fixed on the table.

"I borrowed the money to pay for it, since I don't have any. The dope was supposed to arrive on last night's boat, but Narcotics busted the mule at the harbor."

Suhonen startled.

"So the whole job went to shit. Now, on top of the old debt, I owe another ten grand. And to some heavies, too."

"Who?"

"No, I can't..."

"I can't help if I don't know."

"That fat porker from the Skulls. You know Niko, right?"

Suhonen nodded. He knew Niko Andersson: a true prototype of a gangster. Tormented in school for being overweight, he was driven to crime, then prison and found brotherhood in a gang, where he got the admiration he so lacked. During long stakeout nights, Suhonen had often mused that many of these guys could have ended up in some radical religious sect, but in prison, the gangs were a more powerful influence.

"How much do you owe all together?"

"Well, the two grand from prison has ballooned to eight grand with interest, plus this ten grand. So eighteen grand all together."

Suhonen reflected. He had two grand in his bank account, but he could never raise the other sixteen.

"How'd the two grand turn into eight?"

Salmela chuckled. "Don't ask me about the math, but supposedly the interest keeps running up because I haven't been able to pay. I've got nothing to sell either. Social security pays for the flat and I'd barely get a hundred for this crap."

Suhonen surveyed the room. A hundred was wishful thinking.

"The old debt is for the Skulls. What's the new one for?"

"The Skulls too."

Not good, Suhonen thought. "Who organized the drug deal?"

Salmela looked up from the table. "Can't talk about it."

"Really?"

"A middle man. He promised to arrange the four pounds, but he wanted ten grand in advance. I scraped up some of it from a couple sources and Niko wrapped it all up. I don't know where it went wrong.

We were waiting for her last night and everything seemed fine, but the cops picked her up right in front of the terminal. Don't know much more. Obviously, Narcotics was tipped off."

"Had they been tipped off, they would've arrested her right away in the terminal. That's how it usually works, anyhow."

"Well, that could be, but it doesn't change the outcome."

Suhonen was glad that he and Toukola hadn't arrested her, but had stayed further back among the other travelers. "I can ask around in Narcotics. Won't do you much good now… But she had the whole four pounds?"

"Yeah. Apparently she's made the trip a few times before, too. Tapes the stuff to her sides and just walks off the boat. Simple but effective, they say. Not this time, though."

"Who was the middle man?"

"Some Estonian shithead. Niko knows him."

Suhonen mulled over Salmela's story. According to his friend, the mule should have had four pounds, but they only found twenty ounces on Marju Mägi. Had Salmela been swindled? What role did the Skulls and Niko play in the scheme?

"Well, let's think about it. I have an idea what we can do next, but I need to do some research first," said Suhonen.

Salmela nodded. "Okay."

Suhonen rose and began to clear the dirty dishes off the table. "This pad of yours is quite the dump. I'll just clean a little if you don't mind."

Salmela didn't say anything, just stubbed out his cigarette in the overflowing ashtray. A butt tumbled over the rim onto the table, but Salmela didn't bother to pick it up.

Suhonen opened the window, scraped everything off the table into a couple of yellow plastic bags and began to gather the dirty clothes from the floor into one bag, and the empty bottles and cans into another.

After a good hour, the dishes were washed, the floors swept and the apartment was almost in better shape than Suhonen's own.

He didn't pry any more about Niko or the Skulls. He'd have time to get back to that later.

CHAPTER 8
FRIDAY, 11:50 A.M.
SKULLS' COMPOUND, HELSINKI

The building, originally a two-story warehouse, was situated in an industrial area in north Helsinki. At some point, it had been used as a vehicle inspection office, but now the Skulls owned it. Located just five miles from downtown Helsinki, the former warehouse was still remote enough to serve as their headquarters.

The compound was on the left side of a cul-de-sac. A grove of birches stood behind the building, and further still was Beltway One. On the south end of the street was a filthy sports dome, where junior soccer star hopefuls practiced in the winter. Next to the dome were a few rusty shipping containers, and on the shoulder of the pot-holed street, giant sections of concrete tubing were scattered about. The Skulls' compound was about a hundred yards from the nearest building.

Tapani Larsson drove the BMW sports car through the open gate into the yard, and parked it next to a few cars. He recognized the gang's black Chevy, but the other vehicles were unfamiliar. Larsson had driven Sara from the suite to her apartment in Lauttasaari, where the Skull VP was bunking.

The yard was large enough to suit the needs of a vehicle inspection office. In the back was a test track where the engineers had tested car brakes.

The concrete building was encircled by a chain link fence that seemed too flimsy to Larsson.

He was happy that, rather than continuing to rent, the Skulls had bought the building last year. On paper, it was owned by a fronting company.

The logic was simple: If you own your house, you can't be evicted. They had rented the downstairs garages to a repair shop for some extra income. Larsson parked the Beamer in front of the door.

The downstairs door was locked and Larsson punched in the code—it was still the same. The door seemed flimsy as well, he thought, but maybe that was just because the doors he had seen in the last year and a half were considerably thicker.

Just inside was a former service desk, and directly opposite the entrance was a stairway leading upstairs. At one time, a door had stood there. The walls were white, as offices generally were, though these were much dirtier. Larsson noticed a few posters of various metal bands hanging on the walls. The floor was filthy, as though it hadn't been cleaned for years, and the stench of dust hung in the air.

Still nobody around. Larsson was getting pissed. They had talked about getting security cameras, but he hadn't seen a single one. Anybody could walk right in.

The narrow stairwell was painted black, except for the rough-sawn wainscoting. Photos of the wild parties held there decorated the walls.

The stairs led directly to the second floor. At the top was a pair of saloon doors.

Larsson pushed through the doors, one of which advertised its need for oil.

A bull-like thug looked up from his game of billiards. "Who are you?" he snorted, his broad, flat nose and wide nostrils flaring in unison with his eyes. In comparison to his short legs, his massive shoulders and torso seemed unwieldy.

"The devil himself," Larsson hissed. "You on guard duty?"

The man kept the cue in his hand. "Nobody's on duty in the daytime."

The stairs entered into the middle of a vast, dark room, which was furnished like a Wild West saloon, though the windows were covered with thick black cardboard.

Larsson was still standing at the top of the stairs. A bar opened up to the right, along with several tables, and in the corner sat a large flat-screen TV and an Xbox. The left side was more open: a pool table in the middle and behind it, a small, knee-high stage for bands. In the far left corner was a pinball machine. Larsson knew that the office, which he would soon reclaim, was behind the bar.

"Who are you?" Larsson demanded.

The man set his jaw before answering hesitantly, "Roge." This guy didn't look like someone he should mess with, he thought.

"Roge, huh. You here alone?"

A toilet flushed in the background and a smaller, goateed man stepped into the room from a door behind the pool table. "My turn?" he asked before noticing the visitor at the top of the stairs.

"Two of you here?" noted Larsson.

"You must be Tapani Larsson," the little guy said, advancing. He dried his hands on his jeans.

"And you?"

"Osku, hang-around member. Same as Roge here."

Osku offered his hand, but Larsson breezed past him into the room.

A huge man stepped out of the office behind the bar. "What the hell is…"

Niko Andersson spotted Larsson. "Larsson! The devil himself!"

He pounded over to Larsson and the men embraced, smacking one another on the back.

"Good to see a familiar face here," Larsson said.

"Yeah. Meet Roge and Osku. They've got potential."

Larsson shook their hands.

"Something to drink?" asked Roge, as he squeezed behind the bar.

"I'll take a water."

Roge glanced at the rows of bottles inside the glass-door fridge. "Sorry. No water. We got Pepsi. And diet."

"Sure." Larsson mumbled.

"Which?"

"Doesn't fucking matter."

Roge grabbed the first can he struck upon and hurried it over to Larsson.

"Notice anything?" Niko asked. "We fixed up some things."

"Looks pretty much the same to me."

"Osku, let's get some light in here!" Niko hollered.

Osku walked briskly to the end of the bar and snapped on a row of switches. The lights along the bar lit up in blue and red, and a spotlight illuminated the pictures on the walls.

Larsson nodded. "The downstairs is total shit, though."

"Still working on that," Niko admitted. "We're going to build a coat check down there as well as a guard station."

"A coat check? This some kind of speakeasy?"

Niko laughed. "No. But in case we ever need one, we'd have it. We could install a gun safe too, so we don't have any accidents. Heh-heh!"

"Be a damn church if guns are checked at the door," Larsson muttered.

"What?"

"Nothing."

The saloon doors creaked again, and a short-haired man stepped in. Sami Aronen, the Skulls' weapons expert, bellowed, "Larsson!" The men went through the same patting ritual.

Aronen was a few years older than Larsson. The size of his biceps and the lack of a beer belly showed he was in excellent shape. Close-shaved hair and three-days of stubble capped off his steely looks.

"Good to see you again," said Aronen.

"Same."

Niko and Aronen formed the gang's current nucleus, since half of the members were doing time. Larsson trusted both as much as he trusted anybody.

Aronen had been a member for a couple of years now. He had served in Afghanistan with the Finnish peace-keeping forces some years ago, but was discharged after punching a Swedish officer in a bar fight. When a sergeant hits a captain, he'll take the blame, regardless of the reason.

As luck would have it for Aronen, the Finnish forces were in Northern Afghanistan's ISAF-operation under Swedish command and the loud-mouthed captain happened to be the unit's judge advocate officer—Aronen never stood a chance. He was one of the few Skulls that had never been in prison. For the swing at the Swedish officer, he was fined and received a dishonorable discharge from the Finnish Army, where he had worked as a weapons specialist in several regiments.

Larsson drank his Pepsi straight from the can.

"Larsson, let's sit down," said Niko, gesturing toward the wooden tables in front of the bar. "I wasn't sure when you'd get here, so I asked the others to come over at half past twelve."

* * *

Suhonen was sitting in the same Customs control room at the West Harbor as he had on the previous night. The director of port security had arranged to replay the video of the previous evening's passengers. Then, the undercover cop had seen it live, now he could see it on tape.

Unlike in real life, video allowed him to pause, rewind and fast forward. The previous evening, the police had only been looking for a woman in a red coat, but another mule had also disembarked. Who? They had spotted Karjalainen, the junkie, but what about *after* Marju Mägi?

The director hadn't asked why Suhonen wanted to see the footage again. It had been enough that Suhonen had asked for it. They also had footage of the parking lot, which Suhonen and Toukola hadn't needed the night before. All of the footage was on a hard drive, so Suhonen could switch between cameras and zoom in on passengers.

The director had also shown Suhonen how to print the images. They could be emailed as well.

Before leaving the control room, the director had lamented the fact that facial recognition software wasn't fully functional yet. In the future, cameras would be able to identify people based on their facial structure. Facial metrics—the distance between one's eyes or between one's nose and ears, the length of one's chin measured from the bottom lip—were unique to each person. Every person with a driver's license or passport photograph, for example, would receive a unique facial ID. Computers would be able to match that ID to individuals captured on security camera footage. However, the director knew that the current systems still had a 25 percent failure rate, even under near-laboratory conditions

With corresponding legislation, the technology would be implemented in Finland. He had surmised that the legislation would be passed under the guise of counter-terrorism. If passengers could be positively identified before boarding, those deemed dangerous could be picked up then. It would be even better if the system were integrated with the police database.

That done, it was only a matter of determining who would be deemed dangerous, thought Suhonen. A history of nights in the drunk tank probably wouldn't qualify. At least the shipping lines would make that argument, since they'd lose their best customers.

The footage swirled on the screens. Karjalainen, the junkie, wobbled across the monitor and Suhonen printed off a screenshot. Same with Marju Mägi. The shot could be used as evidence in court, but Toukola probably wouldn't need it. A short while later, Suhonen watched as he and Toukola were trailing Mägi in the concourse. He tried to track Karjalainen outdoors, but the man had escaped the cameras. The outdoor wide-angle lens showed the cops escorting Mägi into the van.

Then Suhonen reviewed the footage of the remaining passengers in the gangway, but saw no familiar faces. Perhaps it would help if people were identified on screen, along with their criminal histories. Perhaps it would be nice if they integrated the software with people's movements based on their cell phone signals, as well as their credit card purchase histories. In principle, this was all fully possible.

Passenger traffic thinned out, then dried up completely. Suhonen hadn't noticed any suspicious passengers. On the other hand, Marju Mägi wouldn't have aroused any interest without the tip from Estonia.

Suhonen pondered the situation. His friend, Salmela, had directly implicated himself in a drug smuggling operation. The twenty ounces already found would earn him the same punishment as Mägi: about two and a half years. Salmela wouldn't survive another prison term—he barely seemed to be surviving on the outside.

Suhonen would have to pump Salmela for more details about his connections to the Skulls.

CHAPTER 9
FRIDAY, 12:30 P.M.
SKULLS' COMPOUND, HELSINKI

Eight men were seated in the main room of the Skulls' headquarters. Larsson sat on a tall stool next to the bar, the others around the tables. Larsson glanced at Aronen, who nodded.

"Except for Steiner, looks like everybody is here, so let's get started," Larsson said in a calm voice. "I've known many of you for a long time. A few faces are new to me, but I can say this: We're all brothers. If that weren't true, none of us would be here. If anyone feels otherwise, then now is the time to leave."

His bald, tattooed head glistening, the vice president scanned his throng of toughs. Nobody moved.

"There you have it. No hesitations, no sideward glances. That is how the Skulls operate. Each of us is an individual, but the individuals constitute one brotherhood. Trust is our cornerstone. Together, we are what we are."

He had mulled over this speech many nights in his cell. There, it had seemed perfect, but now he questioned whether it was too sentimental.

The men's eyes were riveted on Larsson. Good, at least nobody was laughing. If someone had even dared smile, Niko would have slammed the guy to the floor and put a boot through his teeth.

"This is not news to you, but I want to talk about it because it's important. Each of you is my brother. That means that even if my life is going to hell, I can still be happy about your successes. There is no envy amongst us."

Larsson held another pause then continued. "It means that no matter how hungry I am, you'll always get half my food. If someone needs money, I'll give half my own. If someone hits you, I'll hit him back— no questions asked. If someone steals from you, I'll beat the shithead to the ground. There is no right and wrong, only brotherhood. I am ready to die for any of you. And you should be ready to do the same."

"We have plenty of dead heroes, and there will be more. The S.W.A.T team shot Korpela just last year. Kahma and Jyrkkä suffered the same fate a few years earlier. They acted on our behalf without thinking of themselves and fearing nothing. Brotherhood always took precedence. They thought about us. Each of you must be ready for anything."

"Do you understand?" Larsson asked, nearly shouting.

They all nodded emphatically.

"Ready for anything. That's not an easy task. If you're in a situation, think about Korpela, Kahma and Jyrkkä. Korpela was taking care of the firm's business when a traitor ratted him out to the cops. He took one with him."

"Kahma and Jyrkkä were in the same boat. Prison or death were their alternatives. They weren't afraid of the decision. We must *honor* that."

Larsson couldn't take this any further, since he himself had been in the same situation a year and a half ago. A gun in his hand, he had stared down the barrel of a S.W.A.T officer's submachine gun. He could have raised his weapon and gone the way of Korpela, Kahma and Jyrkkä, but chose prison by dropping his piece. That was then. No longer would he be subdued.

"If one of us is locked up, we'll take care of his wife and children. If his family doesn't have money for rent, food or kids' hockey, we'll help. The brother in prison would do the same for you."

"There will be no lies among us. If you fuck up, take the responsibility, and don't pass it to a brother. We will not steal from each other. No empty promises—keep your word. If you have a dispute with a brother that can't be settled otherwise, bring it to me. Nobody will talk to the cops, under any circumstances."

"Any questions?" Larsson asked before continuing.

Nobody spoke. Larsson scanned from one man to the next, his gaze resting on each man long enough for them to feel it.

"If we stick to these principles, things will go well. Now for a few announcements," Larsson said in a more relaxed voice.

"Our president is doing life in Turku. If you happen to be going that way, make sure to drop by. From experience, I can tell you that the place is dull as hell. The inmates are pent up in tiny cells and friends are few and far between. But if you do go there, keep it clean—all conversations are recorded, and, of course, wind up with the pigs."

The audience sat silently, listening to Larsson's address.

"The same applies, of course, to all of our other brothers across the country. Niko has a list of who is locked up where. If you have nothing else to do, then you should hit the road and go see your brothers. You all know visitations have to be worked out with the Gestapo in advance. It's not a good idea to just show up and pound on the door of the brig."

Some tense chuckles rose from the crowd.

"I'll be meeting one-on-one with each of you in the coming week so we can discuss how I can help you in more detail, and how you can help the brotherhood. Be direct and honest with me about any possible problems."

Larsson's voice rose once again. "You are all my brothers and I've got your backs, just as you've got mine and every other brother's."

The speech ended and the men applauded.

* * *

Suhonen was sitting at his usual seat on the window sill in Takamäki's office at the VCU. The detective lieutenant was at his desk; Sergeant Joutsamo sat on the other side.

"Wasn't this case already transferred to Narcotics?" asked Joutsamo.

Suhonen had briefed them on the events of the last couple of days, except for his meeting with Salmela.

"Come on now," said Suhonen. "Our unit knows the Skulls best. We've been going at it with them for the past three years. You should know, of all people," he added.

Takamäki scowled at the undercover cop. Three years back, Joutsamo had shot and killed a Skull named Mika Kahma when the burly gangster had charged her. Takamäki had been there, too. In the same clash, a S.W.A.T. team sniper had dropped

Raimo Jyrkkä, one of the gang's leaders.

"Yes, I know them," Joutsamo said. "As we all do. Complete shitheads."

Neither Takamäki nor Suhonen had anything to add to that assessment.

"But," she continued, "As far as I'm concerned, we don't have the resources to go after them now. Unless we can let the routine cases slide, we just don't have enough personnel. I'd go after Larsson and his goons right now with a horse and a six-shooter, but I just have too much paperwork."

"I don't doubt that," Suhonen said.

"These aggravated assaults, rapes and so-called 'routine cases' are burying us. The cases are backed up so badly that some may never be solved, since we can't even tend to the basics."

"When is Kirsi due back?"

"Next week," Joutsamo replied. Police work paid little, but the vacations were long. This, in turn, hobbled the team's ability to strike quickly. Kirsi Kohonen, a veteran officer in Takamäki's group, had worked through the summer, delaying her month-long vacation until October. Now she was in Australia riding horses.

Suhonen was quiet. He had been the one to recommend the Australian adventure, having taken a several-month sabbatical there a few years ago. He had no qualms with Kohonen. People could do whatever they wanted on their vacations.

"Well, Kirsi will be back soon—that should help."

"But we don't have the resources to take on the Skulls unless Karila can shift our whole unit onto the case," Joutsamo continued.

Captain Karila was Takamäki's boss, the head of the VCU.

"If we're on the right track, he'll give us some slack," Takamäki remarked.

Suhonen cut in from the window sill. "Anna is right. This is a Narcotics case, at least in principle. But we have an opportunity to make it something bigger. Felony extortion is clearly within the VCU's mandate."

Joutsamo turned to look at him. "Do you have someone in the scope who's willing to testify against the Skulls for felony extortion?"

"Well," Suhonen backpedaled. "Not yet, but it's a possibility."

"I'd like to hear the whole story here," Joutsamo said, visibly irritated. "It's a little frustrating to discuss resource allocation here as an outsider when the facts are being withheld from me."

Takamäki turned back to Suhonen.

"Relax, Anna," said Suhonen, a strained calm in his voice. "You know how these gangster cases go. If we had an obvious crime, it'd be easy: Take down the suspect and wait for a confession."

"Quit the bullshit, Suhonen. I don't have time for it."

"Well, then why don't you go solve those train station beatings and let us have a conversation."

"OK, peace," Takamäki intervened. "I can't have two of my best cops bickering like this."

Joutsamo spoke up again. "We're not bickering—it's a matter of priorities. What do you want us to investigate? You have to resolve this, Kari. If you actually turn us loose on the Skulls, I'll promise to shoot half of them before they ever make it to court. In the meantime, I don't want to see a single stabbing, beating or back-seat rape case."

Suhonen thought it best to keep his mouth shut.

The VCU officer responsible for allocating cases across the various units appeared at the door. He was in his forties and wore a flannel shirt.

"Listen, Kari. I've got a seventy-eight-year-old woman, found dead. Based on the report, no crime suspected. She died at home, so just a routine cause-of-death investigation. I've been calling it out here in the hallway, but nobody seems interested. So what now? It's your unit's turn."

Takamäki looked at Joutsamo and Suhonen.

"Nobody interested?" Takamäki wondered. "Hell, I'll go myself."

The case officer raised his eyebrows.

"What, you don't think a detective lieutenant can handle a dead grandma case?"

Takamäki stood up and marched out. Suhonen and Joutsamo glanced at one another. From the hall, they could hear Takamäki asking him, "Where can I find a crime scene bag?"

* * *

The meeting at the Skulls' compound continued.

"Anyone have any issues?" Larsson asked, his eyes wandering over the crowd.

"Something your brothers can help with?"

Nobody answered. The VP's gaze stopped on Osku, the short one with a goatee.

"Osku? Problems?"

Osku's eyes darted over to Niko, who nodded.

"Well, not anymore. The brothers already stepped up."

"In what way?"

"Last Tuesday some guy tried to hit on my girl at the bar, so this morning, me, Niko and Roge dropped by to teach him a lesson in manners."

"What kind of lesson?" Larsson probed.

"A few hooks and kicks to remind him what he's allowed to do and what not," Osku said. Roge sniggered as if to affirm the story. "We busted the window of his car, too, just to make sure he doesn't forget. I think he learned his lesson."

Larsson nodded. "Okay, very good. That's exactly how we do it. We got your back...but in these types of situations we should think about the brotherhood, too."

"Uhh, how's that?" Osku asked.

"Good question," Larsson said without the slightest hint of condescension. "If something isn't clear, ask. There are no stupid questions. Creativity is important, too. What kind of car was it?"

"A red Alfa Romeo."

"Okay. In that case, a creative solution would've been to make the guy sign the title over to us. What do you think? Would've he signed the papers?"

Osku glanced at Roge. "Yeah, I think he would've. It didn't even cross my mind."

"Next time I'm sure it will. Anybody else have anything to report?"

One of the men spoke up. "I'm protecting an auto repair shop over there in Pitäjänmäki. They had a burglary a week ago. Typical breaking and entering. The place was ransacked and some money, cell phones and tools were stolen. The owner asked me to take care of it, and I suspected a couple of local junkies. So I paid them a visit, seized the goods and returned them to the owner."

"Good," Larsson said. "Builds customer loyalty— maybe he'll recommend us to his friends."

Nobody else had anything to report.

"Couple more things. One. From now on, we need a guard on duty during the day as well. Two. This place is a mess," he said, glancing at Aronen.

"Sami's making a guard-duty schedule and cleaning rotation. You can clean it yourself or get somebody trustworthy to do it for you. Questions?"

Nobody had any.

Larsson invited Aronen and Niko into his office. Some business was best conducted behind closed doors.

* * *

Suhonen had heaped his plate with macaroni casserole and salad from the police cafeteria. He found an empty table and sat down.

Hell, the undercover policeman thought. It was a tricky situation. His friend Salmela was tangled up in a dope smuggling operation that Suhonen should probably tell Narcotics about. On the other hand, that wouldn't help the ex-con turn over a new leaf. Salmela wouldn't be able to cope with the two-and-a-half year sentence—he would tie one end of his sheet to the bars and the other around his neck.

He sprinkled salt on the tasteless macaroni and squirted some ketchup on top.

Salmela was a link to the Skulls, but he'd never testify that one of the Skulls' key players had financed the drug shipment. That would earn him a spot in the protective custody ward, where he'd fare even worse.

Salmela needed money. His debt was somewhere in the range of fifteen to twenty thousand. The Helsinki police didn't have that kind of money for informants, but the Interior Ministry or the National

Bureau of Investigation might.

But twenty grand was a lot of money. They wouldn't cough that up for one amphetamine case. Salmela would need to offer something more, but did he have some other interesting chunk of intel? Probably not, Suhonen guessed.

Could he *obtain* intel that was worth that kind of money? Maybe. But the ministry and the NBI weren't the only ones willing to pay for intel. Insurance companies also paid for tips that led to the reacquisition of stolen property.

Suhonen chewed his food as he considered the alternatives. There weren't many.

* * *

The office behind the bar at the Skulls' compound was rectangular: Twelve feet long and about fifteen wide. Black cardboard covered the windows in this room as well. The furnishings were bare. In the middle of the room was a round dark-brown table, ringed by five black plastic chairs. Against the back wall was a worn hide-a-bed, and beside that, a lone bookshelf with a messy stack of magazines. The top issue was a rumpled *Playboy.*

Larsson sat down at the table. Next to a thermos was a stack of paper cups and a folded laptop.

In the corner rested a device that resembled an old minesweeper or a metal detector: a five-foot-long shaft joined to a disc the size of a frying pan. Aronen had swept the room for microphones just before Larsson's speech. He had also done it in the morning, but now checked the room again just to show Larsson that he was working hard.

He didn't find any microphones this time either,

not the police's, nor another gang's.

Aronen plopped down on the sofa and Niko seated himself at the table with Larsson.

"Coffee?" Niko asked. If his plastic chair had had arm rests, his fat backside wouldn't have fit into it.

Larsson shook his head.

"Something else?"

"No," he snapped impatiently. "Tell me about Roge and Osku. Are they trustworthy?"

Aronen deferred to "Dumbo," though he'd never use that name to Niko's face or there would be fisticuffs.

"Yes. I'll vouch for them," Niko said without hesitation.

"You better. What are their backgrounds?" Larsson continued to probe.

"Straight out of juvie. Assaults and theft."

"Drugs?"

"The usual stuff, but they're no junkies."

That seemed to satisfy Larsson. Niko was a simple man, but sometimes that came in handy. Larsson would have sensed it immediately had he been lying to protect his protégés.

"Where's Steiner?"

"Haven't seen him in a week," said Aronen from the sofa.

That didn't surprise Larsson. "On a bender?"

"Don't know—he hasn't been here."

The Skulls' rookies and prospects were at the compound daily for guard duty, but for Rolf Steiner that wasn't required. The white-haired man had been a member almost from the beginning, when the president had recruited him in the pen. Steiner had been in for felony drug trafficking, felony assault, and involuntary manslaughter. He had beaten a low-level pusher to death for pilfering drugs. Steiner had been charged with murder, but his shrewd lawyer had managed to reduce the charge to involuntary manslaughter, shaving years off of his sentence.

"You've tried to track him down?"

Aronen nodded.

"His phone is off. Not sure what he's up to, but he definitely knows you're out. Though I'm not sure if he remembers."

"Well, he'll get here when he gets here," Larsson said and shifted gears. "I hear the cops seized some drugs?"

Niko cleared his throat. "Yeah. Some Estonian bitch got nailed right off the boat."

"How much?"

"Twenty ounces."

"That's not so much."

"No," Niko looked relieved. "The other mule was on the same ship with three pounds. That one made it through."

"Who messed up?

"Don't know yet."

"Who's paying for the lost dope?"

"Now *that* I know," Niko smiled. "The guy who ordered the shipment thinks the cops got all four pounds. He'll pay us for the full load—even for the three pounds that made it, so we'll double dip. Best of all, he won't rat us out."

Larsson laughed. "That's good. What about the Turk?" He was referring to the pizza shop owner who had accused two Skulls of extortion, then let the police plant the secret camera that had put them behind bars.

"Haven't done anything yet. It'd be a little obvious to burn down the restaurant right after the ruling," Aronen said.

Larsson agreed. "But let's not forget it."

"Of course not."

"Every snitch will get what's coming—and hard," Larsson said and paused. His eyes roamed the room. "We need more manpower. Damn pigs have thinned out our ranks the last couple years."

"What do you mean?" asked Niko.

"We need to recruit more. First as prospects and then bring in the best ones. More of these Roges and Oskus."

Niko nodded. "I'll second that."

"How's our financial situation?" Larsson turned to Aronen.

"As far as I can tell, we're okay. Membership dues and interest are coming in as usual. Collections are steady and we're getting our share from other businesses like Gonzales'. Then there are these random dope deals," he said, gesturing toward Niko.

Larsson nodded his head. "Okay, I got a few ideas, but we'll get back to that. Aronen, can you get me twenty grand in cash? I need it tomorrow."

"Okay."

"A couple more things," Larsson continued, glancing about. "This place is fucking dirty. Somebody really has to start cleaning. Niko, will you take care of it?"

Niko looked confused for a second before realizing that Larsson wasn't asking him to actually clean. "Yeah, I'll make it happen."

"But don't put Roge or Osku on it. They should have some status," Larsson smiled. "Right now, housecleaning isn't for our newcomers."

"Okay."

"And those junkers in the yard have to go." The

old inspection stalls were being used by a car repair shop whose owner paid rent for the space and protection.

"Okay," said Niko. "I'll have a talk with him. The shop is a good way to recruit, by the way. One of the mechanics is already a prospect."

"Yeah, good to have them around, but I don't want those junkers out there. Have them get into some kind of custom detailing or something. Something showy. It fits our style," he said. "And one more thing. I want a headstone made up for the bar room, chiseled with the names of every member who's died on our behalf. It should be big enough to leave plenty of empty space."

"I'll take care of it," Niko said dutifully.

Larsson was satisfied. "And if Steiner shows up, tell him to come see me."

"Tell?" Aronen wanted to be sure.

Larsson's eyes narrowed. "Yes. Tell!'" he roared.

Annoyed, he opened the laptop, signaling that the meeting was over. When the men didn't immediately leave, he thundered again, "Get the fuck out!"

CHAPTER 10
FRIDAY, 3:00 P.M.
PASILA POLICE HEADQUARTERS, HELSINKI

Lieutenant Takamäki was sitting at his desk. Friday afternoon had lost its flair after Captain Karila had talked him into covering the weekend shift. Lieutenant Ariel Kafka had been hit with the flu and at least one lieutenant-level officer was required to be on duty.

The stale stench of death lingered in Takamäki's nostrils. Though he wasn't really sure whether the smell was real or imagined, he knew it would last for at least a day.

Nothing unusual had surfaced in the old woman's death. Seventy-eight years old, she had slipped in the shower and hit her head on the tile floor. Takamäki remembered investigating at least a dozen such deaths throughout his career.

The case was typical—the daughter had become worried when mom hadn't answered the phone, went to the home and found her dead.

Every year, about 1,500 of these kinds of cases occurred in Finland. If a person died anywhere other than the hospital, the police were required to investigate.

Takamäki was filling out the cause-of-death form. They had verified the woman's identity with her passport, which was found in the apartment. Her address, the spot where she was found, and the circumstances surrounding the death were routine. Takamäki determined that this was not a murder, suicide, disease or poisoning. The woman had simply died as the result of an accident. The medical examiner would determine the exact cause of death and provide the death certificate. There was no need to notify the family, since they had called the police in the first place.

Takamäki was re-reading his two-page report when Suhonen walked in. As he set down the papers, he reminded himself to read them later to ensure nothing in the text could cause undue pain for the family. Usually, the papers just ended up in the police archives, but relatives had the right to obtain a copy.

"Well?" Suhonen asked. "How did the case go?"

Takamäki shrugged. "Nothing a lieutenant can't handle."

Suhonen rubbed his nose. "A rare reek of death in here."

Takamäki ignored the barb. Detective lieutenants spent most of their time behind their desks.

"Did you have something you wanted to talk about?"

The undercover officer closed the door, indicating that he did. "I have an idea."

Takamäki could have retaliated for the barb, but settled for: "Let's hear it."

Suhonen sat on the window sill and asked if Takamäki had thought about Joutsamo's idea. "Should we bust some Skulls?"

Takamäki's expression conveyed the futility of the suggestion.

"Have you spoken with Narcotics?" he asked.

"Not yet…not even sure I want to."

"How come?"

"That would implicate Salmela." In the earlier meeting, after Joutsamo had left the room, Suhonen had told his lieutenant about Salmela's role in the drug deal.

"Pretty dangerous territory," Takamäki remarked. "Harboring a suspect…"

Suhonen interjected. "No. You don't understand."

"I'm not sure I want to."

Suhonen smirked. "Here's the idea. Four pounds of speed isn't enough to interest Narcotics. For us, though, it's an opportunity."

"Really?" Takamäki hesitated. "Opportunity for what?"

"To get inside the Skulls."

That wasn't enough to convince Takamäki, but at least he wanted to hear more.

"For starters, we have a crime that falls squarely in our court. We could build a case against Niko Andersson for felony extortion of Salmela," Suhonen explained. He had carefully chosen the legal terms in advance to better convince Takamäki. The lieutenant was listening.

"But we're not going to get Salmela to testify because that would implicate him for the drugs."

"Yes, but…" said Takamäki.

"But there's our opportunity."

"Opportunity for what?" the lieutenant repeated, still skeptical.

"If we could get Salmela onto the lower rungs of the gang, he could provide intel to bust the whole gang for something bigger. In the best case, we'd put them all behind bars."

An opportunity indeed, Takamäki thought. At

least it seemed to make sense. Obtaining intel from gangs was a perpetual challenge, and Takamäki wouldn't be the least bit bothered if the whole herd were locked up, even if only for a few years. There was one big "but" in Suhonen's scenario.

"Has Salmela agreed to this?"

"Haven't asked yet."

Takamäki rephrased his question. "Do you think he'll agree?"

"I doubt he has a choice. He's deep in debt and I think we can talk him into it."

Takamäki read between the lines. "How much would it cost us?"

"Probably close to twenty grand. If we could settle his debts and get him into a witness protection program somewhere in Europe, on a beach in Spain for example, then he might very well agree."

"Even if everything went according to your plan and we asked the prosecutor for a suspended sentence, it's still possible he'd get two plus years for the twenty ounces."

"He'll have to take that risk. If he gets an opportunity to get off the hamster wheel, there's a good chance he will."

Takamäki nodded approvingly. "You're right about one thing—it's an opportunity. But like Joutsamo said, we can't take this case on top of all the others. I'll call Captain Karila. Let's see what he says—right after you tell me how Salmela can infiltrate the Skulls."

"He already has—he worked with them on the drug shipment."

"Can't we just smoke them for the amphetamines?"

Suhonen shook his head. "Small potatoes. No

point in blowing this kind of opportunity for that. Of course, the drugs would be part of a larger case."

Takamäki took out his phone and dialed. Suhonen stayed to listen in. Takamäki didn't mention Salmela by name, nor the full details of the drug case. Initially, the captain seemed against it, but Takamäki was able to persuade him with the idea of an informant within the Skulls. Resources and money would pose a problem, however, so Karila directed him to speak with Skoog, the assistant chief of the Helsinki Police Department. Skoog would need to approve any project of this scale anyway, and he could also provide the VCU with a few temporary investigators to tend to routine cases.

Takamäki phoned Skoog immediately. They didn't go into details over the phone. Skoog wanted to meet the following day to discuss the case in person and Saturday worked well for him.

* * *

It was almost nine in the evening and the Corner Pub was packed—as usual for a Friday night. Salmela was sitting at the corner table with his friends Ear-Nurminen and Macho-Mertala when the bartender brought three pints of beer to the table. Even indoors, Salmela wore his leather jacket with the lambswool collar.

"It's on the house," said the whiskered barkeep. "Actually, it's on a certain gentleman."

"Who?" Salmela asked, immediately suspicious. This was the first time that Salmela, or anyone else for that matter, had received table service at the Corner Pub.

"Don't really know. He's on the phone...wants to

talk to you, Salmela. He's on hold...there on the wall behind the bar."

Salmela was puzzled. He had a cell phone. If somebody wanted to talk to him, why didn't they call his cell? And how did they know he was at the Corner Pub?

"Now," the bartender said, turning back to the bar.

Salmela guzzled what was left in his glass and took a fresh one with him. He wouldn't make the mistake of leaving an unattended beer in front of Ear-Nurminen and Macho-Mertala.

The barkeep weaved through the crowd and Salmela followed him behind the bar. "Over there by the door," he gestured. Salmela knew very well where the bar's landline was.

"Hello," Salmela said into the receiver. Through the din, he couldn't hear a thing. He set the beer on a shelf and jammed a finger in his free ear.

"Hello?" he repeated.

"Hey," said a man's voice. "What's up?"

The noise was loud enough that Salmela didn't recognize the caller immediately. "Niko?"

"Correct," the voice said coldly. "When you gonna pay up?"

"I don't have the money."

"That's what I thought. And that's why I paid for the beers."

"Thanks, man," Salmela said hesitantly.

A short silence on the other end. Salmela wasn't sure if Niko had hung up or if he just couldn't hear. "Sorry, I can't hear. Really loud over here," he said to be sure.

"Then tell them to shut up when I'm talking," Niko snarled. His dramatic pause hadn't gone over like he planned.

Salmela glanced at the packed bar. He wasn't about to start shouting at this mob. He strained to listen more closely.

"Okay, I think it's better now."

"I need the money."

"Right, right. Yeah, I'm trying everything," Salmela sputtered, realizing now why Niko had called the bar's landline—the call wouldn't show up on Salmela's cell phone record.

"Not enough."

"C'mon. Don't go jumping to conclusions," he said, glancing around nervously. Maybe he'd been led to the phone just so some heavy could see who to beat up.

Nobody seemed interested in Salmela, nor could anyone hear the conversation.

"Tomorrow morning at nine in front of the Olympic Stadium."

"Niko, I can't get it by then."

"Then just bring yourself," he said, and asked Salmela to repeat the time and place.

The call ended and Salmela emptied his beer with two gulps. Fuck.

The bartender shot him a stern look.

"Everything alright?"

"Yep," he answered calmly. "He bought us another round."

The bartender nodded and lined up three more mugs.

The speakers were blaring Finnish rock: *"You're a news rag in a restaurant, scattered and torn. A card deck in a locker room, wrinkled and worn."*

Precisely, thought Salmela as he gathered up the beers.

Larsson parked the Beamer in the parking lot of an apartment building in the Lauttasaari section of west Helsinki. He'd have to get another set of wheels—this one attracted too much attention.

The gangster boss had received a bullet proof vest and a 9mm Beretta 92FS from Aronen. The hefty gun was strapped under his arm, and with the bulky vest, Larsson's leather coat wouldn't zip up.

The white apartment buildings lay perpendicular to the road. Sara Lehto's apartment was in the one with the grocery store on the end.

Larsson opened the ground-level door with his key and bounded up to the second floor two stairs at a time.

He stopped in front of her door to listen for a moment. Just the TV. He opened the door.

"Hey," he said.

The lights were on but nobody answered.

"Hey," he said, louder, stepping into the living room.

Sara was curled up on the sofa in a pink top and tight shorts, watching TV. The room was sparsely furnished. When she noticed the movement, she startled. "Oh, hey."

The TV was playing the same *Rome* series she had watched back at the hotel. Larsson started to take off his jacket.

"This is really good. I just bought the second season on DVD."

This time it was Larsson's turn not to respond.

"Oh yeah," she went on. "We're out of milk. If you want some for your coffee in the morning, go get it from the store downstairs."

"Huh?"

"Out…of…milk," she said slowly.

Larsson shrugged his jacket back on without a word. If he didn't get his coffee in the morning, the day would go to hell. And coffee called for milk.

SATURDAY, OCTOBER 24

CHAPTER 11
SATURDAY, 8.50 A.M.
KAARTI POLICE STATION, HELSINKI

"I'm not so sure," said Skoog, the Assistant Chief of the Helsinki Police Department. Surly and graying, Skoog was sitting behind a desk piled with tall, orderly stacks of paper. The man worked long days, often weekends too.

Takamäki and Suhonen had explained the possibility of planting an informant inside the Skulls. Salmela hadn't been identified by name.

"What do you mean not so sure?" Suhonen said, irritated.

"It's a hell of a big operation just to ensure the informant's safety. You guys...er, we'd be in deep shit if it fails and the guy gets killed."

"Well, true," Takamäki conceded. In his time, Skoog had run some heavy cases. The chief knew what he was talking about.

"How much manpower can the VCU devote to this?"

"I don't know," Takamäki answered honestly.

"You should," the assistant chief said bluntly, "In the critical phase, I'd bet 24-hour surveillance alone will require over a dozen officers."

Suhonen raked his fingers through his black hair. "Is it really necessary to follow the informant 24-7?"

Skoog's cutting stare fell on Suhonen.

"In ops like this, yes it is. I've led a few of these in

my time."

Suhonen was beginning to regret having made such a big deal out of it. The case could have been handled much more simply, but then Salmela wouldn't be able to pay off his debts.

"But I'm glad you came to discuss it," Skoog said.

Great, Suhonen thought.

"So, what should we do?" asked Takamäki.

"An undercover operation of this scale falls under the NBI's purview," said Skoog. "I'll get in touch with them and set up a meeting for you guys. We'll see what they say. Until then, keep the case on ice."

"Got it," said Takamäki.

Skoog fixed his eyes on Suhonen. "That goes for you especially. No solos. If we're going to take advantage of this opportunity, let's do it right."

* * *

Salmela reached the Olympic Stadium right on time. There'd be no point in making excuses. He didn't have the money and was prepared to pay the price.

His head was pounding hard enough that whatever he had coming couldn't possibly make it worse. He remembered the beers at the corner table last night, but the trip home was a fog. Maybe his friends had walked him home. Luckily, he had remembered to set his alarm for eight in the morning. A cold shower had helped, but only as long as the water had run. It had rinsed the vomit off the shower floor, too.

Across the street from the Olympic Stadium was an Irish bar. Salmela had the fleeting impulse to grab a cold pint for his nerves. It would do him good, but the bar didn't open till nine—still a couple minutes away.

He lit a cigarette, which tasted terrible.

Salmela had flipped up his collar and pulled on a black wool cap. This afforded some protection from the biting wind, but inside, he was shivering.

The Skulls were ruthless, but even they wouldn't kill a laying hen. They'd just pluck it to make a point. That's what Salmela hoped, anyway. Just in case, he had left a letter addressed to Suhonen on the sofa, informing the officer of whom he had gone to meet, and why.

Salmela had considered calling him too, but were the cops to swarm the area, he would surely wind up dead, labeled as a rat.

The wind rattled the cords on the nearby flag poles, but otherwise it was quiet. A couple of young girls in parkas with backpacks slung over their shoulders walked by Salmela. Cars drifted lazily past. The city awakened slowly to Saturday morning.

Salmela paid no attention to the passersby. When his ride came, it would stop right in front of him.

* * *

Sami Aronen's stride was wide like a cowboy's—his muscled thighs made him walk slightly bow-legged. The weapons expert wore a pair of sharp-toed cowboy boots, black jeans and a frayed denim vest pulled over his leather jacket. But he bore no colors. Sometimes those garnered too much attention.

The Velodrome parking lot was quiet. Aronen had left Larsson's BMW at the corner of the cycling stadium and strode over to its wall to take a leak. He checked the time: 8:59 A.M. In one minute, Gonzales would still be on time—in two, he'd be late.

Aronen unzipped his pants and pissed on the wall. He wondered fleetingly how many walls he'd watered like this over the years. This was probably his first cycling stadium, so congratulations for that. So far, the only mosque had been in Afghanistan.

That damned gig. In the end, it had all gone to hell, but it didn't bother him anymore. In the peacekeeping forces, war was like a game. There, he never knew whether his comrades would sacrifice their lives for his. In the Skulls, every man would—without hesitation.

Aronen felt the pressure subside. A quick shake, a zip and he headed back to the car.

Nine on the dot. Aronen had just begun to grumble when a dark blue Volkswagen Golf swung into the parking lot.

He recognized Gonzales, who drove toward him, braked and stopped the car six feet off.

Aronen had always considered Gonzales to be a schemer, but what did that matter? These types existed all over the world, even in Afghanistan. And they always thrived, regardless of their country or form of government.

Gonzales left the engine running and rose from the car. The usual grin and quick lift of the sunglasses. It was his version of the military salute: hand to the temple. The men had known each other for years—before Afghanistan Aronen had moonlighted as a carpenter for Gonzales.

"How are things?" Gonzales asked.

"Alright," he said brusquely.

"Where's…" Gonzales managed to say before spotting the Beamer about ten yards off. "Oh, over there."

Aronen tossed him the keys. "Nice ride."

"Yeah. Larsson like it?"

Aronen nodded. "Little too showy, though."

Larsson had called Aronen at three A.M. and ordered him to switch cars first thing in the morning.

The early morning call hadn't bothered Aronen, since he hadn't been able to sleep anyway.

Gonzales laughed aloud. "Damn right it is—that's the point! But yeah, I get it... What's in the works now that Larsson's back?"

"Durus, iratus, crudelis," Aronen rattled off without a trace of a smile. The Skulls had done some research on the net to come up with their own "Olympic Motto" to counter the famous "citius, altius, fortius," or, "faster, higher, stronger." As expected, the Skulls' Latin grammar was sloppy, but it meant—or at least it was supposed to mean—tougher, angrier, crueler.

"Right, of course. Not surprised at all. That batch of speed..." he started before deciding to change the subject. "...well, this Golf is a little pokier than the Beamer, but she does OK: two-liter engine and a couple hundred horsies. Any problems or need service, just give me a call."

Aronen had to admit—he liked the way Gonzales operated. When the guy made a promise, he kept it. Of course, that worked both ways, too: if Gonzales was promised something, it was kept. To a T, not just in the ballpark. Aronen didn't even have to ask about the car's documents—they would be in order.

But the drug shipment hadn't gone so well, at least in part.

"Glad you brought up the dope. Pretty interesting that the mule got smoked right in the harbor. Know anything about that?" Aronen said.

"I heard about it, but that's all."

"Well, if you hear something, call."

"I'll try to keep me ears open."

"Don't try. Do it. Good news is the other batch turned out to be the good stuff—75 percent pure. We'll be able to cut it four, five times."

Gonzales smiled. "That's what the Russian promised... But, be sure to cut it before anyone uses it. I'll check on that leak... And there's an envelope in the front seat. Twenty grand, just like you asked."

"Good," Aronen nodded. He believed Gonzales, and certainly wouldn't touch the money. You never knew where it would end up or if fingerprints or DNA would be lifted from it.

"Anything else?" Gonzales grinned.

"Nope."

Gonzales took a couple steps toward the Beamer then turned. "I have another deal that should bring in a decent amount. I'll need some help from you guys, but we can talk about that in a couple weeks."

"Oh," Gonzales continued. "And I left a little present in the trunk."

* * *

Niko Andersson rolled down the window and barked at Salmela, "Get in."

The Skulls' matte black Chevy Nova had stopped in front of the Olympic Stadium. Salmela glanced around as though in a last ditch effort to look for help. None was there. He dragged himself to the car.

Roge, the bull, was driving, Niko rode shotgun and Osku was sitting in the back seat.

Andersson had to wrestle himself out of the two-door coupe and tilt the seat forward. Salmela squeezed past him into the back seat.

"Morning," Niko muttered as he sank back into the car.

Salmela didn't respond.

The Chevrolet puttered off westward along Helsinki Avenue.

"You got the money?" Niko asked without

looking back.

Salmela stayed quiet.

"Answer me when I ask you a question!"

"No."

"No what?" Niko sneered.

"No money…to pay my debt," Salmela said quietly.

"You've had plenty of time, and nothing to show for it."

"I tried."

"No excuses."

Salmela fell silent.

The coupe reached the intersection of Sture Street. They passed the Linnanmäki Amusement Park on the right and Roge drove down the hill under the train tracks.

"We've got a problem—and that problem is you," Niko remarked coolly.

* * *

Aronen parked the VW Golf in front of a gas station and glanced at the time: 9:30 A.M. He had some extra time, as Larsson was to be picked up at ten.

The gas tank was full, but a cup of coffee would do him some good. The Lauttasaari Shell was a familiar spot. Aronen remembered the old arcade bar, long gone now. On the far side of the fuel pumps was a stodgy convenience store with a few pedestal tables.

Inside, the ex-soldier poured himself a cup of coffee and paid the 1.50 euros. A young woman next to him was playing slots and the beeping grated on Aronen's ears. He went back to the counter and ordered a hot dog. It was ready in a minute.

Save for the woman at the slots, there were no

other customers. That was good. He wouldn't run into anyone he knew. Lying to his former army buddies about his new gig was tiring. Not that there was any shame in it, much to the contrary, but talking about the Skulls inevitably led to too many questions.

Aronen flipped through a newspaper left on the table, but couldn't focus.

His phone rang. The caller's number was unidentified.

"Yeah?" he growled into the receiver.

"Sami Aronen?" asked a woman's voice.

He didn't recognize the caller. "Who are you?"

A short silence on the other end. "Don't hang up, just listen for a bit. I'm a reporter named Sanna Römpötti and I'd like to chat with you."

Aronen thought for a second. He could've hung up, but curiosity got the better of him—at least for the moment.

"Where'd you get this number?"

"From a police interview transcript. You were a suspect in a pizza shop extortion case and the police had this number in the file."

Alright, fair enough, Aronen thought. Maybe it was careless to keep the same number for so long, but on the other hand, he never used this line for business. "What do you want?"

"Well, since you're the acting boss, at least on the outside, I thought maybe we could talk. So the cops won't have all the say," she said. Römpötti had formulated her strategy in advance. This was probably the only way to get the gangster to talk.

"What kind of story you doing?" Aronen asked. He didn't want to let anything slip about the gang, not even to correct her error about who was leading it. She had done her homework, but apparently didn't know about Larsson's release.

"I'm interested in your organization in general, particularly in how you've ended up at odds with the Helsinki police. It's surprising to me that the police consider you a criminal organization when, at least in the pizza shop case, the court ruled otherwise."

"Uh-huh."

"Will you promise to think about it?"

"Can't promise anything, but I'll get back to you."

"When?"

"After I've thought about it."

"Okay," she said. "I'll text you my number."

The call ended and Aronen turned back to his coffee and hot dog, both now tepid. The woman was still at the slots, and had definitely been listening to the conversation. Whatever. He hadn't said anything suspicious.

His phone alerted him to an incoming text. Aronen hesitated then saved it to his contact list.

CHAPTER 12
SATURDAY, 10:00 A.M.
NBI HEADQUARTERS, VANTAA

The air conditioner was humming quietly. "Think the room is bugged?" Suhonen wondered.

Takamäki grinned and sipped his coffee.

"Wouldn't surprise me at all," Suhonen continued.

The lieutenant wasn't sure if Suhonen was serious or not.

The two men were seated in a clean, blue-themed conference room at the headquarters of the National Bureau of Investigation in suburban Helsinki. Whereas the Helsinki police used flip charts and grungy white boards, the NBI used smart boards and overhead projectors.

The table had space for sixteen. There were no windows to offer a view, but several large dragon trees sat in the corner. The plants were healthy enough that somebody other than an NBI agent had to be watering them. A silver thermos and paper cups rested on the table.

Suhonen was surprised at how much the room resembled the conference room at the Estonian Central Police headquarters.

The meeting had been set for ten o'clock. They had driven here directly from Assistant Chief Skoog's office. Lieutenant Jaakko Nykänen, the head of intelligence for the NBI, had met the men in the lobby and escorted them upstairs. The stout, walrus-whiskered Nykänen was a familiar face. Before transferring to the NBI, he had worked for Takamäki in the Helsinki VCU, though that had been many years ago.

"What do you think?" Suhonen asked, sipping his coffee.

"Tough to say. It'll probably depend on their caseload."

Nykänen came back into the room along with another agent. Each was wearing a gray suit, white shirt and blue tie. The second man, Jouko Aalto, stood just under six feet tall, and had a lean face and neatly trimmed hair. Takamäki had on a blazer and polo shirt, and Suhonen, his trademark leather jacket. His black hair was pulled back in a ponytail.

"Sorry it took a while," Nykänen rasped. About ten years ago, he had lost part of his voice box after being shot in the throat on a VCU raid.

"Is that your uniform here?" Suhonen asked, pointing to the pair's identical outfits.

Nykänen smirked. "Coincidence. Do you know Jouko?"

Takamäki nodded. He had met Jouko Aalto previously, but the man was a stranger to Suhonen.

Nykänen gestured toward Aalto and explained that he was in charge of coordinating the NBI's undercover operations, a part of the intelligence group.

The NBI men took their seats and poured themselves a cup of coffee.

"So, you had a project proposal?" Aalto began in a dry voice. His lips barely moved and his expression was rigid. "Typically, these initiatives would get channeled through the supervisory branches of the police departments to the PCB-committee, where such matters are resolved…"

Aalto rattled off a synopsis of multilateral work between Police, Customs and Border officials, collectively known as PCB. Suhonen was sure his eyelids would start to sag if this Aalto droned on with his bureaucrat-speak any longer.

"We're familiar with PCB," Takamäki interjected.

"Oh, good," the man said, disappointed. "Then I'm sure you know the numbers, too. There are about 1,100 members in 80 different criminal organizations, of which 40 fulfill the organized crime criteria set out by the EU. Annually, about 550 gang members, or half, have a run-in with the police."

"I guess we'll have to improve that," Suhonen remarked dryly.

Aalto continued, his expression unchanged, "My group has undertaken fifteen new investigations this year. Plus, we still have a good thirty open cases."

"Can we get to the point," Suhonen cut in. "Numbers are really interesting, but…"

Aalto shot Suhonen an icy glare. "I only tell you this so you understand that we never say 'no' without a good reason. Most often, we can't just take on new initiatives. We simply don't have enough manpower for them all."

"So, about your case," Nykänen intervened. "Give us the short version."

Takamäki took five minutes to outline the situation once more, but again left out Salmela's name.

Suhonen capped off the summary. "Basically, we have an opportunity to plant an informant close to the Skulls."

"How close?" Aalto asked. "I doubt he'll have any

"substantial rank."

"No," said Suhonen. "He's not in the inner circle, but close."

"What's the end game here, best case and worst case?"

Suhonen glanced at Takamäki then fielded it himself. "I'm not sure I understand. The end game is to put the bad guys in prison."

"Let me paint you another picture here," Aalto said gently. "Recall the Turku bank robbery in '07 and the attempted robbery of an armored truck in Salo. We worked on them for nearly a year and obtained prison sentences of more than 60 years. What are we looking at in this case?"

"Hopefully all of them in the penalty box for long enough that they lose their grip on the streets. And nail the money-men behind the scenes."

"And if that doesn't happen?"

"Maybe two or three guys behind bars for a couple years on drug charges."

Aalto nodded. "There's our best and worst case. Good."

Nykänen spoke up. "This informant. What's his background and what kind of risks are we talking about? And I should probably clarify that I'm not dumb. The intention here is just to make sure we're on the same page."

Takamäki bit his tongue, though Nykänen certainly remembered his second most important maxim: There are no dumb questions. The first was: Never assume.

"The informant is a career criminal who's ended up in deep debt," Takamäki explained. "He participated in a recent drug-trafficking job with the Skulls, but wants out of the game. There's our opportunity. Of course, for his own safety we'll have to bust him for the drugs, which will mean a few years in prison."

Takamäki's eyes wandered from Nykänen to Aalto. He could see the impact of his words as the scope of the opportunity dawned on the agents.

Takamäki went on, "If this informant were discovered, it's almost inevitable he'd be killed."

"So in that instance, our best case can be increased. We'd get at least a couple life sentences," said Suhonen gravely.

* * *

The silence of the forest was broken only by the sporadic curses of four men, which burst forth every time a bent branch snapped back at the next man's face. Osku took up the lead. Following him, in order, were Salmela, Niko and Roge.

The twenty-five mile car trip northeast from Helsinki to the forest in Nuuksio had been couched in silence. A few hundred yards back, the Chevy sat parked at the dead-end of a dirt road, where a trail cut into the woods. The soft floor of the heath forest was waterlogged and soaked through the trekkers' shoes.

Niko Andersson remembered having gone to the same national park some fifteen years ago. Then in grade school, his mom had made him join the scouts, but it had only lasted one fall before a fight got him kicked out. The "fat kid" had fought with the troop leader after having been ordered to wash the dishes. Even then, Niko was very large for his age, and not inclined to obey orders he deemed frivolous.

The trail led them to a rocky expanse, which rose gently up the surrounding hillside. Here, the spruces gave way to pines. In the open, the wind was cutting.

The goateed Osku, wearing a wool beanie cap, glanced back.

"Another hundred yards," Niko panted.

The foursome dodged the watery furrows carved out by ice age glaciers. The pines began to thin out.

The summit of the cliff overlooked a majestic valley, blanketed with spruces, but Salmela's gaze was directed at the rocky ground. Niko continued to the precipice, where the cliff dropped about 100 feet into a deep gorge.

"Beautiful view," he said quietly, digging a 22-caliber pistol from the side pocket of his cargo pants.

The bull-faced Roge smirked, seized Salmela by the back of his jacket and shoved him towards the edge. Holding on tight, he jerked Salmela back. "Whoa! Don't fall."

Salmela didn't utter a sound.

"Open your mouth," Niko commanded.

His lips remained sealed.

"Open your mouth!"

Salmela sank to his knees and opened up. Niko shoved the pistol into his mouth. Salmela was trembling, the barrel clattering against his teeth.

"You understand, of course, that debts have to be paid," Niko said.

Salmela tried to say something, but the barrel of the gun reduced his words to senseless blubbering, like answering a dentist's questions with a drill in your mouth. Roge and Osku remained unfazed as they watched the scene unfold.

"We can't afford to let these things slide. What would we do if nobody paid their debts? You understand, of course."

Salmela looked pale, but tried nodding his head carefully.

"Understand?" He repeated, thrusting the gun barrel downward toward Salmela's chin, then back up. Roge and Osku were laughing.

Niko wished he could get a snapshot of the occasion. A damn fine picture with a gorgeous backdrop. He in the middle, deciding between life and death like…God.

He could go around showing the picture to all the damned clowns who had pushed him down over the years.

The taste of blood filled Salmela's mouth when the gun barrel split his lip.

CHAPTER 13
SATURDAY, 10:05 A.M.
LAUTTASAARI, HELSINKI

Aronen was sitting in the VW Golf in front of Larsson's apartment building. His boss was late, but he didn't care. In the army, he had gotten used to waiting, and he wasn't in a hurry anyway.

On the other side of the street, a dad in a green jacket was putting a hockey bag in the trunk for his son, who was only carrying his stick. Aronen recalled how, as a kid, he had always carried his own bag.

Suddenly he remembered Gonzales' comment about a present in the trunk. He stepped out of the car and circled to the rear. The wind had stripped the leaves and dead twigs off the birches in the yard. The ex-soldier scanned his surroundings with a trained eye. A father in a baseball cap and his toddler were busy at a nearby playground. The dad was feverishly building sand castles, and the tot was close behind, smashing them. That kind of life didn't interest him.

A few others were around, but they ignored him. Aronen opened the trunk to see a yellow blanket. Something was clearly wrapped up in it. He started to unravel the blanket, keeping it inside the trunk.

Footsteps approached from behind: Aronen turned to see Larsson approaching.

"That's a better ride," Larsson remarked, his black beanie cap pulled down over his eyebrows.

"Yeah," Aronen said as he unwrapped the last few folds.

"What you got there?"

"A present from Gonzales." Aronen shifted to the side enough that Larsson got a glimpse of an oily AK-47.

Beside the rifle were about ten small brown boxes of ammo, each holding 30 rounds. The text on the boxes was Russian.

"Nice," said Larsson. "You thank him?"

Aronen wrapped the blanket around the weapon. "No. I didn't see it till now."

He slammed the trunk and Larsson walked around to the passenger side. By the time Aronen made it to the driver side door, Larsson was already in his seat.

"To the compound?"

Larsson nodded.

"Gonzales' money is in the glove box," Aronen said.

Larsson snatched it out and immediately counted it.

Aronen remembered something else. "Oh yeah. Some lady reporter called. Wants to interview us…"

Larsson interrupted. "Really? Interesting. How's she know you?"

* * *

Niko Andersson's stance was wide, but he began to hesitate. The gun was still in Salmela's mouth and Niko continued with his taunting. Roge and Osku stood near Salmela, but safely away from the edge.

Salmela's cell phone jingled in his jacket pocket. Already having accepted his fate, he made no move to answer.

"Goddamn," Niko said and jerked the gun from

between his victim's teeth. He laughed, "Go ahead answer it, then. Dead man's last words."

Salmela didn't smile, just pulled his phone from his pocket. The caller was unlisted.

"Hello."

"Bad time?" Suhonen asked. Salmela recognized his voice immediately.

"How should I put this…kind of," said Salmela, glancing at the gangsters standing around him with the rugged tree-covered fells in the background.

"We should meet."

"Call me later. We'll see if I can make it."

He hung up and slipped the phone back into his pocket.

Niko bobbed his head. "Hmm. Yup. Nicely done. Nicely done."

"What's nice about it?" Roge asked.

"Maybe this Salmela's not such a bad guy."

Osku looked at Niko, dumbfounded. Only a moment ago, the big guy had been ready to shoot the man he was now praising. "Uh… That so?"

"Think about it. I'm about to put a slug in his head and his phone rings. I'm thinking—just out of curiosity—let's let him answer. And *goddamn* if he doesn't keep his mouth shut. Most would've bawled into the phone begging for help, but Salmela just tells 'em to call back. 'We'll see if I can make it…' Fuck. That takes balls…"

"Yeah," said Roge.

"Maybe I'll let you live," Niko said and shoved the gun back in his pocket.

Salmela didn't say anything, just flexed his jaw. The gun barrel had left his mouth numb.

"Who called?" Niko asked.

"Just a friend." Salmela realized his teeth were chattering and he felt weak.

Suddenly, he doubled over and threw up. He didn't have time to turn away, nor did Niko have time to move. The vomit splattered onto the fat man's boots.

Niko took a step back, but stumbled over a pine stump. He had already lost his balance and was reeling toward the cliff when Roge caught him and heaved his enormous body to safety.

Niko exhaled hotly, thanked Roge and turned back to Salmela, who was still on his knees.

"Damn son-of-a-bitch. I'd kill you if I hadn't just decided not to. Shit!"

He wiped the mess off his boots on a bush, then burst into laughter. "Yeah, we'll come up with something for you—I got an idea."

The threesome marched back down the trail. Salmela stumbled along behind them, not wanting to be left in the woods alone. He wiped his mouth and spit blood into the thicket on the side of the trail. He was thankful he had puked—had his fear come out the other end, he most certainly wouldn't be allowed to get back in the car.

* * *

Takamäki was sitting in the passenger seat as Suhonen drove past the massive box stores and shopping malls along Beltway Three. The pair was en route from NBI headquarters to their own in Pasila.

Clouds skirted across the sky and the trees tossed in the wind.

"Salmela had no time to talk, huh?" asked Takamäki.

"Nope. Told me to call back later. Sounded a little nervous. Who knows what he's got going on."

Aalto and Nykänen of the NBI were considering

the proposal to initiate a full-scale undercover operation. Since the decision involved a change in resource allocation, they had needed some time to think about it.

"We've wasted an entire morning in these meetings," Suhonen complained. "And we're none the wiser."

"Well, at least they had *some* value. I've sat in on a few management meetings. Now *there's* something. A giant meeting just to discuss park safety and…"

Takamäki's sentence was cut short when Suhonen's phone rang.

He glanced at the display—an unfamiliar number.

"Yeah," he answered.

"It's Juha. Hi."

Suhonen recognized Juha Saarnikangas' voice, but it sounded strained. The former drug addict had provided a gold mine of leads over the years.

"How are things?"

"Terrible."

"Huh?"

"Shit. You remember Vesa Karjalainen? The junkie?"

"Yeah," said Suhonen. Karjalainen had been on the same ship from Estonia as Marju Mägi, Salmela's mule. Suhonen was intending to go see Karjalainen when he had a chance. "What about him?"

"Fuck," Saarnikangas said.

Suhonen could tell from the background noise that Saarnikangas was walking. A female voice was making an announcement. "You at the train station?"

"Yes. Listen. Karjalainen is lying dead on the bathroom floor of the Restaurant Eliel here. I was supposed to meet him at the bar here this morning."

Suhonen wondered for a moment why Saarnikangas would meet Karjalainen, but he let him continue. The car merged onto the freeway.

"He showed up a half hour late, but I was in no hurry. I was just having some coffee," he explained. "So he comes to the table and I can see right away that he's high as a kite. Can't sit still. He's complaining that he's hot and he feels like shit. Then he takes off to the bathroom. I stay and wait at the table and fifteen minutes later I go to check on what's taking so long. Hell, if I hadn't gone, I would've been waiting a damn long time. He was lying dead in the stall. Obvious OD."

"You call an ambulance?" Suhonen asked, glancing at Takamäki who was listening in.

"Of course, but I didn't give out my name. I just wanted to tell you that I didn't have anything to do with it. There are shitloads of security cameras at the train station, so I'm sure I'm on tape. It was completely his own fault. I had nothing to do with it."

"OK." Suhonen tried to calm him down. "I'm glad you called. Can I get hold of you at this number?"

"Yeah, at least this week."

"You know what he's been up to lately?" Suhonen asked. He intentionally left out the bit about Karjalainen having been spotted leaving the same ship as Salmela's mule.

"I dunno."

"Why'd you guys meet?"

"Uhh," Juha stalled. "He owed me some money and promised to pay up this morning."

Suhonen wasn't sure whether Saarnikangas was telling the truth.

"What kind of dope was he on?"

"Speed. Not sure if he took anything else. The jitters definitely pointed to speed."

"Is there any unusually strong stuff on the streets right now?" Suhonen wondered. An experienced user wouldn't screw up a dose. Most often, deaths from amphetamines were due to overdose, but sometimes they were caused by contaminants.

"Not sure. It's certainly possible, but his heart could've just given out too."

"I'll call you," Suhonen said and hung up the phone. He updated Takamäki on the conversation and mentioned that the lab should run a comparative analysis between the drugs found on Karjalainen and those found on Marju Mägi.

CHAPTER 14
SATURDAY, 10:50 A.M.
SKULLS' COMPOUND, HELSINKI

Aronen parked the blue VW Golf in the yard of the Skulls' headquarters.

"Sami, we need a couple things for the yard," said Larsson. "A proper fence and barriers that'll keep out the pigs even if they roll up in tanks. Same with the front gate."

"Okay," said Aronen.

"You've got the expertise from the Afghan bases, so draw up some plans and pay some firm to do it. They can take care of the bureaucracy if we need permits."

Aronen gazed at the sky and thought aloud, "If we barricade the yard, they'll just come from above in choppers."

"How do you deal with that?"

"The building has a flat roof. Missiles are probably out of the question, but we could put fireproof platforms on every corner topped with piles of tires. Then if we need to, just light 'em up for a smoke screen. And if we could get them from somewhere, we can put a few landmines on the roof. Also, I think we'll need to do something to those windows so they can't shoot tear gas inside."

"In other words?" Larsson asked.

"Strong steel mesh on the outside and replace the windows with bulletproof glass."

"Do it."

Larsson walked to the front door. "And something has to be done about this."

Aronen, the AK-47 swaddled in his arms, looked at Larsson, wondering what the boss had in mind. Preparing for a damn war? At some point, the cops would borrow a few Leopard tanks from the army, slap some "POLICE" stickers on them, and plow through. In that case, they'd need some of those new shoulder-fired anti-tank missiles, which could be fired from inside a building without scorching the room.

"Yeah, we'll reinforce it," he responded nonetheless.

With some dynamite and shotgun shells, they could easily build some IEDs, but the anti-tank missiles would be virtually impossible to obtain. If Larsson's intent was to launch a full-scale urban war against the police, it would be absurd for the whole gang to be holed up in one building. Maybe Larsson just wanted to flex his muscles.

With the AK-47 in his hand, Aronen followed Larsson into the building and they headed up the stairs. Aronen was already counting in his mind how many sandbags they'd need. At least a stack for every window, but that wouldn't look so good. Maybe they could stash them someplace where they could easily be pulled out when needed.

They nodded to the rookie on guard, who had cut his pinball game short when the pair walked in. The men proceeded to the back room and Aronen locked the assault rifle in a metal cabinet.

"So where'd the AK-47 come from?" he thought aloud.

Larsson stared at him, "Ask Gonzales."

Yeah, of course, Aronen thought. He grabbed a

beer from the fridge and offered one to Larsson, who shook his head. Aronen sat down on the sofa, Larsson at the round table in front of his laptop.

"You know everything you do on the computer can be tracked," Larsson remarked. "Everything."

Aronen nodded. Larsson's eyes were fixed on the screen as he tapped on the keys. Aronen had read some article in the newspaper about computer security, but his knowledge of computers was limited to word processing, email and the internet. He wanted to ask what they should do about the reporter, but Larsson would tell him sooner or later.

"Did you know that the pigs use mostly WIFI in their audio surveillance these days?"

Larsson didn't expect an answer this time either. Aronen put the unopened beer back in the fridge. It wasn't even 11 o'clock yet—maybe he could make it to the gym. He got up and decided to scan the building for listening devices first.

Suddenly, a booming voice from the bar startled the men, "Larsson! Dammit! Come outta your mouse hole!"

* * *

Joutsamo was sitting in her chair when Suhonen stepped into the shared office area.

"Well?" she snapped. Lieutenant Kafka had spread the flu to his detectives, so Takamäki had ended up asking his own team to cover. He had promised a long respite for the following week.

"Nothing. Meetings, meetings, meetings and lots of 'let's think about it'—just like the Stockholm PD," Suhonen grumbled.

"Kulta went to check out the bathroom at the train station," Joutsamo said.

"Good."

Suhonen sat briefly at his corner desk, booted up his computer, and stood up again.

"Half day today?" Joutsamo hollered as Suhonen stepped out of the room.

"Coffee or tea?" he turned to ask.

"Neither," she said, and continued to scrutinize her interrogation transcript.

A minute later, Suhonen returned with a steaming cup of coffee. "Little coffee break," he said, but Joutsamo couldn't hear through her headphones.

Suhonen settled in front of the computer and pulled up the information on the deceased Karjalainen. His last known address was in South Haaga. Suhonen knew the apartment building, located behind the Central Fire Station.

He picked up his desk phone and dialed Mikko Kulta, who told him they had indeed found Karjalainen in the lavatory, and that he appeared to have died of an overdose. Nothing indicated foul play.

"Did he have anything on him?"

"Didn't find any drugs. An empty needle, though."

"What about money?"

"Just an empty wallet."

"Okay. Bring everything here."

"Wasn't planning on putting them in the garbage," Kulta said.

Suhonen's thoughts turned to Juha Saarnikangas. The man had said that Karjalainen owed him some money, but none was found. Maybe Juha had raided the wallet when he found the body. Any drugs would have obviously gone the same route.

* * *

Niko killed the Chevy in the side yard of the Skulls'
Compound. The four men got out of the car as a
rusty, beige '80s Opel Cadet was being pushed into
one of the downstairs garage stalls. Salmela had once
owned the same car and he glanced at the plates:
AFR. The letters matched, but the numbers didn't.

Niko walked in front, and behind him was
Salmela, sandwiched between Roge and Osku.

"Well, Salmela, welcome to our offices," Niko
said in a pompous tone.

Salmela didn't expect anyone to offer him a beer
or challenge him to a game of pool.

"Things went so well out in the woods today that I
have a plan to settle your debt."

Salmela watched the animated Niko with vacant
eyes.

"You owe about twenty Gs, so if I pay you, say,
two grand a month, then you'll be paid up in ten
months... No wait, two grand is too much," he
mumbled to himself. "Fifteen hundred, so let's say in
one year we're all square."

"What do I gotta do?"

"You'll clean this place every morning. Vacuum,
dust, pick up the empty bottles and butts, wash the
toilet and all that." Larsson had told him to get a
capable guy to take care of the housekeeping. During
their episode in the forest, Salmela had demonstrated
his trustworthiness.

"I see," Salmela managed. "A year?"

Niko's expression was rigid. "That a problem?"

"No..."

"But you can take comfort in the fact that the pay
is completely tax-free," Niko sneered. "So get to
work. The cleaning supplies are over there in the

corner closet by the bar. If you run out of something or need anything else, feel free to bring it yourself tomorrow."

Salmela's eyes scoured the dim room for the closet.

"Don't touch the windows," Niko said, pointing to the cardboard-covered frames.

Roge chimed in. "But make sure to clean the glass on the pinball machine."

"And one more thing," Niko said. "What happens in here, stays in here. It's a short trip back to that cliff."

* * *

A lanky blond man was sitting on the sofa in the back room, chuckling as Larsson spoke. Rolf Steiner had showed up on his own time.

"You got a problem?" Larsson cut in from the table. Aronen sat further back, observing. The weapons expert was wearing a tank top, and one of his shoulders was tattooed with an arrow pattern in the form of bear claws.

"Yeah," Steiner shot back. "Your bullshit."

"Huh?"

"Just listen to yourself," said Steiner. A long-sleeved Metallica shirt and dirty jeans hung from his lean frame. "None of us have ever talked about branding before. Fuck. What is this, some kind of ad agency?"

Larsson rubbed his bald head. Steiner was a simple guy, but Larsson needed him to buy into the new program.

"Brand is just a word. Hell, forget it. You tell me how to revive this gang."

"Simple. More toughs out of the pen."

153

Larsson nodded. "I agree. But how are we gonna do that? There's about a half-dozen other gangs in there trying to recruit the same guys."

"Let's work out an NHL-style draft with the other gangs."

"What are you talking about?"

"Look. Every gang will get their turn to pick one eighteen-year-old. The weakest group goes first and so on."

Larsson wondered what Steiner had been smoking this time. "Uh-huh," he managed.

Steiner peered over at him with his squinty eyes. "I think you spent too much time in your cell. Read too many damn books."

"Any time in a cell is too much time," Larsson said. Steiner was right, though. Larsson's strategy was simple. Most people had some knowledge of the Skulls, and the more they were feared, the better. That way, recruits would perceive them as a more attractive option.

The Skulls didn't have a problem with name recognition, they were well known. But the quality of their product, at least in Larsson's opinion, was mediocre at best. They had to become more professional. And what about their image? The Skulls were associated with violence, but more so through prison sentences than by being successful at what they did. Larsson wanted to give recruits the impression that this gang was successful, and joining would mean money and power.

"So tell me, why don't we have recruits lining up at the door?" Larsson asked.

"Because we're too boring," Steiner said. "When's the last time we had a bash here—where we invited candidates and prospects? We had one last summer, but it's been pretty quiet since. No? And

154

next time we better have a living buffet."

In a living buffet, a naked woman lies on the table covered in whipped cream and fruit, which the guests get to eat—with the bulk of the goodies piled on her breasts and bikini area.

Larsson was in agreement and Aronen nodded too. "So how come you're in this gang, then?"

Steiner's jaw muscles rippled. "We got a problem?"

"No. I just want to know."

The question was difficult for Steiner and he took a moment.

"It's not because it's fun. Anyone afraid of prison doesn't belong here. We get money, and of course, trust is the most important thing. I have to be able to trust every man here. No betrayals. That's what it's all about. Respect."

Now it was Larsson's turn to laugh. "So that's our brand."

Steiner lunged to his feet and a stiletto appeared in his hand. "You wanna go?" he snarled. He looked serious.

Aronen crept up from the side and kicked the knife out of Steiner's hand. He landed a straight right on the man's jaw and Steiner collapsed on the couch.

"Don't we have enough to do around here without fighting each other?" Aronen said calmly.

No sooner had he said it than Larsson walked from the table and threw a quick left hook into his gut. Aronen instinctively started to strike back, but he managed to stop himself.

"Conversations between Steiner and myself are none of your business," Larsson growled. "Remember that."

Aronen clenched his teeth.

* * *

The Skulls' toilet was literally shitty and it stunk. Salmela had hung his leather jacket in the broom closet, leaving only jeans and a T-shirt. The ex-con scoured the bowl with a toilet brush soaked in detergent. He was no stranger to this, having worked as a custodian in the brig in his younger days.

Salmela breathed through his mouth to keep from vomiting again. The toilet bowl took five minutes and he moved on to the floor and then the tiled walls. Last would be the sink and mirror.

Fuck this, he thought. Well, at least it came clean.

He drank some rusty-tasting water from the tap. The pipes were due for replacement.

Salmela stepped out of the bathroom and wondered what to do next. He caught sight of Niko at the bar, divvying up fifty-euro notes between Roge and Osku, but quickly looked away. Salmela decided to clean the sticky glass on the pinball machine as he had been ordered.

* * *

A fifty-something maintenance man stood in front of the stairwell in his overalls. The light-brown stucco apartment building, located behind the Central Fire Station, was built in the latter half of the fifties. Above the door, illuminated by the light from the stairwell, was a sign with the number 6. The lamp was crooked. The building was situated perpendicular to the street, and in front of the building was a rocky outcropping with a few pines growing on it.

A blue and white Volvo police station wagon pulled up to the front door. Leaning up against the wall was an orange bicycle with a large chain and padlock hanging from the frame.

Suhonen got out of the passenger side. Johan Strand, an immense uniformed officer sporting a mustache, circled back to the hatch and let out Esko, his German shepherd. The dog immediately heeled beside its handler. Suhonen had requested the help of a drug-sniffing dog.

Further off on the outcropping, a man in a baseball cap walking his collie was closely following the events in front of the building.

Strand also lifted out a heavy pipe, about three feet long and six inches in diameter, with hand grips in the middle.

"I see you brought your own key," the maintenance man rasped. Strand nodded, a dark wool hat stretched over his bald head.

Suhonen had explained the matter over the phone so the maintenance man asked no questions, just led the policemen into the stairwell.

The dog's claws scraped on the marble stairs. Karjalainen's apartment was on the third floor. The maintenance man got out his keys, but Suhonen stopped him.

"Let's ring the doorbell first."

It was possible that the police database was out of date and someone other than Vesa Karjalainen was living in the flat.

They heard the muffled chime of the doorbell. Instinctively, the cops took their positions on both sides of the door.

A moment passed before the sound of shuffling came from behind the door. The dog shifted anxiously at its handler's side.

The maintenance man was standing directly in front of the door and Strand jerked him out of the potential line of fire.

The door cracked open a couple of inches. The security chain was engaged.

"Who's there?" a woman's voice asked.

"Helsinki police," Suhonen announced and showed his badge through the crack in the door. A woman with tangled blonde hair and a black hooded sweatshirt peered out. Suhonen estimated her age at forty.

"What do you want?"

Suhonen immediately concluded that they were dealing with a repeat customer. An ordinary citizen would open the door without any further questions.

"May we come inside?"

"Why?"

Suhonen wondered how to put it. He couldn't really say they were looking for Vesa Karjalainen, because if the woman was his wife or girlfriend, he'd end up delivering the bad news. "Vesa Karjalainen?" he uttered.

"Not me," she said.

"Is this Karjalainen's apartment?"

"Sometimes. He's somewhere downtown now."

Suhonen had a warrant signed by Takamäki to search the residence used by Karjalainen. In Finland, the police could search homes based on warrants executed by a lieutenant, with no further authorization from a judge. In principle, even though he was already deceased, the man could be suspected of drug use. Determining the cause of death also granted them the right to search the premises.

"Will you please let us inside? This is an important matter."

The door moved no further than the end of the chain. "*What* is?"

Suhonen's patience was beginning to wane. Given Karjalainen's background with drugs, the woman's conduct was making her look very suspicious. Her listless eyes vouched for that, too.

"Ma'am, I'm sorry. Vesa Karjalainen was found dead this morning in a bathroom in downtown Helsinki. That's why we're here to search the apartment."

The woman closed the door, but the noises inside indicated she had left the entryway. Suhonen guessed what was happening. "Open up," he said.

The caretaker bent down in front of the doorknob. His hands were trembling and the keys clattered to the floor. Strand shouldered the man aside and swung the battering ram into the lock. The door splintered ajar, but required one more blow near the security chain before it burst open.

"Esko! Go!" Strand commanded. The dog shot inside, barking.

Inside, the woman shrieked and shouted, "Call off the dog or I'll kill it!"

Strand went first, a Glock pistol at the ready, and Suhonen took up the rear. The dog was barking and snarling.

The entryway was about ten feet long, and strewn with jackets and bags of garbage.

"The bathroom," said Strand, and Suhonen ducked inside to check it out while Strand went ahead. He noticed some blood on the sink, but no people.

Suhonen heard the dog barking in the kitchen and Strand's bellowing voice, "Please put down the knife."

"Get the hell out of here!"

Suhonen glanced into the bedroom. Stuff was strewn everyone, but nobody there either.

"Drop the knife!" Strand commanded again.

"I'll kill that dog!"

Suhonen came into the kitchen and stood next to

Strand. The woman was wearing black sneakers and a hoodie. Her hair was greasy and knotted. Suhonen revised his estimate of her age to 35—drug use had left its mark, making her appear older than she really was.

"Call off the dog," Suhonen said calmly. He saw an opportunity. She was no career criminal, just scared.

Strand kept the Glock leveled at the woman. "Esko. Heel."

The dog barked once more, then backed up ten feet and sat at his handler's side.

She clutched the knife for a moment longer before it clattered into the sink.

Strand worked fast, twisted her arms behind her back and clapped the cuffs on her wrists. Suhonen pulled a chair out from the kitchen table and sat her down on it.

"What happened?" he asked.

"I'm afraid of dogs," she stammered. "Is Vesa really dead?"

"Yes," he said, sitting down opposite her. "Overdosed and died in a train station bathroom stall."

Tears welled up in the woman's eyes.

"What's your name?"

"Mari. Mari Simola," she managed to say.

"Mari, are there any drugs here?"

"N-no."

Suhonen glanced at Strand. "Search the place."

The woman burst into tears.

"You can probably guess that Esko's not just a K-9, but a drug-sniffing dog as well."

Strand commanded the dog to search. His training had involved a game in which the dog received a reward for finding drugs. He was taught to identify hash first, then other narcotics.

The dog went eagerly to work and soon began clawing and barking at one of the base cabinets in the kitchen.

"What's in there?" Suhonen asked the woman.

"Vesa's speed. I don't know where he gets it, but a couple days ago he got a big shipment. I don't do that shit."

Strand slid open the bottom drawer, and using latex gloves, removed a Ziploc bag of white powder and set it on the table. Suhonen guessed it to be one to two ounces of amphetamines.

"What's your drug of choice?" Suhonen asked.

"Just weed. Can't handle the other stuff."

Suhonen glanced around the filthy apartment. "Where's your stash?"

"There's a couple joints in the bedroom nightstand. Nothing else."

Suhonen and Mari stayed in the kitchen while Strand and the dog continued the search. The woman seemed to be realizing the gravity of the situation.

"Who has Vesa been hanging out with lately?"

"Uuh," she said, staring at the table. "I don't know their names."

"Try to remember."

She looked at Suhonen. "He's really dead?"

Suhonen nodded. "Yes."

Mari thought for a moment. "One of 'em was an ex-junkie named Juha... Saarinen, Saarnivuori or something like that."

"Saarnikangas," Suhonen answered. "Who else?"

Mari looked up at Suhonen. "I told Vesa he shouldn't be hanging out with the Skulls, but he didn't care."

"Where'd he get the speed?"

"I know he went to Tallinn—could've bought it

161

over there. Was it a bad batch? Is that why he died or did someone kill him?"

Suhonen shrugged. "We don't know yet. Is that there from Tallinn?"

"Must be. He didn't have the money to buy it anywhere else. He owed everybody something."

Suhonen was still thinking. "The Skulls that Vesa hung out with. You know their names?"

"I saw 'em once from the window when they picked him up in some American muscle car…it was black. A fat guy and a couple younger ones. I don't know their names."

"Okay," said Suhonen. That was enough—the description matched Niko Andersson's crew. "One more thing. This Juha Saarnikangas and the Skulls. You ever seen them together?"

Mari thought for a moment. "No. Definitely not."

"You know someone by the name of Eero Salmela?"

"Name doesn't ring a bell."

"About my age. Wears a brown leather jacket with a lambswool collar all the time."

"I don't know him. Vesa probably did."

Strand returned to the kitchen with his dog. There were three joints in the Ziploc bag.

Suhonen tried to comfort her, "Esko would protect you in a heartbeat. He's actually a sheep in wolf's clothing: nice to nice people."

"Or nasty to nasty people?" Mari said, trying to force a smile.

Strand commanded the dog to stay and followed Suhonen into the hallway.

Suhonen spoke in a hushed voice. "This was partly my fault—I didn't know she lived here too. I figured this was Karjalainen's pad and we'd just search it for drugs."

"Yea-ah," he whispered. "No big deal."

"We could get her for resisting arrest and drug possession, but as far as I'm concerned, we should just call it post-traumatic stress syndrome, you know, considering her man just died and all."

Strand could see where Suhonen was headed. "She gave you some good intel?"

"Yes... But the truth is she only threatened Esko, so it was more like resisting a canine. We've been trailing Karjalainen and I know those drugs were his. The joints are probably hers, but let's just have the dead guy take the rap for that."

Strand shot him a look as though Suhonen was just trying to get in her pants, but the undercover officer read his mind.

"Come on, are you serious? Honestly, I'm more interested in Esko."

Strand laughed aloud. "Okay. Works for me, but you'll have to court Esko with some nice treats. He likes cheese pizza, and he can't eat that at home. Too much pizza is bad for police dogs too."

"Okay, I owe you one. If Esko ever needs dog-sitting sometime, call me."

"You can be sure I won't."

They went back into the kitchen. Strand took off the cuffs and left with the dog. Suhonen stayed to ask more questions and fixed a pot of coffee for Mari.

CHAPTER 15
SATURDAY, 5:00 P.M.
VIHTI HIGHWAY, HELSINKI

"I'm tired...and hungry," Eero Salmela complained from the passenger seat.

"Not cold though?" Suhonen asked. He was driving an unmarked squad car southbound along the Vihti Highway. They went through a roundabout and stopped at a red light. The rain had started again and the Peugeot's wipers were hard at work. Headlights from the oncoming traffic glared off the wet asphalt.

"That I could've helped with," continued Suhonen, pointing to the switch for the seat-heater.

The light changed and the car moved on.

About a half-hour earlier, Salmela had called his friend and asked to be picked up at a bus stop along the Vihti Highway. That had worked for the Suhonen.

"Let's go for coffee at the Teboil station," Salmela suggested as they approached the new Hakamäen Avenue. The hundred-fifty-million-dollar road and tunnel project had been completed a year ago. It had gotten off to a catastrophic start when a multi-car pileup had shut it down on opening day. Despite the new tunnel, the road was plagued by congestion even more than before. The newspapers called Hakamäen Avenue "Finland's most expensive parking lot." Now, on a Saturday, there was little traffic.

"No coffee shops. We can get you some grub from

a drive-thru or something."

"What's wrong with the Teboil? I like that place."

"I wanna talk in the car where it's private," Suhonen explained. He switched to the slow lane. Two other cars continued onward to the tunnel, but Suhonen veered southward onto Mannerheim Street.

"You smell like detergent," Suhonen remarked.

"New job."

"Congrats," said Suhonen, though he was already wondering how that might affect the plan they had in store for him. "Somewhere north?"

"Yeah," he hedged.

"You selling soap or cleaning?"

"Cleaning."

Continuing past the Teboil station toward downtown, they passed the lofty office buildings of Ruskeasuo and the residential districts of Pikku-Huopalahti.

"What company?"

"None of your business," he shot back.

The trip continued in silence. Suhonen turned on the radio. Radio Rock was on commercials so he changed the station. He let a classic hit from the Rolling Stones play quietly in the background. Suhonen had only been asking about Salmela's work so he could steer the conversation toward the job they'd been planning for him.

"Where can we get some food?" Salmela asked. "I'm fine with anything but burgers. My stomach can't take those additives."

Suhonen drove past a Hesburger and a McDonalds to the Töölö section of Helsinki. Nestled in an old streetcar station was a Turkish kebab place that would do the trick.

"You okay with kebabs?"

"Sure."

The lights turned green and the car lurched ahead. Suhonen figured he could hint at the job opportunity before the restaurant, but he wouldn't get into the details until afterwards.

"How much is your debt now?"

"Fifty less than yesterday."

Suhonen wondered what that meant, but decided not to pry—at least not yet.

After a few minutes, he spotted the Turkish place, situated on the corner of Topelius Street, near the Töölö library. There were no parking spots, but the street was wide enough that Suhonen was able to double-park in front of the restaurant.

"Now's your chance to take that nap," Suhonen said stepping out of the car. Above the windows of the restaurant were thick yellow letters, spelling "Pizza." Functional sign, he thought. Even if the owners change, the sign can stay.

Ten minutes later he returned with two kebabs wrapped in foil and slid back into his seat. He handed the food and plastic forks to Salmela and pulled a bottle of water out of his pocket.

Suhonen started the car and put it in gear. He decided to drive to the soccer fields on the north end of the Hietaniemi beach. Salmela unwrapped his kebab and immediately began forking it into his mouth. The sweet smell of the dressing filled the car.

* * *

Lieutenant Jaakko Nykänen was sitting in his cramped office at the NBI bunker. His left hand massaged his whiskers, and his right rested on the mouse. He was skimming through intelligence reports, which had been uploaded into the database throughout the day. Some of them were just routine police reports. A criminal flagged for surveillance had been stopped for speeding, or say, drunk driving.

Some had more valuable intel: who met whom, for example, or who called whom. Every day, the Finnish police had dozens of ongoing phone-tapping operations. Not every piece of information ended up in the database, of course, but the bulk of the most important ones did. The bigger problem was that they didn't always know which criminals they should have under surveillance, and when.

Nykänen knew—by name—at least a thousand outlaws tied to organized crime. Of those, a couple hundred were hardened criminals. When needed, he could create a computerized diagram of the connections and contacts between selected individuals. The computer was a wonderful tool.

One report in particular had caught Nykänen's attention. He had read it once already, but returned to it again.

According to the report, black market operator Mika Konttinen, aka Mike Gonzales, had met Ilkka Ranta that afternoon. The encounter had been observed in Tampere, at the restaurant in the Ilves Hotel. Working on another case, NBI investigators had followed a different suspect into the same restaurant. They had spotted Ranta and a man, later identified as Gonzales, together.

Ranta was an exceptionally interesting character. The man had made his money during the recession of the early '90s, and even more after the tech stock bubble burst in 2000. During rough economic times, the situation for men of money was even easier than in good times. The fundamental rule for getting rich still applied—buy low, sell high.

That morning, Suhonen had mentioned Gonzales' connections to the Skulls and to some Russian-

Estonian man. Nykänen had forgotten the name and was unable to check it in the computer. Why couldn't Suhonen enter his leads into the database, Nykänen brooded. The police employed too many old-school cops who didn't grasp the importance of sharing information.

In any event, Gonzales-Konttinen could be the key to nabbing Ranta.

Ranta's business practices were known to be tough, and there was plenty of intel on his shady deals. The police had never found anything illegal, even though financial crime detectives and internal revenue agents had combed through his businesses and contracts. Now approaching sixty, the man understood the importance of staying out of the public eye so as not to arouse envy, which always spawned accusations. He drank his expensive whiskey inside his granite-walled home, and his villa in Spain never appeared in the home decorating magazines. Ranta was also connected to state government.

His activities had never met the probable cause threshold, so the police couldn't tap his phone or search his home. Because of his status, the state prosecutor's office was always involved from the get-go in any investigation concerning him. Prosecutors had a much higher threshold of probable cause than the police did. Both at the NBI and at the prosecutor's office, the bosses, who were closer to the political establishment, made all the final decisions on big cases.

Gonzales and the Skulls might just be the Trojan horse they needed to nab the millionaire, thought Nykänen. Damn. If only they'd managed to plant a microphone at the table of the Ilves Hotel. From a technical standpoint, it would have been easy. The hotel had wireless internet, which could pick up a signal from a small mic hidden in an object on the table.

Surveillance could take a while, but if they could use Gonzales to build a connection between the Skulls and Ranta, it would present an opportunity to put the man under closer scrutiny. If they could show probable cause for, say, incitement to felony extortion, the surveillance could spawn leads on his other activities as well.

Nykänen took a swig of lemon sparkling water from the bottle on his desk.

They could launch the case as a joint effort between the NBI and Helsinki police, but it would gradually shift to the NBI, especially if Ranta wound up in the crosshairs. If the case pertained only to the Skulls, the Helsinki PD would take the lead. Most of all, Nykänen wanted Ranta behind bars.

The end game was beginning to look a lot better now, thought Nykänen. But the NBI would have to oversee Suhonen's informant so they could more easily shift the target from the Skulls to the millionaire. Small-time drug smuggling didn't interest Nykänen in the slightest—Ranta would have to be the ultimate target.

* * *

Salmela blew a plume of cigarette smoke through a gap in the Peugeot's passenger side window. The smell of smoke lingered in the car, but Suhonen didn't mind. The remains of the kebabs, the jalapenos Salmela had picked out, and the garbage from the meal were in a plastic bag at his feet.

On any summer night in Hietalahti, scores of people would be about, but now the place was deserted. Rain pattered on the car roof and the wet windshield scattered the light from the street lamps. It would probably pass for modern art at the Kiasma museum if some artist came up with the idea to build a dark room where people could look at a couple of street lamps through a car's sprinkler-doused windshield.

"I thought maybe I'd rob a bank," Salmela said.

"It'd never work. You won't get twenty Gs out of it, anyway. They keep a total of ten grand in the tills and you wouldn't get access to the vault."

"Two banks, then."

Suhonen shook his head.

"Armored truck?"

"Won't work. You'd need a bunch of guys for that."

"Diamonds? We gave it a good try a few years back, anyway," said Salmela.

Suhonen remembered it well. Salmela's gang had intended to hit several jewelry stores in various parts of the city simultaneously, but the scheme fell flat in the planning stages. Preparing for robbery was not a crime, but the NBI had nailed the perps for drug trafficking. As a member of the gang, Salmela wound up in prison too.

"You should've hired some pros from Estonia."

"Haven't you ever thought of switching sides?" Salmela ventured, finishing off his water. "You'd be quite the expert."

Suhonen chuckled. There were certainly plenty of officers—or former officers—who had shifted to the dark side, but they hadn't fared well. Traitors always got harsher treatment than other criminals. "Nope. This works just fine for me."

"Low pay and long hours."

"At least it pays the bills and I choose the long hours."

The banter went on for some time and Suhonen was glad they had plenty to talk about. Perhaps he should hold off on the proposal for a day or two. It was possible he could ruin the whole plan if he pushed Salmela too hard or too early.

Infiltrating the Skulls wouldn't be easy; they'd need a detailed game plan. One idea would be to devise a "robbery" where Salmela would get the money to pay his debt. Maybe that would elevate his status and allow him to penetrate the gang. From the pen, Salmela knew Larsson—the gang's recently-released leader—so it wasn't out of the question. Of course, a fake robbery would be a complicated trick since it would require publicizing false information, but it could be done.

"So, guess where I'm working at?" Salmela asked.

Maybe this could be the opportunity, Suhonen thought. Earlier, Salmela hadn't wanted to talk about it. "You said you were cleaning and I picked you up in north Helsinki, so it's probably some company over there. Judging by the smell of detergent on your clothes it's a pretty filthy place."

"You got that right," Salmela chuckled. "Filthy for sure."

"Well, let's hear it."

"I cleaned the Skulls' shitter today."

"Huh?"

After hearing about the day's events, Suhonen was stunned. Salmela decided not to mention the nature hike in the forest, however, since he didn't want to involve his friend in it. He remembered the letter he had left on the sofa—that would have to be burned.

Suhonen tried to keep a poker face. There was no longer any need for Salmela to infiltrate anything—

he was already on the inside, and in a role where he could access any part of the club house on a daily basis without suspicion.

"So you're their slave now," said Suhonen.

"You could put it that way. But I'm alive."

"They threaten you?"

"No," Salmela snapped. "This is how I'm gonna pay up. It's not completely fair, but it works for me."

Suhonen knew his friend had left something out. Of course, threats had been part of the deal. Somehow he had to get Salmela bitter enough to offset his fear of the gang. Or get him to fear the police more than the gang, but that was a poor alternative, Suhonen thought.

"Listen, Eero," Suhonen began. "You know that Estonian drug shipment that was supposed to get you out of debt?"

"What about it?"

"I asked Narcotics about it. Guess how much speed they found on your mule?"

Salmela was confused. "The four pounds, of course."

Suhonen shook his head. "One and a half."

"What? Not possible."

"She had twenty ounces on the dot. The bags were taped to her sides."

Suhonen reached into his breast pocket and pulled out her mug shot and a document listing the confiscated goods. Salmela turned on the dome light and looked at the picture for a long time. Afterwards, he read the document.

"Fuck. They ripped me off," he snarled. "Damned Estonians. Charge me for four and send me one-and-a-half. Were they the ones to rat out the mule too? If you hadn't said anything, I would've never known."

"There's another piece to this story. You

remember Vesa Karjalainen?"

"The junkie? Yeah."

"Well, he was found dead this morning on the bathroom floor of the train station. OD."

"Not surprising."

Suhonen decided it was time to up the ante.

"I'm going to give you a couple facts. One: I chatted with his girlfriend, and apparently, he was flat broke. Two: the narcotics cops who busted Mägi with the drugs also saw Karjalainen coming off the same boat."

Suhonen pulled out a screenshot of Karjalainen at the harbor and handed it to Salmela, who was still dumbfounded. Suhonen pushed on.

"Three: Just before he died, Karjalainen went to settle a debt with some friend, which is why he was at the station. Four: I searched his apartment myself and found an ounce and a half of speed."

Salmela was floored by what he heard; his ears were red.

"And five: I spoke with Karjalainen's girlfriend during the search. She had nothing to do with any of this, but guess who picked him up just before he went to Estonia?"

"Who?" Salmela asked, raking his fingers through his hair.

"She didn't know their names, but she knew they were Skulls and gave me a description: one fat guy and a couple younger ones. Can you put the pieces together?"

"Son of a bitch!" Salmela was seething. He felt the throbbing start at the base of his skull. "They scammed me and had me foot the bill for everything. Goddamn sons-of-bitches."

Salmela had financed the drug shipment and taken the downside risk. But the Skulls had reduced their risk by splitting the shipment into two. It still wasn't clear to Suhonen whether Mägi had been deliberately smoked so the larger—and possibly stronger—shipment would make it through. Karjalainen's overdose indicated a potent batch. If that was the case, Mägi had been intentionally sacrificed for something she had done in Estonia.

Suhonen was pleased at Salmela's reaction. Now he had only to channel the man's anger in the right direction.

"Fuck," Salmela went on. "I don't suppose you'd care if I take a shotgun to work tomorrow morning and rid this world of those shitheads. Come pick me up around noon and throw me in jail, but let me burn down their goddamned shack first."

That's one option, Suhonen thought, though not such a good one.

"Listen, Eero," said Suhonen quietly. "I have a proposal for you to think about."

Suhonen and Salmela continued to converse in the parking lot for another half an hour. Afterwards, Suhonen drove his friend home to Salmela's apartment, a tall eight-story building on the corner of Sture Street in Kallio.

The rain had picked up and Suhonen stopped the car in front of stairwell F. The curb was packed with cars, so he double-parked. Salmela got out, bade his friend goodbye, unlocked the frosted-glass door on the ground floor and went inside. Suhonen sped off.

Neither man noticed the Fiat Ducato van parked on the other side of the street. Juha Saarnikangas sat in the front seat, the collar of his army jacket flipped up. Some teenage druggie was supposed to bring him two laptops, for which Juha had promised to pay a hundred euros. The kid was late, but it didn't matter anymore. This was much better.

Juha knew both Salmela and Suhonen, but hadn't been aware that they knew each other. That was valuable information.

* * *

It was nearing eight o'clock and Lieutenant Takamäki was sitting on the couch at home. He had been watching Channel 4 news, which was no less depressing than the others: only gloomy economic stories. From a policeman's perspective, that wasn't all bad—recessions reduced alcohol consumption, which, in turn, lowered violent crimes. As understaffed as they were, however, the VCU wouldn't feel a reduction of a few percentage points.

He was thankful that news broadcasts were short.

The forty-eight-year-old Takamäki lived in a townhome in Espoo's Leppävaara district. His wife was out and the older of his boys was doing homework in his upstairs room—or so Takamäki hoped. More likely, he was listening to music or playing video games.

The door opened and his younger son squeezed in with a hockey bag over his shoulder and a stick in his hand.

"Hey," Joonas called out from the door. "Anything to eat?"

"It's on the stove. Stick it in the microwave if it's cold."

Though Joonas had played hockey most of his life, he wasn't talented enough for the Espoo Blues junior traveling team. Now he only played in a recreational league. As far as Takamäki was concerned, three practices a week for a sixteen-year-old were better than six or seven.

Takamäki sifted through the pile of mail on the

table: magazines and bills. Nothing especially interesting. The television was on commercials.

Joonas came into the living room with a plate of food and sat down on the sofa next to his dad.

"How'd your day go?"

"Not bad," Joonas shrugged. "Just hung around at the mall. Oh yeah, got my math test back on Friday. B+."

"Pretty good," said Takamäki. "And practice?"

"Just goofed around again."

"Uh-oh," Takamäki said. Their coach wasn't able to control the group of teenage boys, all of whom had quit the elite team for a rec league. Practices didn't work without discipline.

"He tried to get us to do skating drills, but Ripa and the others said they wanted to scrimmage—so we scrimmaged. But it was pretty weak."

"So Ripa's the boss?" Takamäki said. Through the years, Ripa had played hockey with Joonas from mites onward and had quit the traveling team at the same time.

Joonas shoveled down his chicken pasta without responding.

"Listen, Dad," he began. "I need a new phone."

"Is that so."

An iPhone ad was flickering on the screen.

"That 3G one there. Ripa's got that one."

Takamäki was about to say "is that so" again before deciding to take a more active role. "Where did he get that? Did his dad buy it for him?"

"No, his brother bought it. He gives Ripa money too."

"His brother bought it? Pretty nice brother. Does he have a job? How old is he?"

Joonas chewed his food as he talked. "Osku's a little over twenty and he has a job…sort of."

Takamäki was interested. A guy in his early twenties buys an expensive phone for his little brother, and he sort of has a job. "What do you mean by that?"

"Nothing really. I've never met him, but Ripa bought us Cokes after practice. Apparently, his brother always has a lot of money and has his own car. He's moved out."

"I believe it. If the guy has the money to buy his own car and a phone for his brother, then I doubt he lives with his folks. But what does he do?"

"I don't know exactly," Joonas answered, annoyed. "It's probably connected to your job, even. He hangs out with that gang, the Skulls, and supposedly was in prison. By the way, Ripa said Osku could get us some phones for really cheap, but I figured I'd ask you first."

"That sounds really great. An ex-con selling phones for dirt cheap…"

Takamäki's cell phone rang.

"You could use a new one too. That thing is ancient," Joonas pointed at his phone.

Takamäki glanced at the display then slipped into the hallway to talk. He closed the hall door so his voice wouldn't be heard in the living room.

"Hello."

"Hi, Nykänen here. You at work, or am I bothering you at home?"

Takamäki said he was at home. The NBI agent teased him about the old days when they were both still in the office at eight P.M. every night.

"I'll get to the point. I think you've got something with that case of yours, so let's get going on it right away. We just have to find a way to get the informant on the inside."

Takamäki glanced instinctively through the

patterned glass of the door. It would muffle the sound, but wouldn't prevent his voice from being heard in the living room.

"Suhonen called about that earlier. He said it's taken care of."

"Good. How?"

"Listen, Jaakko. If it's all right, we'll stop by tomorrow morning."

Nykänen understood. "Okay. Too many ears over there, huh?"

"Exactly."

They settled on a time and Takamäki returned to the living room.

Joonas looked at his dad with curiosity. "You working on a good case?"

SUNDAY, OCTOBER 25

CHAPTER 16
SUNDAY, 9:00 A.M.
HOTEL PASILA, HELSINKI

There was plenty of space in the restaurant at Hotel Pasila. Reporter Sanna Römpötti had arrived early and fetched herself coffee and toast from the buffet. The stench of Saturday night's booze still hung in the air over many of the tables, but Römpötti was alert. Last night, she had limited herself to two glasses of merlot, as the meeting ahead promised to be interesting.

Sami Aronen ambled down the aisle from the bar in wide strides and caught sight of Römpötti. He would've recognized the attractive brown-haired reporter from TV anyway, but she had texted him that she'd be wearing a black pantsuit and a white blouse. On her chest was a rather large silver brooch with a black pearl. Römpötti didn't care much for the brooch, as it made her look matronly. But there was a reason for her choice of jewelry.

Aronen greeted her politely, and she suggested that he get some breakfast. He accepted, and hung his leather coat over the back of his chair.

Römpötti couldn't help but notice the back muscles beneath the man's black sweater as he turned away.

She was sipping her coffee when he returned with some orange juice and a croissant. Behind her back, a streetcar rattled past the window.

"I'm glad that this worked out," she began.

Aronen smiled. "When the media calls, the citizens come."

The gangster glanced around: no cameras in sight and Römpötti was clearly alone. If the reporter had backup, they would have to be among the hotel guests.

"Right, right," Römpötti smiled, stroking her hair. She had intentionally left an extra button open on her blouse.

"I just now put the name and the face together," said Aronen. "You were the one on that dance show last winter."

Römpötti laughed. "Yes, I've been hearing about that all year. Did you watch it?"

"I watched part of one and saw the pictures in the papers, of course. In that samba episode—or was it rumba—you had on that short black skirt?"

Römpötti confessed. "I didn't actually choose it myself; they have a stylist who picks the costumes."

"Good stylist, but it can't be that hard to pick out clothes for a body like yours."

"Thank you. But let's talk about you a little…"

"You're much more interesting."

Römpötti cut the flattery short with a stern look then drank her coffee in a way that was just short of flirtatious. The gesture worked every time with men.

"Alright, then," said Aronen. "We're just talking about background info, right?"

Römpötti nodded. "We can do a proper interview on camera later."

"Maybe," Aronen said, smiling again.

Römpötti wondered how to proceed. Aronen's story was an interesting one: from the peacekeeping forces to organized crime. But she didn't want to start with that.

"So, um," she began haltingly. "The police have deemed the Skulls a criminal organization. Is that true?" The question was dumb, but it would help her get the conversation going. Maybe.

Aronen shook his head. "Don't listen to the police. They exaggerate everything for their own purposes. We're not a criminal organization."

"Quite a few members are serving prison sentences, though?"

"It's none of the group's business what people do on their own time. We're not responsible for others' actions."

Römpötti latched onto his statement. "On their own time? Is there a difference then between your own time and the gang's time?"

"Well, you could say that. Maybe you could come visit our offices some time. You'd see there's quite a lot of work involved in maintaining it."

"What do you do on your own time?"

"Whatever I feel like. Right now I'm building a motorcycle."

"Aha. That's interesting. Will you show me sometime?"

"We'll see," he said, withdrawing somewhat.

Römpötti could see it was too early to talk about the man himself. Better to stay on generic topics.

"How does the club fund its activities?" she asked.

"Everybody pays modest membership dues. Just like country clubs."

"How do members make their money? Illegally, according to the police."

Aronen ran his hands over his bristly hair. The questions were stupid, but the woman definitely had style. Nice tits and a thin shirt that was almost transparent. "Yeah, yeah. The cops say whatever's convenient at the time. The club is not responsible for the actions of its members. Quite a few cops have been convicted in the past few years and that doesn't make the police department a criminal organization."

"I suppose not," she said. "You're an interesting character."

"Am I?"

"Yes. How did you end up joining the Skulls?"

He looked her directly in the eyes.

"You ask too many questions."

"That's my job."

"Now it's my turn to ask the questions."

"So ask," she said.

"You want to get a room upstairs?"

Römpötti was at a loss for words.

"If you really want to know what kind of men we are…"

"Excuse me?" she coughed.

"Come on. I can read your eyes."

Römpötti smiled, but her expression betrayed disgust. "Listen, Sami. It's not a terrible suggestion, but…"

He cut in. "If you do it, I'll go on camera. Although afterwards, you probably won't have any more questions. But I'd give it to you tomorrow too…the interview."

Over the years, Römpötti had received numerous similar proposals from politicians, policemen and other officials, but this was the first one from a career criminal. She wouldn't trade sex for an interview, though she knew several of her colleagues who had. To her knowledge, however, none had done so with a criminal.

"Uhh… Listen, Sami. Don't get upset, but I'll have to think about it."

Aronen was silent while he sipped his orange juice. "Well, you thought about it?"

Somehow, she had to get him to do a proper interview. She couldn't give him a flat no. "Not now."

"Why?"

"I have to think about it more. And maybe we should get to know each other better before jumping into the sack."

"Okay with me. But I'm done here."

"Well, how about if I call you."

Aronen stood up and took his jacket. "Okay. Think about it and call me. Thanks for breakfast."

He headed off in the same direction he had come from.

Huh, Römpötti thought. She glanced at the bulky brooch on her lapel. She had feared it would attract his attention, but apparently her breasts had done a better job at that. The purpose of that extra open button had been to keep his eyes off the hidden camera.

Hopefully the camera and microphone had been working. The lens was hidden in the pearl and the microphone just next to it. A wireless receiver was hidden in her purse on the floor.

Not much there, but at least it was something. She'd have to consider whether she could use any of the material, since Aronen had only wanted to talk about background. Of course, he knew he was talking to a reporter.

The proposal at the end couldn't be aired, though it was a good illustration of the gangster mindset. Römpötti was glad there wasn't a second camera to capture her expression when he dropped the proposal. That would have definitely ended up on the big screen at the newsroom's Christmas party.

A waitress came to the table and interrupted her thoughts. "Excuse me. Your gentleman friend must not have been a guest at the hotel and he left without paying."

Römpötti dug her wallet out of her purse. "I'll pay for the both of us."

As the waitress turned away, Römpötti set her purse on the table, opened it and stopped the recorder.

* * *

"How many in the Helsinki PD know about Salmela?" asked agent Aalto dryly.

Aalto, Nykänen, Suhonen and Takamäki were sitting in the same NBI conference room as yesterday.

"Salmela has been the subject of many investigations over the years, so presumably quite a few know him," Takamäki replied. "But nobody except for the two of us knows about his connection to this case. We've spoken with the VCU's Captain Karila, as well as Assistant Chief Skoog about the operation, but we haven't mentioned Salmela by name."

"Good," said Aalto. "For security reasons, from here on out we'll refer to him by the code name Salmiakki."

Suhonen laughed. Salmela becomes Salmiakki? What do they pay these agents for? Certainly not for coming up with good code names.

"Do you have a problem with the code name?" Aalto demanded.

"Not at all. It's genius."

"Good," said Aalto.

Suhonen had briefed them on the main points of his visit with Salmela. Incensed over the betrayal, Salmela—now Salmiakki—was seriously considering cooperating with the police. Everyone considered his custodial job to be a brilliant stroke of luck that would speed up the operation.

"Let's go over Salmiakki's motives more closely," said Aalto, glancing at his papers. "Does he have a desire to clear his conscience?"

"I doubt it," Suhonen replied. I'd guess he just wants to get out of the gang, and now he wants revenge, too."

"Does he have much of an ego?"

Suhonen wondered about the question then realized why Aalto was going through the list.

"I don't think he'll need to be picked up for meetings in a limo," Suhonen said.

"Finland is too small for limos," Aalto said. The Royal Canadian Mounted Police once had an informant from a biker gang whose vanity demanded constant attention. Among other things, the Mounties had to chauffeur him back and forth to meetings in a limousine.

Suhonen had heard about the incident while abroad at a seminar on criminal gangs. Apparently, Aalto had attended the same one.

"Salme... Uhh, Salmiakki is a long-time criminal, primarily running stolen goods. He's divorced, done time, and his son was shot to death in a drug deal gone bad. I believe his story; he wants out of the game, but can't because of his debt. As a result, he has to depend on someone stronger, and since the Skulls betrayed him, the cops can step in."

"Not exactly levelheaded, then," Aalto remarked.

"Not exactly," said Suhonen. "But he's not dumb, either. And don't bother appealing to his sense of justice. For him, the opportunity to break out of his current circumstances will be enough."

Nykänen interjected. "But he understands that

more than likely, he'll wind up in prison?"

"Yeah. We went through that yesterday. Salmela…"

"Salmiakki," Aalto corrected him.

"Salmiakki knows he'll take the rap for the twenty ounces—for his own security. It wouldn't look good if we busted everybody else and he got off scot-free. I promised him we'd make things comfortable for him in prison."

Aalto frowned. "We can't promise him anything."

"We talked about it," Suhonen reworded. "But it's kind of awkward if he's expecting results and all he gets is talk."

"We'll try to help him afterwards, of course," said Nykänen.

The word "try" was a big problem for Suhonen. If an informant put his life on the line for society, it wasn't enough for the police to just "try." The system should have clear rules.

Aalto went down his list. "At any rate, it's clear that we'll be overseeing the case. The fact that Suhonen is so close to the subject is a clear conflict of interest."

Takamäki nodded. "We've talked about that."

"That way we can be sure the situation will be handled professionally, and that the informant has a genuine desire to talk to the police. He won't be doing this just to please Suhonen anymore, but only for the sake of revealing important matters to the authorities. That works for his own benefit, too."

This case might even work out, thought Suhonen. If he didn't believe that, he would never have given up his own informant. True, Salmela's head injury had already driven him to the sidelines, so he wasn't privy to much valuable intel anymore. He spent most of his time at the corner table of the Corner Pub. But

Suhonen's primary concern was Salmela's welfare. The operation would provide a chance, however slim, for Salmela to get out—not through the front door, but through the back.

Aalto went on, "I'll be one of his handlers myself. Another one, a specialist, will come from my own group. Both of us will attend all meetings with Salmiakki. We'll pay all of his expenses in cash and his real name will go in the NBI's safe. Does this Salmiakki happen to have a dog?"

"No," said Suhonen, pouring himself a cup of coffee from the thermos.

"Pity. Walking the dog is always a convenient way to meet. We'll think of something else. For security reasons, it's imperative that NBI agents are the only ones to meet with Salmiakki. Is that clear, Suhonen?" Aalto stressed.

Suhonen nodded.

"I have the informant's address and phone number here. Do you have any idea where Salmiakki is now?"

"I'd bet on three spots. He's either at home, at the Skulls' compound or on the way there," said Suhonen.

"You don't have Salmiakki under surveillance?"

Takamäki shrugged. "No. We don't have enough resources for that. And there's been no need for it."

Aalto's expression was grave. "So let me get this straight. Your informant is at the headquarters of a criminal organization with no security measures?"

"Why should there be?" Suhonen asked. "I don't have time to babysit them all. These guys are criminals—they don't like being followed. They come to me when a competitor tramples on their toes or they want to get back at someone. The third reason is when another criminal is completely out of control and the related police activity is bad for business."

"Pretty old-fashioned thinking," Aalto remarked.

"Maybe so, but that's how you get street intel. Maybe you guys should invest some time in traditional police work yourselves."

Aalto looked over at Nykänen, who seemed uneasy. "The NBI takes care of organized crime. You take care of the street crimes."

Suhonen wanted to ask him where, exactly, organized crimes occurred. If not in the streets and alleys, then where? The NBI could have all the white collar criminals they wanted.

"One more thing we should make clear, so we all understand," Suhonen said. "Under no circumstances does Salmiakki want to wind up testifying in court. We can only use him for getting intel, which will guide further police operations."

Nykänen nodded. "We've been thinking the same thing. With Salmiakki's help, we'll know where to be, and when, but nobody else will know about his role."

"Any questions?" Aalto inquired.

Takamäki cleared his throat. "Meetings. Where and when?"

"Here at NBI headquarters. I'll let you know when," Nykänen said. "Anything else?"

Suhonen drank the last of his coffee. "Are you guys going to be taking the drug case too?"

"No," said Nykänen. "Our objective here is the Skulls and anyone affiliated with them, especially Mike Gonzales. Narcotics will continue to investigate the drug trafficking case. We can combine the cases later as necessary."

* * *

The Skulls' compound was quiet. Salmela was alone at the bar, wiping down the counter. From a custodian's perspective, the previous night had been rather mellow—the place didn't look much different from the way he had left it.

He had arrived at the compound at just past nine. With walking, the bus commute had taken nearly an hour. The previous night, Salmela had skipped the Corner Pub, bought a six-pack of beer and watched TV. He had burned the letter to Suhonen. It was irrelevant now. The conversation with Suhonen replayed continually in his head, but he didn't let it bother him. Nowadays, things just happened, and he didn't have much control over them.

Roge, who was on guard duty that morning, had opened the door. Salmela hadn't earned the code for the keypad yet, and likely wouldn't for a long time.

Roge had wanted to talk about last night's hockey games, but that fizzled quickly since Salmela didn't know the scores. Soon, Roge got bored, turned to his billiards, and Salmela hung his jacket in the broom closet and got to work. The toilet was an easy task now that the first big cleaning was out of the way.

Salmela could tell by the smell of the ashtrays that someone had been smoking weed. A few spent doobies confirmed it. He stuffed the butts in his pocket. By saving a few weeks worth of remnants and rerolling them, he could have a couple new joints to sell. That would fetch him a few euros.

At the corner of the bar was a plastic garbage pail half filled with empty cans and bottles. If nobody emptied it, Salmela planned to do it himself and keep the deposits.

The steady crack of the billiard balls stopped and Salmela looked up. Roge was chatting with a bald, tattooed man whose back was turned to Salmela, but he recognized him as the same Skull he had met in prison.

Roge said something and Tapani Larsson turned to look at Salmela. Larsson nodded and strode briskly toward him.

Salmela considered his options quickly: bottles, both full and empty, were all about, but Larsson likely had a gun, and Roge certainly did. He'd have to make do with words, and if there was trouble, he'd either survive or not. He was powerless. Others made decisions for him, just like in prison.

Larsson approached the other side of the bar.

"Hey there," the man flashed a grin. "I guess we're old friends."

"Yeah," said Salmela. "Helsinki Prison, right?"

Larsson nodded. "I remember you. You did a few jobs for us—and very well."

"Still am."

"Gotta pay your debts, huh?"

Salmela wiped the counter. "I'm thankful I can settle them like this. I do good work."

"Hopefully… One thing—were you here yesterday already?"

"Yeah."

"So you cleaned the toilet?"

"Yeah."

Larsson clapped his hands a few times. "Goddamn. You should get 'employee of the year' for that. The air even smells fresher in here. I don't know what kind of poison you use, but you sure do fine work."

"Thanks." The praise had seemed genuine. There hadn't been much of it in recent months—or in recent years. Come to think of it, not much in the last forty years.

"Hey, Eero," said Larsson.

Salmela was surprised that the gang boss even remembered his first name, much less used it. "Yeah?"

"There any coffee here?"

"Not made. I'm not sure where it'd be. I haven't cleaned the cabinets yet."

"Will you find some?"

"If it's here I'll find it."

Larsson cracked a smile. "Good. I'll have a little milk with mine. And if there isn't any, knock on the office door and ask Roge to go get a truckload. We don't drink Nescafe here," he laughed.

In prison, Nescafe was the most sensible choice because no valuable grounds were lost at the bottom of the pot. Mixed in a cup of hot water, every last drop of caffeine was consumed.

Larsson slipped into the office just as Salmela's phone rang in his pocket. He snatched it up before the first ring was over and answered. On the other end was a man's voice, asking first if this was Eero Salmela.

"Yeah."

"I'm Suhonen's friend. My name's Aalto and I'd like to meet with you."

"Call back later." He'd have to remember to turn off his phone when he was at work.

"I'll call you at about three in the afternoon to give you instructions. Is that okay?"

Salmela glanced around. Nobody seemed interested in his conversation. "Sure."

"Good. I'll get back to you," the man said.

Salmela shut off the phone, put it back in his pocket and went back to cleaning the counter. Oh yeah, the coffee, he remembered.

A black-haired man wearing a white sport coat over a black T-shirt came through the saloon doors at the top of the stairs. Osku followed him in and got a nod from Roge.

The man's eyes scanned the room and stopped on Salmela for a moment.

The goateed Osku directed the stranger to the office door and knocked. Somebody barked something from inside, but Salmela didn't catch it.

Osku opened the door and Salmela heard him ask if it was okay if Mike Gonzales came in.

Apparently it was. The black-haired man disappeared into the office. He heard some brief conversation and Osku ordered Salmela to make a couple of extra cups of coffee.

The door closed, muffling their words. He found a pack of filters in the cabinet and a brick of Presidentti coffee. The coffeemaker was next to the sink.

In the back room, Larsson greeted Gonzales.

"Do you know the guy who was standing by the bar?"

"No," Gonzales replied. "New recruit?"

Larsson shook his head. "New janitor, an ex-con. Name's Eero Salmela. He was in prison the same time as I was. Ask around a bit and see if you can find out what he's up to nowadays."

"In what respect?"

"Just generally. Who he hangs out with, who he meets."

"Sure. I'll put someone on it."

Gonzales drew a small notepad out of his breast pocket and wrote, "Eero Salmela?"

* * *

"So we're off the case, then?" Suhonen asked. Takamäki was taking his turn at the wheel. The rain persisted, jamming up the ordinarily lazy Sunday

194

traffic on Beltway Three.

"Somehow I got that impression when Nykänen said they'd call us if they need us. But let's give them some space. Stay away from Salmela, at least for now."

"Yeah," said Suhonen. "Of course."

Takamäki wasn't very reassured by Suhonen's tone of voice.

"Helsinki PD still has the drug case, of course. I'll probably go chat with Narcotics about that," Suhonen continued.

"And we still have an open investigation on that train station death, was it Karjalainen?"

"Yep. We've requested his phone records."

"Careful, though. Don't give them the opportunity to push the blame on us if something goes wrong."

"If something goes wrong, you'll be carrying Salmela's coffin with me."

The car circled a massive interchange onto Tuusula Road.

"By the way, do you know a Skull by the name of Osku, probably pretty new?" asked Takamäki.

Suhonen looked at the lieutenant. "Osku Rahkonen. New recruit, about twenty years old. Why?"

"What else do you know about him?"

"The database has quite a bit on him, but his background is pretty typical. He's from the Kilo district of Espoo, or at least he's lived over there for some time. I remember reading in some report that his father has a rap sheet for assault and battery. The kid followed in the dad's footsteps, wound up in juvie for aggravated assault, and there he met his buddy Roge, or Roger Sandström. Of the two, Roge is bigger—built like a bull. But I wouldn't say Osku's the brains. I understand neither has much to brag about upstairs, which makes them great candidates for the Skulls. So, why you interested in Osku?"

"His little brother Ripa plays hockey with our Joonas. Supposedly, this Osku has lots of money."

"Wouldn't doubt that," said Suhonen.

"He bought Ripa some fancy phone and now Joonas has to have one."

The car zoomed under an overpass. A lighted sign on a brick building displayed the temperature: 41° F.

"Sounds like more of a problem for dad than for Detective Lieutenant Takamäki," Suhonen chuckled.

CHAPTER 17
SUNDAY, 4:00 P.M.
OLYMPIC STADIUM, HELSINKI

Salmela was fed up. He rounded the north end of the soccer stadium and headed toward the Olympic Stadium. According to his directions, he was supposed to come to the statue of Paavo Nurmi, the famous distance runner who won nine Olympic gold medals in the '20s.

Salmela wouldn't have complained if it weren't for the rain, which only seemed to mock him. Over the phone, a man had told him to go to the Sörnäinen Metro station in East Helsinki, then take the subway downtown to the central train station, and loop through the Kamppi Shopping Center before taking the streetcar to the Olympic Stadium.

The man had introduced himself as Aalto, and told him that they wanted to be sure that nobody followed him. So far, nobody had. And why would they, Salmela thought.

He reached the agreed-upon corner just as a gray Ford Focus pulled up. The driver pushed a button and the window slid down. His eyes met Salmela's. The driver was in his thirties, with neatly-trimmed hair and a baggy blue hoodie. "Get in," he said.

"Who're you?"

"The police are your friends," he said simply.

"Is there a problem?"

"No, that's why I'm here. The situation has been

deemed safe—you should get in now."

Salmela climbed in the passenger side. "How many of you guys are involved in this?"

"Plenty," the driver said and sped off. "As a matter of protocol, we've been watching, and nobody has followed you. I have orders from Aalto to bring you to the meeting place."

The driver turned northbound onto Urheilu Street.

"What kind of a guy is this Aalto?" Salmela asked.

"What kind of a guy does he seem like to you?"

Salmela watched Töölö's pale-green high school drift past on the left. "Pretty damn careful."

"That's just how he is. Doesn't take any risks, which is good as far as I'm concerned. That's why I can't talk to you."

"But you already have."

"Not anymore. You're in the hands of professionals."

They passed the Finnair Soccer Stadium and continued northward. Salmela recalled his meetings with Suhonen. Those had been different—somehow peaceful, even. Often they had met over beers at the Corner Pub, but after his spell in prison, that had ended. Maybe Suhonen didn't think the place was safe anymore.

More recently, Suhonen had always picked him up at some agreed-upon spot and they had chatted at a gas station or some other public place. Last time, Suhonen wouldn't even agree to meet at the usual Teboil café. And now this. Salmela wondered who had changed, he or Suhonen.

They passed the Helsinki Ice Center on the right and the driver continued straight through the intersection. Oddly, having lived in Helsinki most of his adult life, Salmela had never been in this neighborhood before. The buildings looked like they were from the sixties. He wasn't even sure what this part of town was called.

What if this was just a test from the Skulls? Would they check to see if he'd talk to someone he believed was a cop? And if he did, well... Well, what then? He had already been to the cliff in the Nuuksio forest—what else could they do? Except, perhaps, to make his death more unpleasant than a bullet in the mouth.

A painful death was something to fear, but Salmela no longer had anything to look forward to in life. He had no family to live for, nor was there any purpose for the rest of his journey. His own mistakes had cost him everything. His marriage had fallen apart while he was in prison. His son had been shot. He had no friends, save for the guys at the Corner Pub and Suhonen. They were the only ones who cared.

And now, of course, the Skulls and the NBI. Damn.

They passed a hospital on the right. Parked cars on both sides of the street narrowed the lanes.

The wheels were spinning in Salmela's head. He tried to gather his thoughts and quiet the pulsating pain in the back of his head. Suhonen was an old friend and things had always worked both ways with him. He gave Suhonen information the police needed, and in return, Suhonen helped him out from time to time. This exchange was mutually beneficial, and its scale minimal. Salmela had never considered himself a nark.

Now the whole ordeal seemed more complicated. Suhonen had urged him to agree to it—said it would be his ticket to a new life. But was that really possible? So far, he hadn't succeeded. His efforts had earned him a job as the Skulls' toilet cleaner, and now as an informant for the NBI. Escape seemed impossible.

His headache was steadily seizing more space in his skull. Maybe it would pass if he quit thinking, just listened, and did as he was told.

The driver braked and stopped in front of a tan three-story stucco building. Salmela immediately noticed the fire escape scaling the outside wall. It would be easy to burglarize the building.

"That's it. Someone in the stairwell will tell you where to go."

"Okay," Salmela said, and got out.

He dodged the puddles in the front yard and hurried toward the building.

The white-framed entry door was oddly tall. Salmela stopped and wondered whether the door would bring him more trouble or redemption. He wasn't sure, but the Ford standing behind him compelled him onward. He could run, of course. Mannerheim Street wasn't far. There he could catch a bus, and head someplace where nobody was interested in Eero Salmela. But they would find him—if not the Skulls then the police. In the end, there was really no difference between the two, he thought.

He ascended the seven steps and paused briefly in front of the door. Salvation or hell? Unable to decide, he pulled the door open.

A man behind the door startled him. He wore a suit, a short haircut and was holding out his hand.

"Hello. I'm Aalto. We have a lot to talk about. Let's go up to the second floor."

"What's up there?"

"An apartment. It's our safe house—one of many. We can speak privately there. Nobody will bother us or suspect anything. It's completely secure." Aalto headed up the stairs.

Salmela followed close behind.

Halfway up, Aalto turned around. "Are you hungry?"

"Well, a little."

"Good. We have sandwiches up there." He had used the same question many times before in similar situations. He had no real reason to ask the question in the stairwell, but it created a sense of security. Naturally, the informant was nervous. But if the police had time to talk about sandwiches on the stairs, it would calm down the prospective informant. At the same time, it created the illusion that the police were actually interested in the person, not just the information they possessed.

The door to the apartment was ajar and Aalto went in first. This too was pre-planned: an underlying message that the police were looking out for the informant's safety. The informant didn't have to enter a strange place alone with the police behind their back.

Aalto knew that emotions were made of simple things.

The two-room flat was modest, but not barren. In the entry hall was a row of coat hooks and a shallow table. The bedroom featured a double bed, and in the living room were a small dining set and two loveseats. The walls were decorated with a few uninspiring prints. Despite its dreariness, the apartment was clean.

The NBI had numerous apartments across the country for just these types of situations. They could be used to interview informants, to lodge participants of the witness protection program, and even as a base for undercover surveillance operations. Of course, neither the Interior Ministry nor the police were listed as the official owners. The flats usually belonged to fronting companies that then rented the apartments to the NBI, making it difficult for the criminals to identify or locate them. Nearly all of the apartments had wound up in the state's hands after an elderly person died and no next of kin were found. The Interior Ministry and its subordinate organizations, such as the police departments, didn't have the money to buy apartments on the open market.

Aalto invited Salmela into the living room. An older, portlier cop named Lind was seated at the dining table. Fifty years old and sporting a thick mustache, Lind could have been a regular at just about any corner pub. His voice was low and soothing, but his gaze was cutting.

"Hello," said Lind, offering his hand. "Glad you came."

These words too were scripted, ensuring that the cops didn't say, "Glad you could make it," or, "Glad you're here." Instead, he specifically said, "Glad you came." It implied that Salmela had made the choice himself.

Salmela shook hands with the man. Aalto and Lind were in some respects opposites of one another: a stiff suit and a street-smart cop.

* * *

Suhonen knocked on the doorframe. Narcotics Detective Toukola was sitting alone in an office he shared with four other cops. The space was almost identical to the VCU's, one floor up.

"Hey there," said Toukola.

Suhonen had been hoping to talk earlier, but Toukola's evening shift didn't start until four.

"Busy?" Suhonen said as he stepped into the room.

"No, not yet anyway."

Toukola was dressed in jeans and a red hooded sweatshirt. On the night shift, he was responsible for reacting to whatever happened in the field. If all was quiet, he would work on existing cases, fill out overdue paperwork or just drink coffee. Nonetheless, a case could arise suddenly from, say, a routine traffic stop where officers stumbled upon a large stash of dope.

"Hard to say if that's good or bad," Suhonen commented.

"What, are you crazy? Of course it's good."

"I guess."

Suhonen steered a neighboring chair between his legs and sat down.

Toukola looked at Suhonen. "Well? You need more work, or…?"

"How's that Marju Mägi?"

Toukola laughed. "Miss mini-mule? Why you so interested in her? It's not even your case, even if the tip came from you."

"That's exactly why I'm interested." Suhonen relayed the story of how Karjalainen, the druggie who had been on the ship with Mägi, had died of an overdose. He told him about the visit to Karjalainen's apartment, the stash they found, and the conversation with his girlfriend.

"I see," said Toukola, somewhat displeased. "You should've called me. I would've come."

"You were off duty and I don't have the clout to authorize your overtime. Has she said anything?"

Toukola shook his head. "Last time we spoke was yesterday, and she didn't want to say anything. I doubt she will today either. Looks like she'll take the rap for the drugs rather than open her mouth and end up in deeper trouble."

"Doesn't surprise me."

"Me neither," said Toukola. "But now you think Karjalainen was in on it too? Didn't I tell you back at the harbor we should search the guy?"

"Possibly. I can't remember."

"Karjalainen doesn't have the brains to run a four-pound dope smuggling operation. So, who's behind it?" Toukola mused.

Now, for the first time, Toukola was engaged in the conversation. It finally interested him more than surfing the news on the web. He had wound up on a page that flaunted the biggest silicone boobs in Hollywood.

"Good question," said Suhonen. "Don't know."

"This girlfriend of Karjalainen's..." Toukola began, but cut his sentence short. "Shit, you already questioned her and found a couple ounces. What'd she tell you?"

"What do you mean?"

"Come on. A woman with a bag of dope in her apartment, and I haven't seen a single report about it on the computer. We see every drug case in the database and I just looked through them."

"Look under cause-of-death investigations."

"Aha," said Toukola and tapped out something on his keyboard. He found the report of Karjalainen's death and of the amphetamines found in his home. "No mention here of any woman. What'd she tell you about those drugs?"

"That they belonged to Karjalainen. We sent the sample to the lab to find out if it's the same stuff we found on Mägi."

"That will take weeks, at least," said Toukola. He thought for a second and stared hard at Suhonen.

"Why are you here?"

Suhonen grinned. "Just to warn you not to make any mistakes. The case is now connected to a covert NBI investigation."

Toukola pretended to be frightened. "Oh shit, we should be trembling and turning off the computers. He groped around for the desk phone, snatched it up and pressed it to his ear.

"The state prosecutor, please. I'd like to turn myself in for overzealousness. Just don't hand me over to the NBI..."

That got a laugh from Suhonen, but Toukola ended the show. "So where are they going with this and what am I supposed to do?"

"Mägi had twenty ounces, so somebody else has the other three pounds. Isn't that interesting to you? Especially when the dope is so strong that an experienced user ODs."

"Sure, but it'd be more interesting with another zero after the three. You seem to have an idea on where we could find it."

"At least on who we should ask."

"Well?"

"Just before he died, Karjalainen met Juha Saarnikangas. You know the guy?"

"No, but the name is familiar. A heroin addict who's supposedly clean now. Friend of yours?"

Suhonen circled to the window and looked out over the wet landscape. How could it keep raining this long?

"Sort of," Suhonen replied. "I helped him out a couple times when he hit bottom and we've been on speaking terms since."

Toukola knew what that meant: Saarnikangas was Suhonen's informant.

"Should we go after your aspiring informant? If

the guy is in good shape, knows a lot and stays out of trouble, I'd say he's pretty valuable."

In a way, Toukola was right. There was a time when that's how it worked with Salmela, too, but on the other hand, informants had to be kept humble and obedient.

"You want to come with and have a chat with him?"

Toukola looked at the stack of paper on his desk. "You need me?"

"No."

"Why'd you ask, then?"

"Because this Mägi thing is your case. You should know what's going on."

"I trust you. Let me know if you find that three pounds and I'll come get it."

* * *

Roge had a shovel, and Osku, a backpack. The Toyota Camry they had borrowed from the downstairs garage stood fifty yards off on the shoulder of a dirt road. The woods were quiet in western Espoo, about ten miles from the Skulls' headquarters. Raindrops pattered on the leaf-covered ground. The forest smelled of wet soil.

Along with the bag, Osku had a cell phone and a handheld GPS system.

"How 'bout that rock over there?" Roge asked.

Osku gave a nod of approval and Roge set the blade of the shovel at the base of the rock. He scraped the leaves aside, carved out a chunk of mossy sod just bigger than a sheet of office paper, and set it carefully to the side.

The soil in the nature reserve was soft and the work advanced quickly. Roge shoveled the soil into a large black garbage bag. Once the depth reached about two feet, he stopped digging.

Osku, wearing gloves, glanced in his backpack. At the bottom of the pack were four one-pound packages of amphetamines, shrink-wrapped with an additional layer of foil around them. He dropped the backpack into the hole.

Roge dumped soil from the garbage bag into the hole until it reached grade level. With the shovel, he compacted the soil and added some more from the bag. Then he carefully lifted the layer of sod back into place and sprinkled some leaves over the area.

Osku took a photograph of the spot with his cell phone, and saved the coordinates from the built-in GPS system onto the picture. He compared the coordinates in the photograph to those on the handheld GPS unit. They matched. Just to be sure, he stored the coordinates in the handheld unit as well.

The operation had taken fifteen minutes.

A few days earlier the Estonian shipment had been cut to 15-20 percent purity—typical street grade. Out of the three pound shipment, they now had sixteen pounds to sell. Roge and Osku had already dug two similar holes elsewhere. This package was the last to be hidden in the woods.

Osku wasn't sure how the sale would be made, but he guessed the buyer would get the photograph, cell phone or GPS unit, or a map based on one of them. He didn't care. People he didn't even know would take care of that.

The men trudged back to the car.

"Well, that's that," Osku smiled.

CHAPTER 18
SUNDAY, 5:10 P.M.
THE NBI SAFEHOUSE, HELSINKI

To Salmela, everything had seemed to go smoothly at first. The NBI agents had treated him to a sandwich, a soft drink and coffee. The discussion had seemed harmless. They had even offered him a beer from the fridge, but he had declined.

The agents had asked about his life and Salmela had told them everything—from the best to the worst. From his son's shining moments on the soccer field as a twelve-year-old to his wife demanding a divorce while he was doing time.

One of the agents was continually taking notes, which bothered Salmela.

Then the questions had turned to his past crimes, but Salmela only talked about the ones that he could remember being convicted of. He could no longer remember all the details of the cases. The statutes of limitation had been reached in most of the others anyway. Some of the questions were asked twice, with slightly different wording.

The NBI was also interested in his relationship with Suhonen. Who said what, and when. Salmela had dodged these questions. At one point, he had even wondered whether the NBI was actually investigating Suhonen, but then he recalled the Skulls.

The agents took an interest in his time in prison as

well. What cell had he been in? Whom had he spoken with? How had he met the Skulls' Larsson? They wanted to know how Salmela had gotten his head injury. He gave them the same yarn he gave while still in prison: he had tripped on the stairs. In truth, Salmela's enemy had paid a prison guard for the hit.

The agents weren't convinced by his story, but they accepted it.

They pried into the origins of his debt and his recent experiences with the Skulls. Salmela had complained about his headache and was allowed to rest in the bedroom for half an hour. He had assumed that Suhonen had told the agents about those encounters. The rest did him some good and he ate some more. He'd stay quiet about the hike in the Nuuksio forest.

"Alright, then," said Aalto, drawing a hand over his long face. "We've made good progress here and your honesty is encouraging. I think we're on the same wavelength."

Salmela was suspicious of this, but didn't respond. The cops might think they were on the same wavelength, but he didn't share the sentiment.

"You have kids?" Salmela asked Aalto.

"I beg your pardon?"

"I have to trust you, so tell me."

Aalto was taken aback. "Yes. Two little girls."

"What's your wife's name and profession?"

"What?"

"What church were you married in? Where do you live?" Salmela pressed on.

Aalto was irritated. "We can get back to that once we've worked together a while."

Salmela nodded. Clearly a one-sided relationship that wouldn't last.

"Let's get back to the matter at hand," said Aalto.

"We still have a lot to talk about, and we're already in the critical phase."

"What?"

"You're already on the inside," Aalto elaborated.

"What do you mean?"

"Typically, in these cases it takes a long time to get the informant on the inside, but not in your case."

"Okay," Salmela caught his drift. He had a job at the Skulls' compound and the cops wanted intel from there. "What do you want from me?"

"We need to know who hangs out there. Who meets with the bosses, like this Larsson. What do they talk about? If they have parties, we need you to bring us the cigarette butts."

"How come?" asked Salmela, remembering the marijuana butts in his pocket. Hopefully the cops wouldn't find them.

"We can find out who was there by extracting DNA and comparing it to the database. If someone you don't know seems important, bring us his beer glass and we'll get the prints. Of course, if you sense the risk of getting caught, forget it. Don't put yourself in danger."

"Okay" said Salmela again. It seemed simple, yet left him with a foul taste. He wanted out of the Skulls, but now he was being squeezed between them and the police.

"But the most important thing is that you keep your ears open and tell us if you notice any conflicts or tension. If anything really urgent or sudden happens, you'll call my number, but otherwise we'll meet weekly at this apartment or another."

"You have a lot of these, then?"

"Enough," Aalto smiled.

"I don't suppose anyone lives here?"

"No."

Salmela thought for a second. Now it was his turn to ask the questions, "What's in it for me?"

"What do you want?"

"To be safe for the rest of my life."

Both agents nodded their heads. "Your safety is our highest priority."

That was a smart answer, but it didn't convince Salmela.

"These Skulls are brutal. If they find out I've been talking to you, I'm dead."

"They won't find out from us. If you let it slip yourself, all we can do is react, but I can guarantee nobody will find out through us."

"I just can't believe you can actually wipe out the Skulls. They think I owe them twenty grand, so if I want to live, I have to pay up." Salmela paused before continuing. "How do we deal with that?"

"While the state *can* print money, they don't do it for the police," said Aalto. "Not even if we beg. Once we have something to go on, we'll be able to pay you an appropriate amount to help with your financial needs."

The promise seemed nebulous to Salmela. "So you'll only pay when you get something. But if I can't bring you anything, you pay nothing?"

"It's not like that either, but my boss doesn't cut blank checks."

Salmela stared Aalto in the eyes. "So maybe I should talk to your boss?"

"No."

"Why not?"

"He doesn't know who you are, nor do we want him to. Within the NBI, you have a code name that we can't reveal to you. Your real name and code name are sealed in a safe."

"You never answered my question about the debt."

Aalto took a sip from the water bottle on the table. "It's like this, Salmela. Right now, your value is about the same as this water. If I end up sitting at my desk staring at the screen, I won't get thirsty. Coffee will do fine. But if you get me to run, sweat and get my heart rate up, then that's worth something, and you'll get your money. It all depends on you."

Right, of course, Salmela thought. He was regretting his decision already.

"One more thing," he said. "How long you think it's going to take?"

"We don't know. A couple weeks, a couple months, a couple years. If you're in that compound every day, it's bound to yield some intel we can work with."

Salmela felt cold. The Skulls wanted him for a year and the cops for two. His mind conjured the image of a grill at a hot dog stand, with sausages pressed between two iron grates.

One of the agents rose and walked over to the stereo, perhaps wanting something more cheerful to lighten the mood.

A familiar hit sounded from the speakers. The singer's ragged voice belted out, *"You're a beer glass on the bar, glossed by thirsty sips... The black rock of Islam, smoothed by countless lips."*

Hell, Salmela thought. He rearranged the rhyme in his head, *"A losing poker hand, give up the chips."*

* * *

Suhonen pulled his unmarked silver Peugeot into a parking space on the roof of the Prisma grocery store in southern Espoo. He seemed to recall having been to this store before, but wasn't sure. All Prismas were alike—if you'd been to one, you'd been to them all.

The undercover detective didn't know why Juha Saarnikangas wanted to meet in Espoo of all places. Perhaps his informant had some business in the western suburbs or maybe the man had moved. The last Suhonen knew, Saarnikangas had lived across town, somewhere in East Helsinki.

The ex-junkie had asked Suhonen to be at the parking ramp at six. Now it was five minutes till. The store was closed on Sundays and only a few cars remained. Suhonen spotted Juha's white Ducato van near the entrance of the store.

He pulled up to the side of the van. Saarnikangas watched from the driver's seat as Suhonen got out of his car and climbed into the passenger seat.

"Did you move or something?" asked Suhonen.

Juha wiped some crumbs from his ragged army jacket. His dirty brown hair emerged from beneath a black beanie cap.

"What do you mean?"

"What are you doing here in Espoo?"

Saarnikangas grinned. "Friend of mine lives around here. I'm doing a little remodeling for him."

Suhonen was skeptical. A few years ago, while in the clutches of a heroin addiction, the man would have scarcely been able to hold onto a hammer. Though now he could probably manage to hold on, Suhonen doubted the former art student would even know which end was up.

"Plumbing or wiring?"

Saarnikangas ignored the ribbing. "Neither, I'm putting in a parquet floor... You wanted to meet?" Juha looked impatient.

"About your friend Karjalainen."

"Right. I gathered that much over the phone, but

why couldn't you just ask about it then?"

"I want to see your face when you answer," said Suhonen with a steady gaze.

"What's that supposed to mean?"

"Just what I said—if you lie, I'll see it."

Juha forced a laugh. "I figured you guys already had those phone-based lie detectors."

"Those are still in testing at the insurance companies."

"Listen, always nice to chat, but if you have something to ask me, ask it. I gotta run some errands."

"I thought you were laying some parquet."

Juha answered quickly, "Yeah, but I gotta get the wood first."

"Right," said Suhonen. He made an expression that showed he had caught the man in a lie.

"Karjalainen didn't have any money in his pockets. Did you empty them?"

Juha waited a moment too long to respond.

"Don't bother lying. If your hand was in his pocket, we'll get the DNA."

He wasn't sure if that was true, but the important thing was that Juha believed him.

"Yeah, I cleaned 'em out."

"Why?"

"He didn't need it anymore."

"How much did he have?"

"Maybe twenty, thirty euros. Not much."

"Where's his cell phone?"

Juha looked at Suhonen. "That's what you want?"

"What I want is to know what game you're playing."

"Huh?"

Suhonen's expression was hard. "I suspect that Karjalainen was involved in amphetamine smuggling and had contacted you. You say he owed you some money, and suddenly, an experienced doper dies of an overdose in the train station's bathroom. Doesn't that make you wonder?"

"Well, I guess..." said Juha, wondering how Suhonen had found out about Karjalainen's involvement in the smuggling job. "...I sure ain't mixed up in that... So what..." he trailed off. He had seen Suhonen with Salmela, who was also involved in the job. So was Salmela the rat?

But, Salmela shouldn't have known anything about his involvement in the drug shipment, Juha thought. Was the guy just faking his head injury? Maybe he wasn't as dumb as he pretended to be. How much did Salmela actually know? Juha wouldn't have believed that Salmela could have discovered his role in the job—the man had even sought financing from him. But apparently, Salmela knew much more.

"What do you mean 'so what?'" Suhonen demanded.

"Nothing... Just that there's a constant stream of drugs coming over from Estonia."

"How do you know this has anything to do with Estonia?"

Saarnikangas snorted. "What do you mean? Almost all the speed in Finland is cooked in the Baltics and comes over by ship. Besides, Karjalainen told me he'd been over there."

"When did he say that?"

"When we set up the train station meeting. We were supposed to meet earlier, but he'd been in Tallinn. I think he had some woman over there."

Saarnikangas tried to remember when he had talked to Karjalainen, and what phone he had used. Suhonen would doubtless find Karjalainen's number, which would allow him to trace the calls.

The full smuggling scheme wasn't entirely clear to Saarnikangas. Karjalainen, deep in debt, had told him that a woman had given him the packets on the ship in order to spread the risk. Apparently, someone in Tallinn had ratted out the woman as payback for her flings, or so he had heard.

His own role was minor. He had picked up Karjalainen from the harbor, taken the dope, and cut it to street purity. Then, under orders from Mike Gonzales, he had delivered it to the Skulls' compound.

"I see," said Suhonen. "A woman, huh?"

"I believe so."

"I don't."

Saarnikangas had no intention of taking the fall for this gig. There was no point in talking to Suhonen anymore. The cop was just fishing for bits of info and connecting them until, one day, Juha would end up in jail for a stupid drug deal. Then, inevitably, he would be the fall guy, since he couldn't talk about his employers, at least not if he valued his life.

Saarnikangas grew impatient. "Fuck, I don't know. He lived by the fire station and had a common-law wife. They rolled junkies together. Wouldn't surprise me if he pimped her to pay debts. He even offered her to me once."

"You take him up on it?"

"No. Pretty sure that broad's got HIV. I've been lucky and dodged it so far, so I don't want to take the risk. I'm just trying to stay clean and get my life back in order… I've got no part in this except Karjalainen owed me some money, went to the bathroom and died. And I was stupid enough to call you in a panic."

Suhonen didn't respond.

"You need anything else?"

"Not now, but if you want to stay out of jail, don't lie to me anymore."

As Suhonen climbed out of the van, Saarnikangas cursed Salmela under his breath. They had meant to take advantage of the simpleton, but the fool had gone and talked to the cops, and most likely, Salmela had mentioned him by name.

* * *

Joonas was sitting in the kitchen eating the spaghetti his dad had just prepared.

"This is great," he said between gulps of milk from a plastic mug. "What is it?"

"A secret recipe," said Takamäki.

"So… Barelli spaghetti and Ragu sauce."

Takamäki sat down at the table with his own plate. Six chairs circled the table, but two were buried under piles of mail. "Not sure about the brands, but you got the recipe right."

As hungry as the boy was, Takamäki suspected he wouldn't have noticed if the hamburger were raw and the pasta uncooked.

"Can I ask you about something?" said Joonas.

"Of course."

"We went through the principles of business today in econ and learned that the primary purpose of every business is to maximize profits for its owners."

Takamäki wasn't entirely sure that he agreed, but apparently that's how it was explained. "Yeah."

"So, with that same logic, what would you say is the purpose of an ordinary citizen?"

Takamäki wasn't prepared for this kind of conversation, but at this point, he couldn't wiggle out without an answer. "What did they tell you in class?"

"Nothing. That's why I'm interested."

"Well, under that model, I'd say it would be to maximize your own welfare as well as that of your family and friends," said Takamäki. "And the best way to maximize your welfare is to…"

"Don't get into that yet," said Joonas. "Let's stick to the principles. So, let's take a look at you, Dad. What's the objective of a civil servant?"

Takamäki thought for a moment. "To maximize the welfare of society, certainly. A civil servant can't think about himself."

Joonas nodded. "Let's keep going. So, what about a criminal?"

Takamäki wondered if he was walking into a trap.

"Criminals only think of themselves."

"So," the boy paused. "You said the goal of an ordinary citizen is to maximize his own welfare, but isn't that the same objective as the criminal's who only thinks of himself?"

Takamäki bobbed his head vaguely. "As an end, maybe, but the means…"

"Let's not get into the means, let's just stick with the principles."

"These principles…"

Joonas cut him off. "And with the civil servant thinking of the entire society's welfare, which is actually pretty far removed from the interests of its individual citizens. Aren't citizens just tools of the society?"

Takamäki took a deep breath. "As I recall, the conversation started with economics, and how the goal of a corporation is to make a profit. That right there is a banker's philosophy, but in my view, profit can't be the sole objective for business owners. A healthy society benefits business owners, too. What good is a wheelbarrow full of money if you can't buy anything with it?"

"What do the police want, then?" asked Joonas.

Takamäki paused to think. "The police want to eliminate crime, of course."

"So they'd put themselves out of a job."

"Honestly, I'd rather be a florist than a cop. But because this banker's philosophy of self-interest is so deep-rooted in society, somebody has to do the dirty work. The police are society's scrub brush."

Jonas thought for a while, and asked "You think the police should be able to solve all crimes?"

"In theory, that's the idea. But the cost to society…additional taxes, loss of privacy, loss of freedom…would be prohibitive."

"Are you serious?" Joonas blurted out with a broad smile. "Aren't you rejecting your own profession by saying that crime has to be accepted?"

To hell with this philosophical talk. Philosophy was the furthest thing from a homicide detective's mind when trying to sort out which of the drunks in an apartment had been sober enough to manage to sink a knife in another one's chest.

His mind wandered back to the police academy dorms and the debates they had had on the same topic. Over countless beers, they had hashed it out till the wee hours. One day, they had even asked a police academy instructor, who had one piece of advice: If the conversation gets too difficult, always remember that a cop's toolbox includes a billy club.

"Want some more spaghetti?"

"Sure, but answer my question."

"Here's my answer: Eat, do your homework, clean your room and then I'll take you to hockey practice."

"Do I get an iPhone?"

"No. By the way, have you been in touch with Ripa?"

"Why?"

"Just asking."

"You interested in him or his brother?"

Takamäki chuckled, but his voice took on a serious tone. "If his brother is really in the Skulls, then I'm interested, particularly if he kills somebody or gets killed himself. Hard to say which will happen first."

Joonas said nothing.

"It's your decision, but if you ask me, I'd tell you to stay away from that Ripa and his brother."

* * *

Saarnikangas backed his van up to a brick-red shipping container at a construction site in western Espoo. Two men in overalls appeared and opened the shipping container first, then the back doors of the van.

Apart from those three, the construction site was quiet and nobody was about in the surrounding area. Hemmed in by tall trees, the place looked even darker in the steady rain.

A small sign on the shipping container stated that a two-story office building was under construction. The sign didn't list the general contractor, just a name and phone number.

The men began loading cardboard boxes into the van. Saarnikangas opened the driver's side door, thinking he'd walk back and watch, but the ground was muddy and he didn't want to dirty his shoes. In any case, he would just get in the way, and besides, it wasn't his job.

He didn't know where the goods had come from, or even what they were, but he doubted they were being stolen from here. Such a large amount would be noticed immediately.

He suspected the shipping container was being used as a temporary warehouse to store stolen supplies and tools taken from other sites. Construction sites suited the purpose well. Transporting goods was part of the business, so people loading a van didn't attract attention, even on a Sunday night.

The van shuddered as the boxes hit the floor. The transfer took fifteen minutes.

One of the men came to the passenger side door with a single box. A sticker on top read, "Handle with care," in English.

"Careful with this one," he said, and placed it on the seat with his massive hands.

Juha was tempted to look inside the box, but it was bound with so much tape that it would be impossible peek in.

The doors slammed shut and the men disappeared. After sputtering for a while, the Fiat Ducato roared to life.

Juha swung onto the road and dug a cheap cell phone out of his pocket. It had been given it to him expressly for this job.

The man answered immediately.

"Hey," said Juha. "Where should I take these?"

"Go to Kivihaan Road first," said Mike Gonzales, and gave him the exact address of an apartment building. "There's a remodeling job there. A guy will come out and get the stuff he needs."

"Should I ring the doorbell, or how does he know to come out?"

"Ring the doorbell," said Gonzales. He rattled off two more addresses in Maunula and Oulunkylä. After that, he said, the van should be empty.

"There's some kind of special package here?" Juha said as he pulled onto the ramp to Beltway Three.

"Give it to the guy in Maunula. He'll take care of it from there."

"Sounds good."

"One more thing," said Gonzales. "You know a guy named Eero Salmela?"

An oncoming car had its high-beams on and Juha flashed his brights back. "Why?"

"A friend asked me to check on him."

"Can I ask what friend?"

"No. Obviously you know the guy."

"Sure... I know him. I actually just heard something a little disturbing about him."

"What?" Gonzales asked eagerly.

Juha pictured Salmela's face. There was something pitiable about the guy, especially after his last prison term. The blow to his head had been another to his IQ. But Juha still remembered how, when he was in the depths of his heroin addiction, Salmela had treated him like trash. And now the asshole had squealed to Suhonen about the amphetamine shipment. He deserved to eat shit for it.

"Kind of a touchy subject," said Juha. "But according to my info, Salmela's been in touch with the police."

"Dammit," Gonzales hissed. "You sure?"

"Yes."

"Not just gossip?"

"No. It's for sure. With a Helsinki cop named Suhonen."

Gonzales thanked him. "You'll be paid well for this. This is important info."

Juha slipped the phone back into the breast pocket of his green jacket. Tough luck for Salmela, but he'd been asking for it. Just like Suhonen.

* * *

The room was dark, and the display on the cell phone lit up before it rang.

Lying on the bed beneath the covers, Suhonen slowly became aware of the ringing. As he awoke, he wasn't sure whether he had been sleeping for a while, or had just dozed off. Then, realizing the noise was the ringer of his number-two phone, he groped for the lamp and snatched the phone off the nightstand. He glanced at the clock on the display: 1:37 A.M.

"What's the matter?" he answered, having seen the caller already.

"Did I wake you up?" asked Eero Salmela.

Suhonen felt like cussing him out, but only managed to repeat, "What's the matter?"

"Actually... It's nothing, but..."

"But what?"

"I have a bad feeling about this gig."

He sounded relatively sober. "How so? Something happen?"

Suhonen sat up in bed.

"Just nervous. I can't sleep."

Shit, watch a skin flick and fall asleep to that, thought Suhonen, but he bit his tongue.

"That's normal. I've been nervous too."

"I'm pretty much convinced they're gonna see right through me tomorrow."

"They won't know a thing. You've already been there a couple of days—you're like a piece of furniture."

Salmela laughed. "Speaking of furniture. Did you know they brought a headstone in there?"

"A headstone?"

"A big slab of granite with a bunch of names on it."

"Uuhh. What names?"

"Pretty sure they were dead gangsters, but I didn't want to stare. Jyrkkä, Kahma and Korpela were on there. Tomorrow I can dust it and look closer."

Suhonen remembered the names well. All three were Skulls who had been killed in firefights with the police.

"Those are gangsters. No need to worry about it," said Suhonen, though he wondered why they had a headstone at the house.

"But what the hell is with the gravestone?"

"They want a memorial for their dead and it suits their sense of humor."

"I'm not sure I wanna know what they come up with next."

"Listen, your case is in good hands at the NBI. You're in no danger. Tomorrow, just do the same thing you've been doing, and things will take care of themselves. This is routine stuff."

"That so?"

"Yes, of course. I think I know what kind of info these agents want—you don't need to rush."

Salmela paused briefly. "I'd rather be working with you. That dry-ass suit with the NBI scares me. He doesn't know a thing about this stuff."

"Yes, he does," said Suhonen, surprised at his own impulse to defend Aalto. But assuring Salmela was important for the success of the operation. "They're professionals. Just do as they say."

"I don't believe you."

"This is your chance to get out of your mess. Take care of your job and the NBI will take care of you. Everything will go just fine," said Suhonen. "Catch a few hours of shuteye. You'll feel better in the morning."

"Promise?"

Suhonen didn't really know what he was promising, but answered nevertheless, "Of course."

MONDAY, OCTOBER 26

CHAPTER 19
MONDAY, 9:15 A.M.
SKULLS' COMPOUND, HELSINKI

Salmela dumped the contents of an ashtray into a plastic wastebasket. He considered whether he should sneak the butts out, as the NBI agents had instructed, but recalled Suhonen's advice and decided against it.

Salmela's gait was calm, much like it had been in prison. There, it had been best to blend in with the masses so as not to attract attention. The zipper on his sweater was pulled all the way up and he wore a pair of jeans. Standing in the middle of the bar room, he glanced around, but nobody seemed to pay him any attention.

The janitor went from one table to another, gathering ashes. There were less butts than yesterday, and no doobies, at least not yet.

In five minutes, the job was done. Next, he decided to wipe the tables. He grabbed a rag from the bar, rinsed it under the tap and began wiping the nearest table.

His eyes returned occasionally to the headstone behind the bar. The granite slab gave him goose bumps.

The bull-like Roge and the goateed Osku stepped out of the office and closed the door behind them. They didn't even look at Salmela.

"Where'd he say the car was?" asked Roge as they walked toward the stairs.

"Weren't you listening? The Käpylä ball fields. In the gravel parking lot on the north end."

"And what time we gotta pick it up?"

"Three!" You better pay attention or Larsson is gonna whack you."

Roge's expression was serious. "I remember the dope is in a beige Opel."

"Betcha it'll have some fuzzy dice," said Osku.

"You drive it outta there, then," said Roge as they reached the stairs.

Osku shook his head and Salmela heard them settle the matter with a game of "key, file, and bars". The file wins over bars, but loses to the key. And the key doesn't work on bars.

Salmela moved on to the next table and wondered what car the men were referring to. He repeated it in his head: a beige Opel with dope on the north end of the Käpylä ball fields at three.

He looked at the clock: 9:30. Cleaning would take another couple of hours. After that he could call.

* * *

Suhonen was sitting at his workstation studying a spreadsheet of Vesa Karjalainen's phone records. He didn't know whether the junkie had had any other phones—he had found out about this one from the man's common-law widow.

The date, time, cell tower, and of course, the callers' and recipients' phone numbers were in columns on the spreadsheet. On suspicion of drug-trafficking, the District Court had allowed Takamäki's team access to all of Karjalainen's phone records from October 15 until October 25. The data began a week before Karjalainen had left for Tallinn. The cut-off date, as requested, had been yesterday, but the last recorded call was on the day of his death.

Suhonen was no fan of fiddling with computers, but he couldn't really ask the other detectives to help. They had plenty of their own cases. Had it been a homicide, he would have just gotten someone else to do it. Joutsamo was good with computers, but even Suhonen knew the basics of spreadsheets. If he needed to create a graph, though, he'd have to ask for help.

Suhonen quickly scanned the data. Initially, there had been about ten calls a day, many of them to his common-law wife's phone.

Apparently, Karjalainen hadn't brought his phone to Estonia, since the data had a one-day hole on the date that Suhonen had seen him at the harbor. After that, the calls resumed, as before, at a rate of about ten per day.

Suhonen had checked a few of the numbers in the police database, but they were all pre-paid cards, which were inherently anonymous.

The last call on the list had been placed three days ago, on the day of Karjalainen's death. The time was 9:20 A.M. and the call was fielded by a cell tower in northern Helsinki. The recipient had been downtown, which didn't help him identify the owner of the phone.

Suhonen suspected that this just might be one of Juha Saarnikangas' numbers, though it wasn't one that he knew about. Maybe Karjalainen had called the ex-junkie to say he was running late for the meeting. Saarnikangas had called about the death a little after ten.

Suhonen found four more calls between the same two phones. Of those, one was dated before the trip to Estonia, and three after. All of them, with the exception of the last, were initiated by the phone that

Suhonen suspected was Saarnikangas'.

This call data in itself didn't connect Saarnikangas to the drug case. Had Karjalainen called him from Tallinn, or from the ship on the return trip, it would be a different matter.

On the other hand, now Suhonen had a number, which could very well belong to Saarnikangas, and which his informant had wanted to keep secret. Using that, he could reconstruct Saarnikangas' web of connections.

Right, but connections to what, Suhonen thought. To other anonymous numbers, of course. Suhonen knew Takamäki had worked out an arrangement with Narcotics for Homicide to obtain all phone records in these types of drug-related deaths. They had also agreed that if any of these grew into larger drug investigations, Narcotics would take the lead.

So in order to obtain additional phone records, Suhonen would need permission from Narcotics. A mere cause-of-death investigation did not grant the right to obtain phone records, but drug cases did.

Suhonen scanned the numbers prior to Karjalainen's trip across the gulf, and one captured his attention. It seemed familiar. He took out his phone, scrolled through the directory, and found what he was looking for: Vesa Karjalainen had called Narcotics Detective Toukola two days before his trip to Tallinn.

* * *

Toukola let out a tense laugh. "Uuh. Well, yes, he was my informant."

Suhonen was sitting on the end of Toukola's desk. "Tell me more."

"Or maybe that's too strong a word. He certainly

wasn't able to give me any real intel, but he kept us up to date with word on the street."

"Why didn't you tell me earlier?" Suhonen demanded.

"I told you back at the harbor that I knew him and had busted him for a few pounds of weed. Didn't you read between the lines?"

Suhonen shook his head. It hadn't occurred to him. "What about the mule? Mägi?"

"Hasn't said a word. We finally had to let her take a shower today. I've completed the interview transcripts so now we're just waiting for the lab analysis on the drugs and we'll send the files to the prosecutor. What about the other three pounds? You find them yet?"

"No. Probably never will."

Toukola stared at Suhonen for a long time. "Have you told me everything? What's this all about?"

Suhonen skipped the first question. "As I said earlier, the chance to bust the Skulls."

"But that's in the NBI's court now."

"Not the drug case."

"That's mine," Toukola replied. "Why can't you let it go? I'd think you'd have plenty of assaults, rapes and the like. You know these cases well enough to know what can and can't be achieved. Mägi is locked up, Karjalainen's dead, and the NBI is taking care of the rest of it. Had we found forty or fifty pounds, we could lean on her a lot harder, but we're only dealing with four."

"Karjalainen's stash was obviously strong, and it's probably already been cut to fifteen, sixteen pounds."

Toukola ignored the comment. "If later it becomes evident that this shipment was part of some larger operation, which I wouldn't doubt at all, then we'll combine Mägi's share with it. As is, this case isn't going anywhere further."

"So the drug case is closed."

"Yup," said Toukola. "I already spoke with my boss. We're not pursuing it anymore with the NBI on the case."

Really, thought Suhonen.

* * *

Salmela put the cleaning supplies in the closet and took out his lambswool leather jacket. He shrugged it on and glanced around one last time. He was alone on the second floor.

He grabbed the garbage bags and headed downstairs. All the while he had the feeling that, at any moment, someone would press the barrel of a pistol against the back of his head and stop him. Reaching the first floor, he stepped outside. The dumpster was on the side of the building and he carried the bags there. He realized that gathering the butts would actually be rather easy. He had only to dump them into a separate plastic bag hidden inside the larger garbage bag, and at this point, he could slip the smaller bag into his backpack. The same method would work for glasses with fingerprints. If he needed to, he could "accidentally" break some first.

Maybe Suhonen had been right after all. He could get used to this, but under no circumstances could he get careless.

Salmela noticed that there were fewer cars in the yard. He wondered if business was slow at the downstairs garage. Had the recession caught up to them as well? It certainly shouldn't have. The shop was connected to the Skulls, and criminals didn't feel the pain of economic woes. The downstairs also had a storage room for many of the gangsters' bikes.

He'd have to clean it one of these days.

Salmela walked casually out of the gate, not yet daring to take out his phone. It had been off all morning in his jacket pocket.

The walk to the bus stop was a good three hundred yards. He should call soon. He repeated once more in his head: Roge and Osku will pick up a beige Opel with drugs on the north end of the Käpylä ball fields at three o'clock.

Four facts. Roge and Osku. Beige Opel. At the Käpylä ball fields. At three. Sure, he'd remember.

* * *

Sami Aronen had pulled aside a corner of the cardboard covering the window and watched Salmela hurry down the sidewalk. "Well, there he goes," he said.

Tapani Larsson and Rolf Steiner stood a few yards further back by the pool table.

"Nobody was waiting?" asked Steiner.

"No," Aronen replied. "I doubt even they'd be that stupid."

"The only thing dumber would be for them to pick him up at the front door."

Aronen left the window and joined the others. "I guess now we'll see if Gonzales' rumor is true."

"You think Salmela even heard them?"

"Of course he did."

Steiner raked his blond hair. "You never know with these old ex-cons. They've learned how to not hear anything, or otherwise they drink themselves deaf."

"Trust me—he heard," Aronen said.

Larsson slammed his fist against the edge of the pool table. "Fucking cops piss me off. I get it when the S.W.A.T. team charges in through the front door, or when they snoop on the phones. But they recruit some old yard bird to spy on us? The cops have to play by the book when it comes to raids and surveillance, but it doesn't get any shadier than this nark business. Just the idea of it pisses the hell outta me."

Aronen could see that Larsson wasn't kidding.

"If they wanna know what goes on here, they should stop by for coffee and a chat," Larsson went on. He snatched a billiard ball off the table and flung it hard against the wall. The ball ricocheted off the wall before clattering to the floor.

Aronen and Steiner were quiet.

"And then there's this fucking Suhonen. Goddamn!" he shouted. "Of all the shit faces down at homicide, he's the shittiest. First he serves me up a prison term by acting like an ex-con. Then as soon as I get out, he plants a fucking rat in here. Not gonna happen. Definitely not. He was number-one on my hit-list, but now he takes the whole top three."

"The bastard is so nosy he'll walk right into it. Everything's set, and our new recruits acted their part like true stars," said Aronen. "What should we do to Salmela?"

"Dead man walking," Larsson replied.

Steiner nodded. "You can say that again."

"Should we get going?"

Larsson checked the time: 12:15. "Not yet. I'm not gonna sit there for four hours. It's good enough if we get there by one."

"But what if Suhonen goes right away?"

Larsson thought for a moment. "True. The weasel might just do that. You're right—let's go."

According to the plan, the trio would secure their

alibis by sitting under a security camera at a north Helsinki mall's coffee shop all afternoon.

* * *

Sanna Römpötti was seated at her desk in the newsroom. Monday looked to be a slow news day with no court hearings, nor anything else on her itinerary. The reporter had spent the morning calling nearly twenty acquaintances in the Police Department, the Ministry of the Interior, and the Department of Justice. Returns were slim. No news on the loose, apparently, or at least it wasn't falling into her trap.

Four other reporters were at work, and all were on the phone. Three managers were standing in the middle of the office, cradling coffee cups and trading fall vacation stories.

Maybe now would be a good time to pursue the Skulls' story, thought Römpötti. It had snowballed into a larger project and she was debating between doing a series for the evening news or a longer one for their news magazine program.

The pieces were beginning to come together, but they still didn't form a complete picture. The secret footage of Aronen's interview in the Hotel Pasila was a success, but he hadn't contacted her, nor had he answered her calls. It seemed he didn't intend to open his mouth until she opened her legs.

She had compiled a file of every Skull member that included their convictions. Almost everyone had a record, but that fact was not newsworthy. It would've been surprising if only a few of them had been arrested before.

She had taped an interview with Jaakko Nykänen, the NBI's chief of intelligence, but had gotten only superficial comments. Nykänen had stressed the growing threat of organized crime, but true to his habit, he didn't mention any gangsters by name, even when Römpötti brought up some of their case histories.

Römpötti had also asked about the differences in interpretation between the police and the courts. The police considered the Skulls to be a criminal gang, but in the latest cases, the courts had dismissed the prosecution's requests for additional penalties based on membership in a criminal organization.

The police had their interpretation and the courts another, Nykänen had explained. Römpötti had grilled him harder, of course, but his responses on this topic were just as round as the others. The ball rolled back to the reporter.

It appeared that she would have to interview Takamäki. She might get stronger opinions from the VCU lieutenant, especially if she succeeded in provoking him.

Who else would know something about gangs, she kept wondering. Reports from the Legal Policy Institute were every bit as long as they were broad. The National Penal Agency's organized crime team had plenty to say, but once the camera was rolling, they turned their backs and fell silent. Same with the prosecutors.

Had the gangs already gotten a grip on public officials and injected fear into them? What right did the police have, then, to blame ordinary citizens for not daring to testify against organized crime in court?

That could be another angle entirely: Why didn't anyone dare speak publicly about the Skulls?

Naah, she thought. Not newsworthy. They could run something like that in a longer magazine story, but a news story would need a point.

Römpötti decided to get some coffee and drink it at her desk.

* * *

Salmela was standing alone at the bus stop. He realized his hands were trembling as the charge from the morning's excitement drained away.

Now that there were no ears around, he slipped his cell phone out of his pocket. It took both hands to turn it on.

He waited for the cheap Nokia to boot up then scrolled back and forth through the directory. Of course, neither of the numbers had been entered under their real names. NBI's Aalto was just "Jouko," and a single "S" signified Suhonen. Salmela looked up the road. Cars flowed down the long stretch, but no buses were in sight.

Which one should he call? Salmela hesitated. Aalto had mandated himself as the contact, but there was no trust—that would take months to build. Something about Aalto bothered Salmela, though he wasn't sure what it was. It seemed that he was only a tool to Aalto, nothing more. With Suhonen, it had always been different.

And was this even worthy of a call? All the two gangsters had talked about was picking up a car. Maybe they were just bringing a stolen car to the garage to be stripped down. That would hardly interest the NBI. Even so, Aalto's orders remained on his mind.

What if he didn't call at all? That was also a possibility.

The bus had not yet come and Salmela's thumb roamed over the numbers. Finally, he chose one and pressed the call button.

A familiar voice answered promptly.

"How's it going?" asked Suhonen.

CHAPTER 20
MONDAY, 2:20 P.M.
KÄPYLÄ, HELSINKI

Kristiina Ahlfors, dressed in a red hooded sweatshirt and a black knit hat, was pushing a stroller northward along Mäkelä Avenue. Ten minutes earlier, she had passed the Velodrome Cycling Stadium. In the stroller, her two-year-old girl, bundled in a green snowsuit, was taking a nap. After swimming at the nearby pool, Kristiina had decided to walk to Käpylä.

She could have ridden the bus or streetcar home, but the rain had finally ceased, and she wanted to drop by the store on the way home. Their swimsuits were in a bag, hanging from the stroller.

Throngs of automobiles surged past as the traffic lights allowed. Two streetcars, one after the other, rumbled along Mäkelä Avenue's central tree-lined track.

Later, in police interviews, Ahlfors couldn't exactly say what had attracted her attention to the two men. She guessed it was because, ordinarily, people went to the ball fields in sports gear, but both of these men were wearing dark, heavy clothing. She couldn't describe the men further, except that one was wearing a worn leather jacket.

She stopped to look around. On her right was a small fast food joint, and behind it, a gas station.

The explosion rocked her eardrums and she pitched to the right. At first, she didn't know what had happened. Had it been a tire on a passing bus?

The toddler bolted awake and began to cry in fear. Ahlfors bent down next to the girl and tried in vain to calm her. But the child seemed alright.

Ahlfors turned to look toward the ball fields, where the explosion had come from. There, she saw a column of black smoke rising about twenty yards into the air. Higher up, it spread out into a mushroom cloud that recalled an atomic bomb.

What in the world had happened? Her daughter was still wailing as Ahlfors rooted her cell phone out of her purse and called the emergency number 112. She was the first of dozens of callers to report the explosion.

* * *

Officer Tero Partio accelerated toward Mäkelä Avenue, the sirens on his cruiser howling. Some of the traffic had stopped, and Partio weaved between the cars. Half of the police cruiser was in the oncoming lane.

"There," said Esa Nieminen from the passenger seat, and waved a finger at the column of smoke. Partio's first thought was a car fire, since the black smoke indicated burning tires, but dispatch had reported it as an explosion.

Partio passed a few stopped cars and ran a red onto Mäkelä Avenue toward downtown. There was a gap in the hedge about a hundred yards up, and the officer guided the vehicle down the slope into the park.

A parking lot, a building with dressing rooms, and open grass fields were on the left. Partio immediately noticed that the windows on the building had been broken. On the right were a few trees, and beyond those, a gravel soccer field.

The car—or what was left of it—was in flames about a hundred yards up in the parking lot. Partio gunned it down the hill. He stopped about twenty yards from the blaze and shut off the sirens before getting out. Some trees stood between him and the flames.

In these situations, over-eagerness was dangerous. He had to think first. Nieminen stayed in the cruiser to give an initial report to dispatch. Since dispatch had given radio orders to all Helsinki units, there was no need to ask for back up.

The flames rose ten feet into the air. As Partio had anticipated, the bulk of the smoke came from the tires. Since the demolished car was alone in the parking lot, there was no danger of the fire spreading.

Once out of the car, the officer immediately detected the pungent stench of explosives. This was clearly a bomb—almost nothing was left of the car. Through the smoke and flames, only its blackened carcass was visible.

Further off, he noticed a white sports dome on the hill, slowly collapsing. Apparently, shrapnel from the car had torn a hole in it. Howling sirens closed in from all directions.

Partio took a couple steps to the side and surveyed the scene. He could make out two crumpled figures behind a small shrub, which had blocked his sightline from the cruiser. He ran in to get a closer look, and once within ten yards of the first, he could see that it was a man.

The man's leather jacket was torn to shreds and his wounds were severe. The face was burned and the blistered skin had peeled off. His hair was smoldering and his features were impossible to recognize. Partio also noticed the man was missing his left hand, which lay on the pavement about fifteen feet off. Partio checked the man's pulse carefully using the one intact wrist. He was still alive.

An ambulance pulled into the park through the opening in the hedge and Partio waved it over.

He proceeded to the second heap. This man was dead. The face was just a mass of flesh. Both legs were severed and a metal chunk was jutting out of his chest.

The sight was gruesome, but Partio had seen so many dead bodies that it no longer affected him.

As the ambulance came to an abrupt halt and the EMTs leaped out, Partio returned to the first victim.

"This one's still alive," he said. "The other's dead."

"Got it," said the medic, and knelt down beside the first.

Partio went back to the squad car and Nieminen got out.

"What's the situation?"

"One dead, one still alive. Report it to dispatch and go have a look at the dressing rooms. See if anyone there is injured."

"Roger," said Nieminen, and got back in the car.

Partio circled to the trunk, took out a camera, and began to photograph the scene as another squad car and a fire truck pulled up.

Partio took photographs of the dead body and the victim that the medics were working on. The dome had flopped down entirely and he took a photo of that as well.

He circled to the other side and noticed a cell phone lying in the gravel. Though he didn't touch it, he noticed that it was still on.

As he approached the phone to take a closer look, he spotted a familiar blue symbol in the background

of the display. A sword with a lion's head handle—
the official emblem of the police.

His heart sank as he realized that the casualties
were fellow officers. Goddamn, he muttered.

* * *

Salmela strode down Helsinki Avenue toward the
Corner Pub. The zipper of the ex-con's lambswool
leather jacket was pulled to the very top. The street
was very familiar to him. Salmela had come to the
conclusion that the number of loitering bums here
was pretty much constant. When one died, another
replaced him. The same went for the bars. Over the
years, Salmela had been to them all—both those that
had failed and those that had risen as replacements.

He passed a clock store that had barricaded its
display window with thick bars. For some reason, the
shopkeeper wanted all the clocks to read the correct
time: it was 3:45 P.M. Salmela wondered if Suhonen
had found anything in the car at the ball fields, and if
he had, whether it would affect his assignment at the
Skulls' compound.

He came to an old shop with TVs and radios
displayed in the front window. Salmela stopped in
front of the window and stared at the screen, on
which flickered a wide-angle view of the Käpylä ball
fields. In the upper corner, it read: Breaking News.

Salmela rushed inside and listened to the
reporter's newscast, *"According to the latest reports,
one man was killed in the explosion and another was
critically wounded. The explosion appears to have
occurred inside an automobile."*

The jumpy picture showed CSI techs in white
coveralls scouring the gravel fields on all fours.
White tarps attached to a scaffolding about fifteen

feet high were already surrounding the car. The broadcast was being filmed from the top floor of the parking ramp at the Pasila exhibition hall, which was the nearest spot that hadn't been roped off.

Salmela watched with his mouth agape.

"Crazy story," remarked the graying shopkeeper, who had come up alongside him.

Channel 3 Reporter Sanna Römpötti, dressed in a black blazer, appeared on the screen and continued, "*I should emphasize that this has not been verified, but according to our sources, both men caught in the explosion were police officers. Again, this account has not been verified. At this stage, we have no information about the cause of the explosion.*"

Salmela's eyes were glued to the screen. The female reporter continued with details on the time and the number of emergency vehicles, but Salmela wasn't listening anymore. It all seemed surreal. The picture snapped back and forth from the newsroom anchor to a field reporter and any eyewitnesses, or at least earwitnesses that they had found.

"You alright?" the shopkeeper asked.

Salmela snapped out of it. "Uhh, yeah." he said. When the broadcast cut back to the studio, Salmela walked out the door.

Outside, he pulled out his phone and dialed Suhonen's number. It went straight to voicemail. He tried to call Aalto with the same result—straight to voicemail.

Salmela glanced around, but nobody seemed to notice him. He tried to think about his situation. No sense going home—that wouldn't be safe. He didn't have enough money for a hotel. He'd have to find one of his friends and crash at his house for the night. The guys would be at the Corner Pub, and a couple beers would take the edge off.

Jesus, what had happened? What had he done?

* * *

Römpötti hopped into the satellite truck to warm up for a while. The wind was gusting on the roof of the exhibition hall parking ramp, but at least it wasn't raining yet. The back of the van was packed with monitors and other electronics. One of the screens showed a live feed of the accident scene, still veiled by white tarps. The operator sat near the monitors in an office chair. Römpötti plopped down in the passenger seat and pumped some coffee from a thermos into a paper cup.

Her fingers soaked in the warmth of the coffee. Thin leather gloves didn't suffice for these cold conditions, but they looked better than mittens on camera. She couldn't wear a hat either, at least not unless the temperature dipped below zero degrees Fahrenheit.

Römpötti sipped her coffee as she scanned the screen on her laptop. With a wireless connection, she was able to access the production program. She was back on the air in eight minutes. Something new to report would be nice, but the cops had been tight-lipped. Their initial statement had been brief: An explosion had occurred, and of the two victims, one had died and one was injured. One of Römpötti's friends at dispatch had tipped her off about the victims being cops. She had called again, but the friend hadn't learned anything more.

Something about the incident seemed peculiar to Römpötti. Car-bombs per se were nothing new— Helsinki had been rocked by a few. She recalled the 1994 explosion in the parking lot of Pasila Police

Headquarters. Though the police had a suspect, the case still remained unsolved, as nobody had dared to testify against organized crime. At that time, the cops had been the target, but the circumstances of today's incident were still unclear. Another car bombing had occurred downtown in the summer of 2002—a contract killing.

At a loss for new info, she considered mentioning those stories in her next spot. But viewers wanted new information, not just recaps. Römpötti's phone rang. The caller was unidentified.

"Yeah?" answered Römpötti briskly. Occasionally, these types of incidents stirred up some strange people who were best dumped at the outset. She had no time for them.

"Sanna Römpötti?" a man asked.

"Yes?" She said, unable to recognize the voice.

The man paused briefly. "It's Sami Aronen, from the Skulls."

For a moment, Römpötti was confused. Why was Aronen calling her now? "Oh, hey Sami."

"I suppose you're kinda busy."

"If you've seen the news, you know why."

"Yeah. Listen, I have some information for you about that."

Römpötti nearly dropped the phone. One of the top men in the Skulls wanted to give her a lead on a breaking story. "What's that?" she said in a voice that seemed to have fielded hundreds of similar offers.

"I know the police think we're behind this, but that's not the case."

Römpötti wasn't surprised. "No?"

"Nope. I don't care if you make their suspicions public, but I don't want our denial to be aired at this point."

"Why are you telling me this?"

"You look just as good in person as you do on TV," Aronen said without the slightest hint of comedy. "The cops have been working on some kind of an undercover operation against us and they think we did it. But as I said, that's not the case. If you wanna air what the cops think, be my guest."

Römpötti was confused. Typically, people suspected of a crime would want to minimize or clarify their role. But here was Aronen, tipping her off that the gang was a suspect, yet not wanting to publicize a rebuttal. Suddenly, it occurred to her to record the conversation.

"I'm not sure I understand," she said as she glanced at the operator. He was holding up four fingers—four minutes until she was back on camera. "Why would the police suspect you if you had nothing to do with it?"

"Listen to what I'm saying," Aronen's voice was tense now. "They've been running an undercover operation against us and they think we're behind the bombing. The truth will come out later, but for now, you can say the police suspect us of being involved. That's a true statement."

The operator raised three fingers.

"Okay. I'm on camera in a minute. Thanks for the lead." Römpötti tried to think of how she could say it on the air. Needless to say, the police wouldn't confirm any suspicions at this stage; they seemed to have ceased all communications with the outside. Undoubtedly, the entire police organization was in chaos as the different branches scrambled to figure out who would investigate what. Maybe she could say something like this: "According to our sources, the bombing may have been connected to organized crime. Reportedly, the Skulls motorcycle gang is a prime suspect."

Römpötti took a gulp of coffee and climbed out of the van into the cold wind. The camera operator, dressed in a thick parka and knit hat, waved her in front of the camera.

The top level of the parking ramp was surrounded by a five-foot-tall concrete wall, so the cameraman had set up two plastic crates for the reporter and him to stand on. That way, the scene of the accident, and not just the concrete wall, would be visible in the background.

She cleared her throat. In her hand was a small notebook, where she had written her keywords. Stepping onto the crate, she asked the camera man if everything was ready.

* * *

It was still several minutes before the meeting would begin. In the corner of the conference room at Helsinki Police Headquarters was a television, the volume at a whisper. Several officers were conversing in subdued tones as the NBI's Jaakko Nykänen, dressed in a gray suit with his walrus mustache bristling, stepped inside.

The VCU conference room had been made into the command center for the investigation. About thirty officers, some sitting in front of their laptops, others standing beneath the cold fluorescent lights, were gathered in the room. Nykänen remembered dozens, if not hundreds of meetings that Takamäki had led in this room. Dammit, he thought.

The news broadcast came on and Nykänen told someone to turn up the volume. He hadn't had time yet to see how the media was handling the incident, but now he had a minute and a half before the meeting would start. Nykänen grabbed a half-liter bottle of water from the basket on the table, opened it and took a swig. Sanna Römpötti appeared on the screen.

First, Römpötti spoke about the victims and the fatality, and alluded to the Pasila Police Headquarters bombing of fifteen years ago. Nykänen remembered it well, since he was still in the Helsinki PD at the time.

"Again in 2002, a car bomb exploded downtown. Car bombs don't choose their victims," the reporter said. *"So it's not clear yet whether the bomb was intended for police, or whether it was an accident."*

That Römpötti had obtained accurate information about the victims' profession was no surprise to Nykänen. Almost immediately after the incident, that information had spread to dispatch, and within minutes, throughout the police station and beyond. If Römpötti hadn't known it by now, she could hardly call herself a crime reporter.

But Nykänen perked up when she said the words *"According to our exclusive sources..."* What could this possibly be? Every now and then, these tidbits were useful to the cops too, as long as reporters did their job well. More often than not, however, it was the other way around—reporters revealed information that shouldn't be made public.

Römpötti looked straight into the camera. In the background, gray skies and broad soccer fields stretched from one end of the screen to the other.

"...there is a possible link between the bombing and organized crime. Police suspect that the Skulls motorcycle gang was somehow involved in the explosion. Though this information hasn't yet been verified, it came from a source close to the investigation."

Nykänen stared blankly at the screen as Römpötti

launched into the Skulls' background. Her words fell on deaf ears as the NBI lieutenant struggled to think of where the leak had come from. How in the hell could anyone have known that they suspected the Skulls? Was Römpötti merely speculating in the heat of the moment? He knew she was working on some story about the Skulls; she had just interviewed him a few days ago. But this leak was far too precise.

Several of the officers in the room glanced over at Nykänen. He wondered how many cops knew about their Skull investigation. A handful at most, and of those present, only a few. His eyes roamed the room. Many there had just found about the Skulls' involvement from the broadcast—that was apparent. But who in the hell had leaked this?

His irritation nearly surpassed his grief. He tried to concentrate. In only a short while, he would have to conduct an important meeting to kick off the investigation.

Grief and irritation fostered anger, which Nykänen couldn't afford. He had to stay cool and push his feelings aside. Even though he knew this, it seemed too much to bear.

* * *

Larsson and Steiner were on their third round of whiskeys, while Aronen had settled for coffee. That didn't bother him—best if someone was sober. It had been no different in Afghanistan.

"Goddamn, this is a good day. We hit Helsinki Homicide—and hard," Larsson grinned and raised his glass. In the corner, a television showed Sanna Römpötti gesturing toward the shrouded scaffolding.

"Good whiskey will make my day, any day," Steiner remarked. After three o'clock, the Skulls' core group had proceeded from the mall's coffee shop to the restaurant. Aronen had assured their alibi the moment they walked into the shopping center when a security guard noticed the gang symbols on his vest. The guard hadn't let the three men out of his sight since one o'clock. That was better than any security camera footage. Two guards had followed them from the coffee shop into the restaurant. That didn't bother Larsson today. The guards sat near the entrance, far enough away that they couldn't hear the conversation.

"Steiner, I'll show you where the iron crosses grow," Larsson grinned.

Steiner just sipped his whiskey—he had heard that a few times before.

"Well, what now?" asked Aronen.

Larsson swirled the ice in his glass. "Let's think about what the enemy's gonna do. That's what they taught you in the army, right? Sooner or later, the cops are gonna raid our place and probably arrest us, but they won't have anything on us. No evidence. Even if they lean on their rat hard enough, he might testify that he overheard Roge and Osku talking about the car. But they were only supposed to pick it up. There's nothing more he can say. And if the cops twist his words around, we always have the security footage from the bar room to prove him wrong. That bomb was intended for us. The stupid cops just stumbled in at the wrong time."

Steiner cut in. "The pigs will never admit that they were stupid."

"So we're suspects for now, but in the end it'll work in our favor," Larsson said. "The cops can't touch us."

CHAPTER 21
MONDAY, 4:00 P.M.
PASILA POLICE HEADQUARTERS,
HELSINKI

NBI Lieutenant Nykänen scanned the detectives in the VCU conference room. With room for only about twenty at the table, many were standing. Not surprisingly, their expressions were somber, but as was always the case when the victim was a colleague, they were highly motivated. Nykänen glanced at his watch: four o'clock sharp. Time to start the meeting. The TV flickered in the corner, but the volume had been turned off. The whispered conversation in the room had slowly reached a low hum.

Since several important attendees were still missing, Nykänen encouraged everyone to help themselves to the VCU's beverages and rolls. Nobody knew when they'd eat next.

Several policemen took him up on the offer. Someone checked his watch, as if to draw attention to the fact that time was ticking.

Of Takamäki's team, Sergeant Joutsamo and Officer Kulta were there. Initially, they had feared the worst for Suhonen, but had been informed of the victims' identities soon after the explosion. Both were from the NBI: Agent Lind was dead and his boss, Lieutenant Aalto, was critically wounded.

Nykänen continued to wait for the key attendees, without whom there was no point in starting. He twirled the tips of his mustache with the fingers of his right hand.

Coffee and rolls distracted the crowd for a few minutes before the officers turned expectantly toward Nykänen. He couldn't suppress such a mob much longer without frustrating them. They were all professionals, and they hadn't come to wait, but Nykänen had to hold off.

"Nykänen," barked Skoog from the door. The assistant chief of the Helsinki police beckoned with his finger. "Step out here for a minute."

He addressed the crowd. "We'll be five minutes. Get some coffee…or something."

Skoog marched into Takamäki's office with Nykänen close behind. Inside were NBI Assistant Chief Majakowski, Takamäki sitting at his desk, and Suhonen, planted on the windowsill as usual.

"We have to make a decision about who's going to lead this," said Majakowski. "Our alternatives are Helsinki, the NBI, or another jurisdiction, say Espoo."

Nykänen looked at the others and nodded. He had assumed that the case would stay with the NBI, since one of their own had died in the explosion. The other had lost his hand and remained in critical condition.

"As far as I'm concerned, we can handle this case just fine," said Nykänen.

Skoog coughed. "It's not about who is *able* to handle the case. It's about whether there are any conflicts of interest. Could the media or the minister of the interior get the impression that one of the departments is investigating their own?"

Suhonen couldn't believe his ears. What the hell did he mean "their own?" An officer was dead. It made no difference which department investigated the case—that kind of thinking hampered effective police work. But he said nothing.

"Nykänen…Takamäki…Suhonen." Majakowski addressed them. "Is there a possibility here that the case is going to bite us in the ass?"

"Excuse me?" said Takamäki.

"Don't play dumb. This has been a sensitive operation all along and it was initiated by the VCU. Has everything gone by the book? In other words, is it possible that either the NBI or the Helsinki police will end up being investigated here?"

Takamäki glanced at the others with a sour expression. "Actually, we don't have to answer that. By law, we're not required to say anything that could be self-incriminating. In other words, if that's your starting point, I think Espoo is the only alternative for leading the investigation."

"Dammit, Takamäki," Majakowski hissed. "Don't play the martyr here. Those victims were my men. Lind was a hell of an agent and Aalto one of our best undercover operatives. I only wanna know where we're headed here."

"The fact that the victims were NBI agents doesn't disqualify the NBI," Nykänen chimed in.

Suhonen shook his head. Evidence was fading by the second, and here were the bosses fighting while thirty investigators were sitting in the conference room chomping at the bit.

"Takamäki, as far as you know, is there any reason to suspect that the police have done anything illegal in this operation against the Skulls?" asked Skoog.

Now the question was worded correctly, thought Takamäki. "No."

"What about you, Suhonen?"

"Nope."

Skoog continued around, "Nykänen?"

"Nothing suspicious within police ranks. I'm more interested in the informant's motives. Why did he set this trap?"

"Was it a trap?" asked Suhonen.

"Looks like one to me. And what's more, I'm pretty damn interested to find out how our suspicions toward the Skulls were already on the news five minutes ago."

"They were?" Takamäki wondered.

"Yes. Römpötti just said it on a live broadcast. I don't…"

Suhonen clapped his hands together once. "Hey, we can think about that later. Right now we should let the detectives loose and figure out who did what."

Skoog and Majakowski nodded. The undercover cop was right. The assistant chiefs looked at each other and shrugged their shoulders. It made no difference to either who would take the case.

"We can take this one, if it's okay," said the NBI's Majakowski.

"Alright, that's fine," said Skoog. "Your men— you lead the case."

Nykänen, Takamäki and Suhonen looked at one another in amazement. If it was that easy, then what was the point of the whole meeting in the first place?

"That settles it. Captain Honkala from the NBI will head the investigation," said Majakowski. "And you three stay out of this. Not just because the informant is close to you, but also because these kinds of cases can stir up misconduct investigations. If Honkala has questions, answer them. But aside from that, you're off the case."

"What about the informant's identity?" Nykänen interjected. "It can't be revealed."

"That's up to Honkala. If the informant is guilty or

suspected of a crime, then he surrenders his protection."

Takamäki slammed his hand down on the table. "Okay. Done deal. Nykänen and Suhonen, let's go downstairs for coffee and donuts. I doubt you others can make it with that big meeting coming up."

Someone knocked on the door and pushed it open. "Hi there," said a thin man in a gray suit, standing over six-foot-six. Suhonen had heard that Honkala's nickname was "Stretch," but he hadn't imagined him to be this tall.

"Glad you came, Honkala," said Majakowski.

Takamäki was astonished. So this had all been pre-arranged, and the only purpose of this little meeting was to fish for possible illegalities committed by the police. It looked like the bosses were just covering their own asses. Hell, judging by their willingness to waste time on drama, Majakowski and Skoog seemed more interested in their own careers than in solving crimes.

* * *

Ten minutes later, Nykänen, Takamäki and Suhonen sat quietly at the table in the police cafeteria. Takamäki had treated them all to coffee and donuts.

None of them were worried about the investigation—Captain Honkala was a skilled investigator with the talent to solve even the most complicated crimes.

"Okay, let's go through this," said Nykänen, taking care to keep the frosting off his whiskers. "Salmiakki's role?"

Suhonen sipped his coffee. Since everyone at the table knew who they were talking about and the cafeteria was practically empty, there was no need to use the code name. "Salmela was at the Skulls' compound in the morning. He overheard about the car and relayed the information to me."

"Why you?" asked Nykänen.

"We've known each other for thirty years. He only met Aalto the day before. I have to admit I thought about going, but I figured I shouldn't mess with an NBI investigation, so I called Aalto. At first, he couldn't get a hold of Lind, so he asked me if I wanted to come along. I told him I'd go, but a bit later, he cancelled on me. Said they'd take care of it themselves."

"It's a terrible thing to say, but it's a good thing you didn't go," Takamäki said.

Nykänen spoke up, "Okay. I buy that Salmela had good intentions." He took a big bite of his donut.

"I think so. Given the shape he's in, there's no way he could lie to me," said Suhonen.

Nykänen swallowed before continuing, "Right, but what about the Skulls. Was it a trap?"

Takamäki interjected, "If it was a trap, they're onto Salmela. Is that possible?"

"Not through us," Nykänen replied. He turned to Suhonen.

"Larsson knows me from an old extortion case. Yes, I've met with Salmela many times recently and over the past few years, but I can't think of any particular incident that would've revealed our relationship."

Nykänen shrugged. "If it was a trap, they found out about Salmela somehow. And how in the hell was Römpötti able to report on the Skulls an hour after the explosion? We have a serious leak somewhere."

Nykänen quoted her as closely as he could remember. She had stated that the information was based on a source close to the investigation. The crux of the broadcast remained in his memory, *"Police suspect that the Skulls motorcycle gang was somehow involved in the explosion."*

Takamäki shook his head and dialed Römpötti's number. The line was busy.

"What if the trap wasn't meant for us?" asked Nykänen.

Takamäki set his coffee cup on the table. "Then it was meant for them. Somebody wanted to attack the Skulls, which would indicate some sort of underworld war."

"They've been dealing with the Estonians, who have a long history of bombings, at least in the nineties." Suhonen pointed out.

"You mean that Zubrov...the one you saw about a week ago with Mike Gonzales?" Nykänen asked.

"Hard to say. I really don't have anything on Zubrov. In any case, if someone is gonna bomb the Skulls, they have to be pretty big. I haven't heard anything about any recent gang rivalries."

"It's certainly not impossible," Nykänen replied. "But it's unlikely. I haven't heard anything either, though Estonia's not exactly within earshot."

"What were Aalto and Lind supposed to do with the car?" asked Takamäki.

Nykänen hunched his shoulders. "Just put a tracking device on it. They weren't supposed to go inside, not even in the trunk."

"So," Takamäki went on. "Apparently, the Opel had some kind of tamper-sensing detonator, or else someone was watching from a distance and detonated it remotely. But the techies will figure all that out. They'll rake up every last scrap off those gravel fields."

Suhonen stood up and asked if anybody wanted more coffee. A minute later, he returned with three full cups.

"Was Lind married?" he asked, sitting down.

"Only to his job," said Nykänen. "He divorced ten years ago and his wife had custody of their son. Drank too much for a couple years, but pulled himself together when he was a few inches shy of getting fired. Aalto has two girls, two and four years old."

Takamäki imagined the scene in which dad came home from the hospital and his little girls asked why his hand was missing.

"I contacted the hospital," said Nykänen. "Aalto could lose one of his eyes too, if he makes it at all."

Daddy, how come your other eye doesn't move? Explosions often caused serious brain damage as well. Aalto might not even remember his daughters' names.

Suhonen changed the subject. "What about the car. Anybody have any info on that?"

"They recovered a license plate beginning with 'AFR,' but it wasn't the car's actual plate. It was one of those old '80s Opel Kadetts that were all over the news when that eighteen-year-old swerved off the road and killed four of his friends."

Takamäki started to pull the pieces together. "So most likely, the Skulls were onto Salmela and the car was a trap."

Takamäki's phone rang suddenly. The caller was Römpötti.

"I have to take this," Takamäki said and answered the phone.

The other two listened in.

"Hey there," she chirped. "Thank God you're alive. I was worried…"

"Doing just fine," he interrupted her. "Listen, I have one question."

She laughed. "I have more than one for you."

"Answer mine first. You mentioned the Skulls on the news. Where'd you get that information?"

She paused. "You know I can't answer those kinds of questions."

"Yeah, I know. But this is no petty misdemeanor. We're talking about murder and attempted murder," Takamäki snapped. The seriousness of the crime would allow him to subpoena her, especially since it was potentially leaked from inside the police force. "Let me rephrase the question in a way I know you can answer."

"Go for it."

"Did it come from a government source or somewhere else?"

Römpötti cleared her throat. From the wind in the background, Takamäki could tell she was still outside. "I'll answer that if you tell me whether it's true."

Takamäki thought for a while. She had already broadcast the allegation, so there was no harm in confirming it off the record.

"It's true, but don't quote us. 'Our exclusive sources' will work just fine," he said, then waited.

"The lead didn't come from the police or any other government source."

"Are you positive? This is very important. Don't lie to me here."

"Trust me. I never would, and hopefully you wouldn't either," she replied. "That's all I can tell you about my source. No more. If you want to override my confidentiality, you'll have to take me to court."

Takamäki laughed. "Sanna, that's not how we do it. I believe you and that's enough."

The call ended and Takamäki turned to the others.

"Maybe you overheard, but the lead didn't come from the police or any other official. It came from somewhere else."

"That confirms it was a trap," said Nykänen.

Suhonen's eyes met Takamäki's, then Nykänen's. "The Skulls weren't after the police. Larsson wanted me."

"What do you mean?" said Nykänen.

"Larsson was furious at me for locking him up. He must've somehow connected Salmela to me. There's no way he could've known about the NBI's involvement without a major mole in your organization. So, one plus one equals two."

"Plus one is three," said Nykänen. "How many people know both you and Salmela and have also worked with the Skulls lately?"

Suhonen had one candidate, but he didn't say anything. Juha Saarnikangas knew both of them and was involved with the drug shipment, too. The man was playing hardball; if he had turned to the dark side, Suhonen could easily start a rumor about him being a nark.

"Where's Salmela now?" asked Takamäki.

None of them knew.

"We should probably look for him," said Takamäki.

"But we're off the case," Nykänen said.

Takamäki and Suhonen looked at Nykänen.

"I'll speak with Honkala," Takamäki decided.

* * *

The press conference at Pasila Police Headquarters began at 6:30 P.M. So many reporters and photographers were attending that the Helsinki police press secretary had decided to move it to the station's lobby. About fifty chairs had been brought down from upstairs, but still, many reporters were standing.

Though the NBI was leading the case, Pasila Police Headquarters was still serving as the command center.

The elevator chimed and Honkala ducked out in his gray suit and a matching blue tie. His shirt was a gleaming white and he had hastily straightened his hair in the elevator.

Camera flashes exploded from all sides as Honkala strode to the table. Though there were chairs, he remained standing. At least three TV networks and two radio stations were broadcasting live. On the table were about twenty microphones and recorders, and on top of that, numerous soundmen were moving about with long microphone booms for the live broadcasts. The photographers bristled every time the soundmen stepped in front of the cameras.

"The purpose of this press conference is obviously clear to everyone. Today, at 2:20 P.M. a car bomb exploded in the parking lot of the Käpylä ball fields. One person was killed, another critically wounded. Both individuals were agents for the National Bureau of Investigation. The incident is being investigated as a murder and attempted murder. At this time, we will not disclose the names of the victims, nor any details about their assignments," Honkala began.

"The forensics investigation is still ongoing, and we don't yet have any information about the type of explosive or the detonation mechanism. The police have several leads on the motive for the explosion, but for reasons pertaining to the investigation, I can't discuss them at this time. For the same reason, I can't say why the agents were interested in the car."

Without a second's pause, Honkala looked straight

into the TV camera in the center, "The police are asking for any leads or observations from the public as well as any information on a 1980s beige Opel Kadett. The license plate found does not belong to the car," Honkala said, but nevertheless, he recited the number twice.

The captain gave a hotline number to call with information. He announced that he wouldn't be taking any questions, and that the next briefing was scheduled for noon of the following day at NBI headquarters. Then he marched, unfazed, through the crowd of shouting reporters into the elevator, where an officer stood holding the door.

* * *

"Let's go," Salmela said to Ear-Nurminen as the televised press conference came to a close. The picture cut to an anchorwoman's follow-up, but the Corner Pub's bartender turned the music back up, drowning out the sound of the TV.

"No work, booze, an axe and the kin. A snowdrift, the cops and the final sin," crooned Eppu Normaali from the jukebox.

"What's the hurry?" asked Ear-Nurminen. A single glance at Salmela was all it took to see that the man was serious. Nurminen finished off his beer as Salmela buttoned up his coat.

"Let's grab a six-pack at the store on the way," said Salmela. That was fine with Ear-Nurminen, who had offered him a couch for the night. At first he had wondered, but hadn't asked any questions. Salmela would have done the same if, for some reason, Nurminen had wanted to spend the night on his Salvation Army sofa.

Salmela was pondering the AFR-license plate as

they stepped out into the cold air. Damn license plate. That made the situation even more complicated.

* * *

"Fuck!" Larsson hissed. The lanky man on TV had just ruined what should have been a victorious moment at the Skulls' compound.

He, Steiner, Aronen, Roge and Osku had been watching the press conference on a fifty-inch big-screen in the main room. After the conference, reporter Sanna Römpötti had speculated on the cause of the explosion and the Skulls' involvement, but that wasn't the reason for Larsson's anger.

"What the hell?" he swore again. "Those were NBI agents? How is that possible? This was supposed to be a Helsinki PD operation."

"Very strange," Aronen remarked.

"That fucking Suhonen is still alive," Larsson ranted.

Steiner sat on the sofa and drew a small cigar box from his pocket. He took out a joint, lit it up and took a long drag.

"So what?" he asked, sending forth a stream of smoke.

Larsson scowled at the blond-haired man. "I want that shithead dead, but the fact that the NBI is after us is pretty damned interesting too."

"You can say that again."

Aronen's remark earned him a sharp look from Larsson. Stating the obvious angered him.

Steiner nursed his joint quietly. "The NBI, Helsinki VCU, Espoo PD, the Sheriff of Lapland... Same difference. They're all packed with the same dickheads."

Even if he was right, Steiner's attitude irritated

Larsson. "Go get Salmela. I got some questions for him."

Steiner stared at Larsson. "Only if you drive."

Larsson fingered the 9mm in the pocket of his leather jacket, but let it be. "Let's go."

"I'll drive," said Aronen. "The last thing we need is for you to end up in jail for a DUI."

Larsson waved him off. "The pigs don't have time to bother with DUIs right now."

Aronen tried to remember how much Larsson had drunk. A few shots and a beer…sure, he'd stay on the road.

Larsson turned back to Aronen. "You pick up Niko at the harbor. The ship from Tallinn is docking at seven."

"What's he doing in Tallinn?" asked Roge.

"Pleasure cruise," said Larsson as he followed Steiner out. "We'll take care of this."

CHAPTER 22
MONDAY, 7:20 P.M.
PASILA POLICE HEADQUARTERS, HELSINKI

"Well, I've got a little time now," said the NBI's Captain Honkala as he sat down at the table in the VCU break room. Takamäki had stopped into the conference room earlier, but the captain had been busy.

It seemed to Takamäki that the legs of his chair had been cut down as, even while sitting, Honkala's head hovered well above his own.

"Any progress?" asked Takamäki, gazing up at the other's face.

"Nothing substantial. Forensics is looking further into the explosives. Apparently, it was stolen construction dynamite or something of that sort."

"Judging by what little was left of the car, I'd bet there was five, maybe seven pounds of the stuff."

Honkala nodded. "Round about there. The detonator is a tougher nut to crack, but we should find out within a few weeks, maybe a month."

"Were you briefed on our undercover case?"

"More or less. There was an ongoing investigation into the Skulls, and you guys planted an informant named Salmiakki."

Takamäki outlined the conversation he had had in the cafeteria with Nykänen and Suhonen, that this could have been a revenge bombing aimed at the

Helsinki VCU.

"It's an interesting possibility. We should track down Salmiakki."

Nobody else was around. "We can dispense with the code name game now," said Takamäki, pausing for a moment. "Suhonen and Nykänen left an hour ago to look for Salmela."

"Really. I thought…"

Takamäki cut in, "Salmela has been Suhonen's informant for years and he knows his friends. If the man is still alive, Suhonen will track him down."

"But…"

"The Skulls are probably after Salmela, so we've got to get him under police protection. The best man for the job is Suhonen."

"Is it possible Salmela is working with the Skulls, perhaps by force?"

"Anything is possible, but it's not probable. It's more conceivable that they fed Salmela a false lead."

"The Skulls will certainly deny any involvement."

"Of course, but we'll worry about that then," said Takamäki. "We're not going to solve this case on confessions. Somehow, we have to nail the Skulls for this. Of course, the ideal would be some forensic evidence linking them to the bombing."

Honkala backed off. "Well, let's see where the investigation takes us. And if your guys find Salmela, tell them to bring him here. If he doesn't come voluntarily, arrest him on suspicion of accessory to murder."

* * *

Helsinki Avenue was lively, especially for a Monday evening, and people were loitering on the sidewalks. Suhonen had noticed a few shady characters, which, on any ordinary night, would have captured his attention, but he didn't have the time for them now. Nykänen was behind the wheel of a dark green Toyota and Suhonen was riding shotgun.

Suhonen and Nykänen had checked Salmela's apartment, as well as a few other places where the guy might be hiding. The informant wasn't answering his phone.

They drove past the metro station, westward toward Töölö.

"What about the Corner Pub?" Nykänen suggested.

"If we go there, half the town will know we're looking for him. Too many guys over there know I'm a cop."

"What if I go?"

"You don't know him and his friends. They know you, though."

Nykänen took his foot off the gas and watched a man in a leather jacket walking down the sidewalk. "Well, I've seen his mug shot."

"That's not what I meant, I..."

Nykänen chuckled. "Yeah, I got it."

Nykänen had been interviewed on TV as an NBI agent, which complicated his ability to go undercover.

"Let's go anyway," said Suhonen. "We're sure not getting anywhere here."

After a few minutes, Nykänen parked the car in a semi-legal spot across from the Corner Pub. The giant stickers on the windows of the bar promised a pint of beer for €2.50 all day long.

The officers stepped inside and Suhonen headed past the bar into the back room. He immediately spotted the bony Macho-Mertala at the corner table, wearing a ragged jean jacket over a plain white T-shirt.

A younger man with dark hair was sitting across from him. In all likelihood, Macho was blathering on about his old robberies, which at this point had gone from grocery stores to appliance stores and would eventually turn into jewelry stores.

"Hey," said Suhonen, startling Macho-Mertala.

"Shit! Don't sneak up on me like that. You'll give me a heart attack."

You'll get one anyways, thought Suhonen and sat down in an empty chair. Nykänen took a seat beside him.

The younger one looked inquiringly at the two.

"The police," Macho-Mertala explained.

The man took his beer and made tracks.

"No need for threats, blackmail or bribes. Let me guess," said Macho. "You're looking for Salmela."

"How'd you guess?"

"You're not the first. A couple gangsters were here a half-hour ago looking for him, too. At first, I thought they had come back."

"What gangsters?" asked Nykänen.

"They didn't leave their business cards, but if I had to guess, I'd say they belonged to a certain gang. Pretty sure the baldy was Tapani Larsson."

"And the other?" asked Nykänen.

Macho took a swig from his mug. "White hair, thin face. That enough?"

Nykänen nodded. If the first was Larsson, the other was Rolf Steiner.

"What did they want with Salmela?" asked Suhonen.

"Probably the same as you guys—wanted to know where he is."

The officers waited for him to continue, but he

only sat there, casually sipping his beer.

"So where is he?"

"He took off a while ago with Ear-Nurminen. Not sure where they went. Maybe to his place."

"Does Nurminen still live over there on Siltasaari Street by the Kallio church?"

"Yeah. Hasn't been evicted. But you're a good thirty minutes late."

"You got Nurminen's number?" asked Suhonen.

"Yup, but it's not gonna help. I tried calling both of them, but neither has his phone on," he said, sounding bored.

Suhonen turned to leave, but Mertala stopped him. "You think it was worth twenty euros?"

Suhonen dug a wrinkled blue note out of the pocket of his jeans.

* * *

Nykänen fired up the car and stepped on the gas, not wanting to end up behind the approaching bus. From Helsinki Avenue, he swung left at the next intersection toward the fire station.

"Thirty minutes is a long time when the trip only takes three," said Nykänen.

Suhonen held onto the hand-hold over the window as Nykänen floored the gas pedal. "Wonder what the Skulls want out of Salmela now."

The acceleration proved pointless—directly ahead of them was a stopped streetcar, and another approached from the opposite direction. No way to get around them. Nykänen drummed on the steering wheel as the passengers filed on and off.

"Apparently enough that both Steiner and Larsson are after him."

They continued along behind the streetcar to the

corner of a park, where Nykänen swung right past the fire station. In front of them was the gray-granite Kallio church, built in the early 1900s. The massive building accommodated 1,600 people, but the last time Suhonen had been there—at an old ex-con's funeral—only four were in attendance: Two of the dead guy's friends, himself, and the pastor.

"Pull up slowly and park in front. Let's look around a bit first."

At the corner, Agricola Street led to the left and directly ahead rose a six-story white stucco building.

"Not this one—the next one down on the right," Suhonen directed. Nykänen coasted down the hill and double-parked. Though the street was quiet, the curb was packed. The eight-story building, built in the sixties, seemed too new for the streets of Kallio. Suhonen bounded up the entry stairs, which were tucked into a recess. He noticed a gap between the doorjamb and the glass door. With a credit card, he slipped the lock aside and pulled it open. From the street, it appeared that he had simply used a key.

"You got a skeleton key?" Nykänen smirked. Suhonen could sense the man's uneasiness.

"Doesn't work on too many doors anymore, now that the maintenance guys have learned how to do things right."

The stairwell was dark and Suhonen snapped on the lights. Both men checked their weapons instinctively. They didn't want backup; they'd take care of this one on their own. When Nykänen was still with the VCU, the two had occasionally worked as partners.

Though Ear-Nurminen lived on the fourth floor, Nykänen and Suhonen opted for the stairs, which skirted the wall on the right-hand side. The climb took a few minutes. The stairwell was clean, as was the fourth floor landing. Surprisingly, the tag on the door actually read "Nurminen."

The door was ajar and a light was on inside.

Suhonen took up his position to the side of the door with Nykänen just behind him. He slowly opened the door and peeked inside. Nobody. Suhonen recalled that the apartment was a studio. The bathroom was in the hallway on the left, and the only room was around the corner on the same side.

Suhonen pulled out his black Glock and went in. He gestured for Nykänen to check the bathroom and continued on to the living room. Behind him, he heard Nykänen open the bathroom door. The worst thing he could encounter in the living room would be two bodies on the floor. The second worst thing would be Salmela and Nurminen on their knees with Larsson and Steiner holding pistols to the backs of their heads.

The same quick peek around the corner. The room was messy and nobody was there. Huh, thought Suhonen as he advanced into the room. A bed, a plastic dining table and a TV were the only furnishings. There was nothing on the floor but clothing and newspapers.

The search was over quickly. "Nobody in the living room," he hollered.

"Come in here," Nykänen shouted back.

Suhonen hurried back to the hallway and entered the bathroom.

Nykänen didn't need to say anything. In the bathtub lay a fat, naked man. It wasn't Salmela, who was substantially thinner. The man's face had been beaten so badly that Suhonen wasn't able to recognize him as Ear-Nurminen.

The bathroom was covered in blood and some had pooled at the bottom of the tub. Countless lacerations covered his body. There was no point in speculating on the cause-of-death without forensics. Oftentimes, knife wounds only became evident once the blood was wiped away, especially when there were multiple stab wounds.

The amount of blood, however, proved that Nurminen had lived for some time during the attack. Had he died on the first stab wound, his heart would have stopped pumping blood.

"Dead," said Nykänen. "No pulse."

"Alright. Let's not mess up the prints anymore—give forensics a chance."

The men withdrew into the hallway. "They can't have much of a head start. I'm sure that butcher job took a while, and if their lead at the Corner Pub was half an hour…"

Suhonen dug out his phone. "That half an hour was Macho's drunken guess. In reality, it could be more."

Nykänen eyed the bloody corpse from the door.

"That there looks like Steiner's work. You remember what he served those seven years for?"

"His girlfriend."

Nykänen nodded.

"Think Salmela was here?"

"No. That looks like torture. If Salmela was here, they wouldn't have had a reason for it."

"Steiner doesn't always need a reason. You think he talked?" Nykänen wondered.

"Tough to say. Most do and Nurminen sure would've. Based on this mess, I'd guess he didn't know where Salmela was, but the Skulls didn't believe him."

He glanced at the body and noticed a piece of paper lodged between the man's arm and the side of the tub. Not wanting to touch it with his hands, he grabbed two knives from the kitchen drawer, slipped back into the bathroom and plucked out the note.

In large shaky letters, it read, "RAT."

The officers examined the note. "How do we know Salmela didn't do this? That's a possibility," said Nykänen.

Suhonen shook his head and phoned Takamäki.

* * *

A blue Audi A4 rounded the west side of the circular Ympyrätalo building at the edge of Hakaniemi Market Square and stopped at a red light.

The men had been largely silent since they left the apartment. Larsson was behind the wheel and Steiner sat next to him. The driver fumbled a joint out of a metal box and lit up. Larsson cracked a window as the sweet smell of marijuana filled the car.

"Didn't exactly go as planned," said Larsson, offering the joint to his buddy.

"What was the plan?" Steiner replied coolly. "I thought the whole point was to find the rat. I know that cauliflower-eared fool knew where he was."

Larsson knew it was fruitless to start an argument with this junkie, but he went on, "He didn't know anything more. If he did, he would have talked... I believe his story. Salmela was there, but he went to get some pizza and beer."

"Well, maybe we should have stayed and waited for him to come back."

"Yeah, and wait for the cops too, with all the racket we made."

The lights changed and Larsson turned northbound onto Hämeen Street. "That pizza joint was practically across the street. The little shit probably smelled a trap and took off."

They had both taken five minutes to clean up their tracks, and they had worn gloves so there shouldn't be any prints. Their beanie hats kept loose hairs from falling, so hopefully no DNA was left at the scene. At some point, they'd have to destroy their clothing, so no fibers could be linked to them, though both were wearing jeans, which had such a common fiber as to render them useless as evidence.

Emptying a fire extinguisher into the car would wipe out the prints in it. Had they had more time, they would've taken the body along and properly disposed of it.

On the other hand, the "rat" note made the murder look like Salmela's work. Two friends got in a fight and Salmela made a break for it.

In Larsson's opinion, killing Nurminen was stupid. Roughing him up would have been enough, but Steiner had gotten out of hand. The stop at the Corner Pub wasn't very smart either, but he hoped the Skulls' reputation would keep anyone from talking to the cops.

At any rate, now they had to finish the job.

CHAPTER 23
MONDAY, 7:40 P.M.
PASILA POLICE HEADQUARTERS, HELSINKI

Honkala stared at Takamäki. "Shit."

"Brutal and bloody enough that it'll be prosecuted as a murder," Takamäki remarked. Finnish law divided homicide into three categories: murder, manslaughter, and killing. Murder, which carried a life sentence, was reserved for premeditated or particularly brutal acts causing serious danger to the public.

Five detectives sat at their computers in the VCU's conference room. Investigators from the NBI, Helsinki, and the neighboring Espoo police departments streamed in and out, reporting the latest news. The head of each investigative branch received the intel, sorted it out and then relayed the main points to Honkala. Takamäki was somewhat envious of how well the system worked. This was how he would have wanted the VCU to work, but they only had the staff for it in exceptional circumstances. This case was exceptional and was getting more so at every turn.

"The name was Kauko Nurminen, you say?"

Takamäki glanced at Joutsamo's printout of Ear-Nurminen's rap sheet and handed it to Honkala. "Minor stuff. A former burglar, but he's been more focused on drinking and shooting the breeze lately."

Takamäki had already described the victim's condition, as well as what Suhonen and Nykänen had told him. A team from forensics was already on the way.

"So the duo that was kicked off the case is now on the hottest trail."

"How should I put it? Suhonen and Nykänen make a dynamic team. More often than not, they'll end up on the right track."

Honkala chuckled. "The dynamic duo. Yes, of course."

Takamäki was glad that Honkala had loosened up his tie over the course of the evening. Managing an investigation involving nearly a hundred officers with a tight tie would have been too much. If nothing else, the blood supply to his head would be disrupted.

"And the two top dogs at the Skulls are our prime suspects?" asked Honkala.

"According to them, Larsson is second-in-command. The president is doing life in Turku. Steiner, well, he's a psycho. Never know what to expect from him. But you're right in that these two hold the most sway with the Skulls right now."

"What grounds do we have for suspicion?"

Takamäki repeated Suhonen's story and explained how Macho had told them that the two Skulls had come to the Corner Pub looking for Salmela, and how he had directed them to Nurminen's apartment. Takamäki also told him about the note found in the bathtub, which got Honkala thinking.

"There's always the possibility that Salmela killed his buddy for ratting on him," Honkala noted. "Let's not forget about that."

"Of course not. We'll follow every lead, but the one from the Corner Pub makes these two Skulls prime suspects."

"We should take this Macho in for questioning before he finds out what happened to his buddy. After he finds out, we won't get anything out of him," said Honkala as he glanced around the bustling room.

"Listen, Kari. Would it be possible for you to take this Ear-Nurminen angle?"

"Fine with me, but is that going to be okay with the bosses?"

"Let them hash it out among themselves later on. We have crimes to solve here."

"Good call. And I can use Nykänen and Suhonen?"

"We'll need Nykänen back at the NBI tomorrow. Otherwise, I don't see why not. Let them have at it. It'll do Nykänen good to be back in the field and away from the coffeemaker for a while."

Takamäki looked at Honkala. "I'm guessing you have the S.W.A.T. team on standby. When are you looking to raid the Skulls' compound?"

"You're thinking *now*?"

"For two reasons. First: we might get some forensic evidence for the bombing. Second: I'm thinking about this Nurminen's murder. The top brass at the Skulls are suspects, so it's possible we'll find them at the compound. We have plenty of probable cause for a search warrant."

"We'll have to hit Larsson's and Steiner's apartments at the same time," Honkala said.

"I'll dig up the addresses. You let the S.W.A.T. team know so they're ready."

* * *

Salmela paid no attention to the cars hurtling past on Hämeen Street in Kallio.

"Can you help me out?" Salmela asked over the phone as he walked down the street.

"What do you need?" asked Juha Saarnikangas.

"A place to crash for the night. I gotta figure out some stuff…can't go home right now."

"Why not?"

"I'll tell you later. Help me out," he begged. The ex-junkie was the only one he could think of who could help—even if Saarnikangas didn't have a fat wad of cash in his pocket.

"Where are you?"

"On Hämeen Street. If nothing else, I've got a door code for a basement nearby that should still work. But can't you help me out?"

Saarnikangas promised to look into it and call him back shortly. He hung up.

A couple of minutes later, Salmela reached the unemployment office building. Its entry lights glared off the pavement. A car turned onto Hämeen Street and slowed down as it came abreast of Salmela. He turned abruptly into the courtyard of the unemployment office, picking up the pace. The car sped up and followed him in.

Salmela glanced back at the car. In the dim lighting from the entryway and the street lamps, the shadowy faces of Larsson and Steiner were visible. Larsson had a phone to his ear.

The parking lot of the courtyard had room for about thirty cars. Salmela looked about frantically for an escape route, but he was cornered. He stopped in his tracks in the middle of the parking lot.

His swirling thoughts brought him back to the cliff in Nuuksio. There had been no escape there either. He didn't stand a chance—struggle was futile. Fate usually proved more merciful than a fight.

The car stopped a few feet short of him. Back at

Ear-Nurminen's place, luck had struck when he spotted Larsson and Steiner walking into the building from the window of the pizzeria. He had known better than to go back. Salmela had taken off walking—he didn't dare run. He had passed the fire station along Agricola Street. Then the streets had seemed too dangerous, and he ducked into a bar for a beer.

For a moment, the familiar surroundings had made him feel safe, but then anxiety struck. He thought about calling Suhonen, but the officer had only caused him trouble recently. That wasn't the right answer, and he couldn't just sit there in the bar, waiting for the inevitable. He had to keep moving. The labyrinthine streets of Merihaka had crossed his mind and he headed in that direction. He might be able to find some unlocked door to a warm cellar and sleep there for the night. That had its risks, though. Security guards made their rounds, and getting caught could land him in jail. He had hoped Saarnikangas could've provided refuge, but now it didn't matter.

Salmela stood in the headlights, resigned to his fate as Larsson and Steiner climbed out of the car.

* * *

"Shit," Nykänen said as he gunned the car through the tunnel under Merihaka. "This is hopeless."

"You have any better ideas?" asked Suhonen.

The NBI lieutenant mulled it over. Technology couldn't help—they had no way to use GPS tracking, phone records, wire taps or any other means of pinpointing the target. Nykänen's thoughts wandered back to the nineties, when he had been chasing violent offenders in the same manner. If somebody ran, walked in a peculiar manner or fit the description, they were stopped and questioned. They had criss-crossed the city by car, watching for anything suspicious. Now, it seemed a complete waste of time.

"No."

"Let's take a spin through those parking ramps," Suhonen suggested. He recalled an old case that had given the parking ramp a grim reputation. A homeless bum had beaten a tax official to death with a roofing hammer. The VCU had dumped countless hours into solving the case. When he was drunk, Salmela had bragged a few times about how he could break into the Merihaka cellars if he ever needed to.

They weren't the only ones on the prowl anymore. To help in the murder investigation, Takamäki had dispatched five squad cars to patrol the streets of Kallio for Larsson and Steiner. The patrol officers had been given a description of Salmela as well.

Nykänen swung the car right into the first entrance to the concrete ramp. There were lots of cars, though the corporate spots were empty. Nykänen drove at a crawl through the ramp, but nobody was in sight.

On the left, an escalator ascended to street level.

"Can't get up there by car," said Nykänen.

"Sure we can, but not through there."

They came upon a concrete wall and Nykänen turned left. The route through the ramp led back to the same entrance they had just descended. On the right was a vast parking lot.

"If someone wanted to hide here, we wouldn't have a chance of finding him."

"Unless he was nervous enough that he couldn't sit tight," said Suhonen, his eyes scanning the cars. He was ready to burst out of the vehicle in a foot pursuit at any moment.

"Right or left?"

"Left. Let's go back to Kallio and comb the streets for another half hour. Then let's start leaning on a few people and see what we can find out."

* * *

Larsson raised the gun and pressed it against Salmela's forehead. "Goddamn bastard!" he hissed.

Larsson was amazed that Salmela didn't respond. He didn't cry, beg, complain or even soil himself.

"Pull the trigger and let's get outta here," Steiner said, standing beside the door of the car. He took a swig from a water bottle. Smoking weed always made him thirsty. The parking lot was empty.

"I'm not gonna shoot this pathetic asshole here. That'd be too nice," Larsson said and lowered his weapon.

Steiner took a step forward and a knife appeared in his hand. "If you can't do it, I will."

"No, you won't. Get in the car—both of you!"

Steiner stared at Larsson, who was obviously serious. Salmela obeyed at once and headed toward the car. Larsson followed close behind and Steiner groaned. Drawing this out further would not bode well.

Salmela settled into the back seat and Steiner slid in next to him. Larsson climbed into the driver's seat and whipped a U-turn in the parking lot. He didn't say a thing. In the back seat, next to Salmela, Steiner twirled a bloody knife in his hand.

CHAPTER 24
MONDAY, 9:00 P.M.
SKULLS' COMPOUND, HELSINKI

Beneath their helmets, the S.W.A.T. officers were wearing black ski masks. The first in line next to the wall was Jack Saarinen. Though Jack wasn't his real name, it had stuck because of his appearance, which was uncannily similar to TV's "Jack Bauer" of *24*.

All twelve of the officers in the stack were decked out in black. The majority of them held MP5 sub-machine guns, though a couple had shotguns. Jack was also wielding a ballistic shield. The street lights cast the dark shadows of the policemen onto the concrete wall of the Skulls' headquarters.

The S.W.A.T team's vehicles were parked a couple of hundred yards away and the team had crept in from there. They had snipped an entry hole in the flimsy fence. Back at police headquarters, they'd gone over the blueprints and the plan was clear—a surprise attack would give them the upper hand.

Just behind Jack, officer Jarmo Eronen waited. He had a heavy battering ram to bash open the lock on the front door. If that didn't work, a third policeman had a shotgun equipped with a lock-slug at the ready. Instead of a regular cartridge, it was loaded with a heavy metal slug that would destroy any ordinary lock.

Jack thought this was a perfect location. Far away from any residences in the middle of an industrial district. Almost like training.

The order came over his earpiece. "Let's go," said the calm voice of Turunen, the S.W.A.T. team's commander. Each officer was wearing a headset with an earpiece and microphone.

Jack lifted the heavy ballistic shield off the ground and quietly covered the remaining distance to the door.

Eronen ducked out of line, came next to Jack and studied the door and lock. It would be too time consuming to pick and they didn't have the code for the keypad. Eronen swung back the hulking battering ram. For the moment, the element of surprise was still theirs, but not after the racket he was about to cause.

The ram smashed into the lock and the door bounced open.

The entryway was dim, but not completely dark. No need for night-vision. Jack took up the lead behind his shield and the others followed in a tight line.

A squad car pulled up to the curb with its lights flashing and two officers and a German shepherd joined the others.

The S.W.A.T. officers had flipped on their laser sights. Through the window of the shield, Jack watched the red specks dancing in front of him.

The entry was empty and the stack of officers proceeded up the stairs. A glimmer of light came down the stairwell, telling Jack there was no door at the top of the stairs, or at least it wasn't closed.

"The top of the stairs is open," he reported over the radio. They continued halfway up before Jack stopped. Eronen dug two canisters, each slightly longer and thinner than a beer can, from the cargo pocket of his pants, pulled the pin out of the first and hurled it through the doorway to the left. Immediately afterwards, the second one flew to the right.

"Police!" Eronen shouted.

The officers shielded their eyes as the stun grenades exploded. The brilliant flashes of light would blind anyone on the upper floor for about five seconds, and the 180 dB blast would slam their ear drums shut.

* * *

Niko Andersson was sprawled on the sagging office sofa, his body hardly able to fit. After hearing the crash downstairs, he struggled to his feet and hurried into the main room, where Roge and Osku were already on their feet. None of them knew what to do. The intruders were likely already on their way up, so they couldn't go down the stairs.

Osku hurried to the window, pried the cardboard aside and saw the squad car at the curb with its cherries flashing. He pulled out the AK-47 assault rifle that had been stashed behind the sofa. There was no need to load—a full magazine was already inserted with a cartridge in the chamber. He pushed the safety all the way down, setting it on full-automatic.

Niko and Roge, standing behind the bar now, were holding their handguns. Osku was positioned opposite them, near the pool table. Just as he was preparing to unleash a barrage of bullets out the window at the cruiser, a shout came from the stairwell.

"Police!"

Osku glanced at Niko, who raised his gun.

In the corner of his eye, he saw an object fly about ten feet from him, bounce off the pool table and land on the sofa behind it. Another one hurtled toward Niko and Roge.

The explosion was deafening and the image of the instant before the blast was seared into Osku's eyes. He blinked frantically, struggling to locate the top of the stairs, then swung the assault rifle in that direction.

Fuck, thought Osku. With his vision and hearing off line, it was the only thing going through his mind. If they were coming up the stairs, they'd be at the top right around now. He raised the weapon to his shoulder and squeezed the trigger hard.

Fragmented thoughts swirled through Osku's mind. This was just the situation Larsson had been talking about. Surrender to no one. Fight fire with fire. That was all that mattered. Only that.

Osku couldn't hear the shots, but he felt the rifle bucking against his shoulder. The rounds departed toward the doorway. In a few seconds his vision would recover. A second magazine lay on the sofa waiting its turn. He could find it by groping around with his free hand.

Osku felt the lurching of the gun as the AK-47 spit out a volley of shells toward the doorway. He could see nothing but the ghosted image of the stairwell, and he paused briefly as the white light gave way to red. After that, he squeezed the trigger once more. The rifle fired the final bullets from the magazine.

* * *

The S.W.A.T. team poured up the stairs after the stun grenades. Despite having plugged his ears, Jack Saarinen's were ringing. Just as he reached the top, a bullet ricocheted off his shield. The impact twisted his wrists, but the shield stayed put. He swung it toward the muzzle flashes and tried to retreat, but Eronen, who was charging forward just behind him, stumbled and collapsed on top of him.

On the left, somebody unleashed another volley of shots. Jack couldn't tell where the bullets were going, nor could he move with Eronen lying on top of him. He turned his head in the other direction, where the bar was supposed to be.

Jack watched as a fat man behind the bar took a bullet in the forehead and half his face vanished. Where had the shot come from? Were the police shooting or was it the assault rifle? He wasn't sure, but he didn't think he had heard an MP5—all the shots had come from an assault rifle.

He concluded that the hit had come from the shooter on the left. After that, the bullets zipped past well wide, but soon, the barrel swung back toward the door. The assault rifle rattled off another series of shots. The flash bangs had disoriented the man enough that he didn't know where he was shooting.

Jack tried to draw his pistol, but it was impossible with Eronen on top of him. The helpless officer could feel his partner shifting around.

Downstairs, Eronen had ditched the shotgun and picked up his MP5. He spotted a man blindly firing next to the pool table and swung the barrel of the gun toward him. The red dot quickly found his face, then his forehead. Jack felt the muffled shudder of Eronen's MP5 submachine gun.

The man with the assault rifle collapsed to the ground. Jack knew that he was killed instantly. Eronen shuffled to his feet and Jack followed. The remaining officers piled in, stepping over the heavy shield. Jack drew his pistol from his belt holster and advanced into the room.

Little by little, Jack's hearing was returning to

normal and he detected a faint whimpering on his right, like the whine of a dog. Eronen was kneeling down, pressing his knee into a muscled gangster's spine. He twisted the man's arms behind his back and slapped the cuffs on his wrists.

"Anybody else here?" Eronen shouted.

The whimpering continued and Jack realized it was coming from the man lying on the ground in cuffs.

The officers quickly checked the upstairs rooms, but found nobody else. These three had been the only ones in the building, and of those, two were now dead.

Jack snapped on the safety to his weapon and shoved it back into its holster.

The unit leader grabbed Jack by the shoulder and looked into his eyes. "You alright?"

He was still dazed, but nodded. "Yeah."

The unit leader put up his thumb and grinned faintly. "The guy emptied the entire magazine blind. Shit!"

Jack heard the report through the earpiece. "All clear. No officers down. Two assailants dead and one under arrest. The other unit is checking the lower level."

The S.W.A.T officer pulled the helmet off his head and peeled the knit ski mask off his face. He lowered himself into the nearest chair. Only then did he notice one of the rear-guard officers dousing the flaming sofa with a fire extinguisher. Apparently, the flash bang had ignited the fabric.

Jack began to cough from the smoke. His face was drenched in sweat, which he wiped away with his hood.

* * *

Takamäki stood in the yard of the Skulls' compound, talking on his phone. The air had turned cold and the occasional fleck of sleet fell to the ground. Soon, it would freeze and the sleet would turn to snow, he thought.

A half-dozen squad cars and an ambulance were parked in front of the building.

"Two suspects are dead, and one under arrest," Takamäki said into the phone. He'd been following the raid from the command vehicle a couple hundred yards away. As soon as they had gotten the "all clear," the van had pulled into the yard.

"What happened?" asked Honkala.

"The S.W.A.T. team went in and one of the Skulls opened fire with a Kalashnikov. The Skulls' bullets killed one of their own and an officer shot the guy with the AK. The third was arrested."

"Who were they?"

"The fatalities were Niko Andersson, a full-fledged member, and Oskari Rahkonen, a prospect. This Osku is the one who shot Niko with the AK. Roger Sandström is under arrest."

Takamäki recalled his son's stories about Osku's little brother Ripa. A tragic event for a kid who idolized his older brother. The incident could affect him in two ways: either it would embitter him or it would frighten him. Difficult to say which way Ripa would swing.

Honkala paused. "So Larsson and Steiner weren't in the building?"

Takamäki's mind returned to the matter at hand. "No. We have no information on their whereabouts. I've been notified about the raids on their apartments. They found Larsson's girlfriend, Sara Lehto, in his flat, and Steiner's was empty. They're bringing her downtown and forensics is going through both apartments."

"Son of a…," Honkala growled on the other end.

Takamäki glanced around the industrial area. So far, nobody but the police had arrived. "We raised quite a ruckus here, so I suppose the media will be here soon. We should probably make some kind of a statement."

"Yeah. We'll put something together. I'll call you when they have it roughed out."

The S.W.A.T. team filed out and the forensics team, decked out in white coveralls, was holding a briefing in the yard.

"We'll also need to inform the state prosecutor so he can evaluate the S.W.A.T. team's conduct in connection with the fatalities."

"We'll take care of that too," said Honkala. "Have you heard anything from Nykänen or Suhonen?"

"Not for a while now. They would've called if they found anyone."

"Pity," said Honkala. "The undertaker's tally for the day is two thugs, a police officer and a civilian. This has got to stop."

Takamäki sighed. "You said it."

TUESDAY, OCTOBER 27

CHAPTER 25
TUESDAY, 3:20 A.M.
SUHONEN'S APARTMENT, HELSINKI

Suhonen awoke to his ringing phone. He groped around for it on the nightstand, coughed once, then answered.

"Hello."

Suhonen heard the sobbing first. "Help me."

"Who is this?"

"Salmela," the man whispered.

Suhonen bolted upright in bed. "What's wrong? Where are you?"

Salmela's voice over the phone was quiet and halting.

"They found me. The assholes found me…"

"Who?"

"Larsson and Steiner. They got me… But I got away… Hold on…" He fell silent.

Suhonen waited. After about twenty seconds, Salmela whispered again. "It was nothing. They're looking for me."

"Where are you?"

"In the woods. Not sure exactly where. There's a road nearby. Come pick me up."

Suhonen got to his feet and looked at the dark streets out the window. "I'll come if I know where to find you."

"There's some school over there. Probably that Russian school. I think…"

Suhonen cut in. "You're somewhere around the intersection of Beltway One and the Hämeenlinna Highway."

"Yeah," Salmela whispered. "There's some road…yeah…now I see it. I'm in the woods northeast of there. I see a kind of greenish house and a bus stop."

"How'd they find you?" Suhonen asked, pinching the phone between his shoulder and ear as he pulled on his jeans.

"Over on Hämeen Street. In the courtyard of the employment office. They just appeared out of nowhere in a car. What happened to Ear-Nurminen? I don't suppose he…"

"Nurminen's dead. They killed him."

"Goddammit!" He lowered his voice again. "I saw 'em go up the stairs. I didn't dare go back."

"Good thing you didn't. What happened after they found you?"

"Hold on again…" said Salmela and the line fell silent.

Suhonen pulled on his sweater. "What's going on?"

"Nothing. Just a car. I don't really know for sure. They drove me here and started grilling me. I don't really know, but at some point they left me alone and I got out the window."

"Go somewhere safe and hide. I'll be there in a silver Peugeot in about fifteen." Suhonen paused to consider his options. Were he to notify dispatch, the place would be crawling with cruisers and sirens. That could make Salmela's situation even worse. It would be better if he picked up Salmela first and then sent in the troops to look for Larsson and Steiner.

There was no time to explain the situation to the lieutenant on duty, Takamäki, Nykänen, nor Honkala.

Every one of them would order him to wait. Waiting was not an option. The second Salmela was in his car, the tables would turn. His hiding spot was only about a ten-minute drive away. Suhonen pulled on his leather jacket in the entryway.

"Listen," said Salmela. "I didn't know anything about the bomb."

"I believe you," said Suhonen, twisting his feet into his shoes.

"And that license plate. That Opel was at the Skulls' compound a couple days ago. I saw it in the yard."

"Huh?"

"Yeah, that agent said on TV that the license plate was AFR-something. Almost the same as my old Opel. I saw it in the Skulls' garage."

"Lay low," said Suhonen as he stepped out the door of his building. "I'll be right there."

* * *

The wet asphalt glowed in the pale light of the streetlamps. A thin layer of snow lay on the shoulder of the road and in random patches elsewhere.

Suhonen parked his silver Peugeot at a bus stop on the shoulder and got out. According to the sign, route 47 stopped here. The green wooden house that Salmela had mentioned was on the left, and near that were several three-story white brick apartment buildings. The one-story buildings of the Russian-Finnish school were further back on the left. To his right was a dark thicket.

This was the spot. Salmela was nowhere in sight, but the rows of street lights formed a bright tunnel from which it was impossible to see into the dark forest.

Suhonen wondered if he should shout for Salmela, but if the gangsters were still out there looking for him, it probably wasn't such a good idea. He lingered a while, but when Salmela didn't show, Suhonen tried his phone.

Salmela didn't answer, but a text message came shortly.

"Can't talk. Hundred yards from bus stop. Red warehouse on the right."

Suhonen read the message and wondered why Salmela couldn't talk. Was the situation that dire?

Best to go check it out. He swung back into the car and headed down the narrow road. A good hundred yards up on the right was a narrow wooded road with no signs.

He hesitated a moment, then swung the car onto the dirt road. Spruces flanked both sides of the road, which was covered in enough snow that he could tell no cars had been through lately. In the headlights up ahead, he saw the road curve gently to the right and end at a red wooden hut the size of a shipping container. There were no windows, at least not on the front. The wooden clapboards ran continuously from the foundation to the shed-style roof.

Suhonen drove closer and waited to see if Salmela would come out. If the other side had a window, anyone inside would be able to see the glow from his headlights. But the little building seemed deserted. Suhonen wondered what kind of warehouse this was anyway. The location was strange. He knew that in the winter, snow was dumped in a nearby lot. Maybe the hut was used for that somehow.

He stopped the car next to the hut. There was enough space in the yard for him to swing the car around.

Suhonen stepped out and listened. The woods

were quiet.

"Salmela," he whispered. Nobody answered, not even the trees. Suhonen had no intention of shouting.

He waited there for a minute to let his eyes adjust to the dark. The zipper on his leather jacket was open for easy access to his Glock, which wasn't drawn yet. Suhonen felt that a drawn weapon was a sign of fear. He wasn't afraid of the dark, nor the unknown. Had he been, he may as well have applied for a desk job.

He could see into the woods now, at least somewhat, and he circled the hut. As he reached the gable end, he noticed the red paint flaking off the walls. Aside from that, the building was in surprisingly good condition. He peeked around the corner. The back side had a door, and a small lone window on the far end, close to the eaves.

Suhonen rounded the corner quietly. Only a few yards separated the building from the forest.

He continued on to the door. There were two alternatives: either go straight inside or shout for Salmela. Suhonen thought briefly, drew his pistol, and without warning, jerked the door open.

Salmela was kneeling on the floor. A piece of silver duct tape covered his mouth, but his eyes were directed to Suhonen's right. Suhonen turned to look, dropped down and raised his weapon. In the corner, Rolf Steiner stood grinning, a pistol in his hand.

Suhonen fired and the shot was deafening. The bullet hit Steiner in his right thigh and he fell to the floor.

"Shi-it," Steiner moaned, clutching his bleeding thigh.

Suhonen kicked the man's fallen gun into the corner and his eyes darted around the room. It was some sort of tool shed, or at least it had been, for all that was left was a vise, a couple of stools, some electrical equipment and ropes. Other than Steiner and Salmela, nobody else was there.

Suhonen looked at the gangster. Blood was spilling onto the floor beneath his leg and the man was cursing in pain. With his gun off in the corner, Steiner seemed harmless, but "seemed" wasn't good enough for Suhonen. He quickly checked the man's pockets and tossed a bloody knife into the same corner, next to the gun.

Suhonen knelt down in front of Salmela and jerked the tape off of his mouth. His hands were apparently tied behind his back.

"You alright?" asked Suhonen.

"Watch out," Salmela managed to say, but Suhonen knew it was already too late. He felt the pressure of cold metal against the back of his head. Apparently, his ears were still ringing so loudly he hadn't heard the door open.

"Hello," said Tapani Larsson coldly. "Drop the gun and put your hands behind your back."

Suhonen weighed his options. Larsson was directly behind him, but Suhonen was kneeling, and wouldn't be able to turn quickly enough to surprise the gangster. Larsson would surely pull the trigger, and even if Suhonen managed to dodge the bullet, Salmela was in the line of fire.

"Larsson, just shoot him and come help me," Steiner groaned from the corner.

"Just wait," Larsson commanded. "Hands behind your back, Suikkanen."

"Suikkanen" referred to Suhonen's alias, the same one he had used a couple of years ago when he arrested Larsson for extortion.

Suhonen lowered his weapon to the floor and started to stand up. But the barrel of Larsson's gun did not yield, and he was forced to kneel again.

"I'm sure you know how to work these," said Larsson as he handed Suhonen a pair of cuffs with his free hand. The barrel of the gun never left his head.

If he was going to try something, he should do it now, thought Suhonen. But he had no chance. No matter what, Larsson would be able to pull the trigger.

Suhonen put his hands behind his back and cuffed himself. Larsson hastily tightened them. At no point did he give Suhonen an opportunity to surprise him.

"Get up," he commanded, and Suhonen stood up.

Without delay, Larsson shoved him into the wall, and the cop tumbled to the floor. Unable to use his hands to break his fall, his shoulder struck the cement floor hard.

"Help me," Steiner wailed.

Larsson went to his brother's side. His jeans were soaked with blood, which was now pooling on the floor. Larsson checked the man's pulse—it was racing.

"You'll be alright," he attempted to comfort Steiner.

"You said he'd give a warning first, not just shoot. Fuck… This is the last time I agree to anything like this. Next time you can be the fucking decoy… Fuck… He pulled the trigger instantly… I should've shot his face off… once he came inside." Steiner spoke haltingly.

That's what the cops had always done before, Larsson thought. They always gave a warning. Their plan had been for Suhonen to arrest Steiner, and then for Larsson to surprise the cop. Even though the plan hadn't worked out, for Larsson, the result was just as good.

True, Steiner's leg looked bad. The bullet had

apparently ruptured a large vein in his thigh, and he could bleed to death. Larsson considered his options, but they all led to the same conclusion. Steiner needed urgent medical care. He had to protect his brother—it was his duty to get the man to a hospital.

But on the other hand, now he finally had the chance to punish Suhonen. Every night in the pen, he had dwelt on revenge. But it would have to wait. A bullet in the back of the head would be fine for the rat, but too painless for the pig. Salmela should be kept alive for now, since executing him in front of Suhonen would intensify the agony.

A choice, that's what this was about. Fuck, Larsson thought. Suhonen had to die and he would, but not so easily. He wanted to see the pig cry and beg for mercy. That's what revenge was about. Domination and power. For the victim to be totally at your mercy and devoid of any hope. Larsson wanted to see him a desperate, blubbering mess—trying to cut a deal. But all in vain, for Larsson wouldn't agree to any deal. He would only watch as each glimmer of hope faded away. This wasn't about Suhonen dying, it was about *how* he would die. A quick death would be far too easy for this long-haired, leather-jacketed pile of shit. The man had to be crushed, but that would take time. Time that, because of Steiner's leg wound, he didn't have.

Larsson got up, walked to the corner, and grabbed two stools, which were slathered with white paint. He twisted a leg off of each one and set both stools in the middle of the room. He took a hank of rope off the workbench and threaded it through a hook in the rafters so that the end of the rope dangled at the level of the workbench. How fitting that there were two of these hooks, he thought. The hooks were meant for lifting heavy equipment in the shed, and could easily carry a man's weight.

Larsson yanked Salmela to his feet and forced him into a kneeling position on the wobbly stool. Salmela struggled to keep his balance. His feet and hands were bound with zip ties. Larsson strapped them together with a second tie, so that his hands and feet were bound together behind his back.

Next, Larsson tied a noose around Salmela's neck, pulled the rope taut and tied the other end to the bench, which was bolted to the floor.

Salmela swayed back and forth in an awkward-looking position. If he lost his balance, the rope would strangle him.

"Goddammit," Steiner moaned in the corner. "My eyes are getting blurry."

Larsson turned to Suhonen with the gun in his hand. "Get up. Don't try anything or I'll kick the stool out from under your rat-friend here."

Apparently, Larsson didn't intend to kill them immediately, thought Suhonen, as he braced himself against the wall and shuffled to his feet. His shoulder throbbed and Suhonen wondered if something had broken in there. That, however, was the least of his problems.

Larsson commanded Suhonen to kneel on the other stool, which creaked ominously as the three remaining legs strained under his weight. He quickly wrapped a zip-tie around each of Suhonen's ankles and strapped them together with a third. The fourth he used to link the zip-ties to the handcuffs so that Suhonen's feet and hands were bound behind his back in the same position as Salmela's.

Suhonen, too, got a noose around the neck, which Larsson pulled tight, then tied to the workbench.

"Rolf," said Larsson as he turned to his friend. "I'll get the car. Hold on a sec."

Larsson left and a couple minutes later, Suhonen heard the car pull up. Larsson came back into the shed, went to the corner and grabbed Steiner's gun and knife. Then he helped his moaning brother to his feet.

"Let's go. I'll help you," said Larsson.

At the door, he turned to Suhonen and Salmela. "Try to stay alive until I come back. I won't be long—then we'll have some fun."

Larsson closed the door and after a few seconds, Suhonen heard the car start.

The contorted position was extremely awkward. It forced the neck forward, which tightened the noose. The missing legs on the stools were on the front-right, so the men had to keep their weight on the left side.

Suhonen didn't dare move on the wobbly stool.

They couldn't hear the sound of the car anymore, and Suhonen shouted, "Help! Help us!"

"No use," Salmela said. "The nearest house is a hundred-fifty yards away on the other side of the highway. Nobody's gonna hear us."

Salmela was right. Besides that, the door was closed and the woods would muffle any sound.

Larsson had left Suhonen's phone in his pocket, but there was no way he could get to it. In the pocket of his leather jacket was a key ring with a key for police cuffs. Even if it worked on these cuffs, that too would be impossible to get.

"I'm sorry," said Salmela. "I really did get away for a while, but maybe they just wanted me to call you."

"Maybe."

"That text was from Larsson."

"It doesn't matter now. This doesn't look good." Defying his balance, Suhonen turned his gaze as far toward Salmela as he dared.

Salmela's voice was calm. "Why drag this out? One little slip and it's all over. I'm ready."

CHAPTER 26
TUESDAY, 4:45 A.M.
TÖÖLÖ, HELSINKI

The blue Audi A4 turned right off of Mannerheim Street onto Eino Leino Street, sped through an intersection, and swung left.

Many of the cars in Töölö were still covered with snow, but the pavement was wet. An old woman in a brown fur coat was stepping into the crosswalk, but quickly shuffled back to avoid being hit.

"Stay awake," said Larsson, poking Steiner in the shoulder as the man nodded off. "Don't fall sleep."

"Dammit," Steiner wheezed. "I'm so tired."

"We'll be there in a minute. Fight!"

The front seat was drenched in blood. Larsson wasn't sure how much blood Steiner had lost, nor how much he could lose before dying.

Larsson had wondered if he should drive to the Töölö hospital or the one in Meilahti, and had opted for Töölö, since the drop-off would be easier. The emergency room there was open twenty-four hours a day. The quality of the care couldn't be that different, he thought. After passing Sibelius Street, the 1960s red brick building appeared on the right-hand side.

Larsson's loaded Beretta lay on the center console. Steiner's gun and stiletto were in the footwell of the back seat.

The entrance to the ER was deserted. A traffic sign nailed to a grimy telephone pole forbade parking, but stopping was permitted. The second floor of the building formed a fifteen-foot deep canopy over the entrance.

Larsson swung the Audi under the canopy and up to the front door. It was almost five in the morning and there were no ambulances or doctors on smoke breaks. That suited Larsson just fine.

He pulled up to the glass doors and stopped the car. On the way there, he had considered just shoving Steiner out and taking off. But the man was barely conscious now, and he'd likely crack his head on the sidewalk if Larsson pushed him out.

Larsson left the engine running and got out of the car. He rounded the front end to the passenger side and hauled Steiner out. The man mumbled something, but Larsson couldn't make out the words. Well, at least he was alive. Nothing else mattered. Larsson laid him down in front of the door and glanced into the lobby. The lights were on, but the hallway was empty. Quickly, he returned to the car and got back inside. He pushed in the clutch and threw it into first.

He glanced through the glass doors again. Still nobody. Wouldn't security be interested in a car and a half-dead man lying on the ground? Wasn't somebody monitoring the security cameras? Couldn't anyone be relied on anymore?

Apparently not, thought Larsson, and doubt began to sink in. Nobody had noticed—not doctors, not nurses, not the security guards. Steiner could die at the door of the hospital.

He spotted a doorbell next to the glass doors. There was no choice but to ring it, he thought, and he stepped out of the car.

The explosion in Käpylä had made for an extraordinary day. Officers Tero Partio and Esa Nieminen were working overtime on top of their double shift, and it was beginning to wear on them. Some of the patrol officers on the night shift had been tied up in the previous evening's raids, and earlier in the evening, their lieutenant had radioed for volunteers to pick up an extra shift. That was fine with Partio and Nieminen and, of course, the lieutenant. So far, they had been on duty for seventeen hours straight.

At first, the explosion had made for interesting work, but slowly, it had become a mind-numbing chore. Partio and Nieminen had secured a corner near the Velodrome. It had been uneventful—one man had stopped at the corner to let his dog urinate. Not a single reporter or cameraman to provide a little variety.

Later in the afternoon, their lieutenant had convinced the army to lend some conscripts for guard duty, so Partio and Nieminen had been able to return to their normal duties.

Tero Partio could feel the weight of his eyelids, but he tried to concentrate on driving. He passed a large mural on Runeberg Street and turned onto Töölö Street. In the back seat sat a mugging victim, whose hand was in need of stitches. A mugger had tried to take the forty-year-old man's wallet at the ATM, but the victim hadn't given it up. For that, his palm was slashed with a knife.

"Last call of the night," said Officer Nieminen.

"Yeah. I suppose we've done enough serving and protecting for one day," Partio remarked. This was a routine call. The medics had stitched the victim's wound, but had had to respond to another call. As they were nearing the end of their shift, the officers had agreed to bring the victim to the emergency room.

The cruiser approached the ER and Partio spotted a car at the entrance and a man fumbling around. What the hell, he thought. Not this again. It looked like a drunk driver had brought his buddy to the hospital with a self-inflicted knife wound. If the driver blew over .005 on the breathalyzer, it would mean at least another hour on duty.

The situation looked suspicious, and Partio let off the gas. He saw a bald, tattooed man circling from the passenger side of the car to the driver's seat. Where were the nurses, he thought. Something was wrong.

"This doesn't look right," said Partio. "Heads up."

Nieminen was half-sleeping and bolted upright.

The squad car's engine roared as Partio stepped on the gas, and the car swerved into the emergency room drop-off. The Audi, idling in front of the door, was five yards off, perpendicular to the police car. Partio slammed on the brakes and heard a bump from the back seat. That didn't concern him. He yanked up the emergency brake and swung out of the car.

The bald tattooed man was opening the door of the Audi as Partio raised his gun and shouted, "Stop! Police!"

The baldy hesitated a moment, but apparently judged the situation hopeless.

"Put your hands up!"

"Fucking pig. You'll regret this," he said, then turned and put his hands on the roof of the car.

Nieminen had already gotten out and was kneeling next to the man on the ground. "Bad leg wound here. Looks like he's been shot."

Partio kept his gun trained on the driver of the Audi. He was about to tell his partner to alert the hospital staff about the wounded man, but just then, a stout male nurse in a white coat came out of the entrance.

The glass doors opened outward. "What's going on here?" the man asked, looking at Partio's drawn gun.

"This man has been shot," said Nieminen. "At least for now he's more your client than ours."

Partio felt there was something familiar about the men, but he couldn't put his finger on what. They both looked like criminals, in any case. "Check him before they take him in."

As the nurse went to get a gurney and some help, Nieminen patted the man down for weapons.

"Nothing," said the younger officer.

Larsson was standing with his hands on the roof of the car. Nieminen walked over and scanned the interior of the Audi. "Partio, there's a gun in there... And another one in the back seat with a knife."

Partio kept his gun sight locked on Larsson. "Okay, that makes three weapons then."

Larsson said nothing. The nurses wheeled a gurney to where Steiner lay and muttered something about a possible gunshot wound.

"Sorry," said Partio to Larsson. "You guys look familiar. Why don't you tell us your friend's name so they can patch him up."

Larsson didn't respond. With Nieminen's help, the nurses counted to three and hoisted Steiner onto the gurney. A dark red blot remained on the concrete.

"If you don't tell us his name, they can't treat him," Partio bluffed. He had to get the bald man to talk.

"Rolf Steiner," Larsson mumbled.

"What's that? I didn't hear."

"Rolf Steiner!" Larsson bellowed loud enough for both Partio and the nurses to hear.

Now Partio remembered. That was the Skulls' resident maniac and this other must be Tapani Larsson, the gang's second-in-command. I'll be damned, he thought. He'd been hearing about these guys over the radio all evening, but fatigue had numbed his brain.

The gurney was wheeled inside and Partio told Nieminen to go along with the patient.

"Alright," said Nieminen. At the entrance, he turned and glanced toward the Audi. "You'll manage?"

Partio nodded and the nurses disappeared inside.

Larsson turned to look at Partio. "So you think you can manage me," he sneered. It occurred to Partio that the guns were still inside the car.

"Stay where you are, please," said Partio, his gun fixed firmly on the target.

"Please, please, please. What the hell are you squealing about, pig. I don't please anyone."

Partio wondered if Larsson was psyching himself up for an attack. Perhaps sending Nieminen away had been a mistake. Suddenly, he realized he had made another. He hadn't told Nieminen to call for backup. The next screw-up could be fatal.

"Get on your knees, please," Partio commanded.

Larsson turned away from the car and took half a step toward Partio, who was rooted in a wide firing stance next to the squad car. The span was about ten feet, an adequate distance. Larsson wouldn't be able to surprise him with one motion, but he shouldn't be allowed to slink in any closer.

"You're afraid of me," Larsson said, and remained standing. "There was a time when you would've bashed me in the back of the knee with a nightstick and then choked me with it. Now you just wave that piece of Austrian plastic at me. What's gotten into you guys?"

"On your knees. Now. Please."

"Jesus Christ, didn't I already tell you to quit that *please* shit?" Larsson took another half-step forward.

Partio backed up a couple of feet. "On the ground now, or I'll put you in there next to Steiner."

Larsson was amazed. He had thought the cop would just continue with the warnings. That's what they were taught to do. Verbal judo and the like, but now the cop had clearly threatened to shoot. Maybe taking off wasn't such a good idea after all. You never knew about these types. Still, they'd never shoot a fleeing man in the back.

"Yeah, right. If you shoot an unarmed man, you'll be charged and lose your badge," Larsson shouted. If he only had his gun, he could test his speed. But it was inside the car.

Partio pulled the trigger. The bullet struck the back door of the Audi and made Larsson flinch. The shot echoed down the street. A small hole surrounded by chipped paint had appeared in the car door.

"On your knees. Now. Please. The next one won't miss."

Larsson stalled for another moment; at least this guy wasn't afraid to shoot. "No," he said.

Officer Nieminen dashed outside with his gun drawn. He saw Partio holding his gun and Larsson still standing by the car. "Everything okay?"

"Pretty much. Call for backup first and then put the cuffs on this piece of shit."

Nieminen marveled at his partner's choice of words. He certainly understood who the piece of shit was, but Partio had always, even in the most difficult situations, been calm and overly courteous. Nieminen took out his radio and notified dispatch that there had been a threatening situation at the Töölö emergency room. Shots had been fired, but the situation was under control. He then asked for additional units. "10-4" said the dispatcher, and the first sirens were audible before Nieminen could make it over to Larsson.

"Well, shithead," Nieminen growled. "Here are your cuffs."

He twisted Larsson's arms behind his back, and forcefully slapped the cuffs on the man's wrists. Nieminen knew the impact was painful, and would leave bruises for weeks, but the gangster should have complied in the first place.

"Anything else?" said Nieminen.

Though Nieminen was directly behind Larsson, Partio kept his gun aimed at the gang boss.

"I told him to get on his knees, but he didn't."

Nieminen pulled a telescoping baton out of his utility belt. With a quick snap, the spring steel club extended to about a foot and a half. Without a word, Nieminen struck Larsson in the back of the knees. The bald man fell to his knees with a grimace.

"Anything else?" asked Nieminen with a wooden expression. He glanced over his shoulder as the first squad car swerved around a distant corner with its lights flashing. He patted Larsson down, but didn't find any weapons. Partio had no doubt that if Larsson's gun had been in his pocket, rather than in the car, he would have tried to use it.

"That should be about it," said Partio. Suddenly, he remembered the mugging victim in the back of the squad car. "That guy with the gash is still in the back seat."

Nieminen still had the baton in his hand and he

tapped Larsson lightly on the ear with it. "I'll watch this piece of shit—you take him inside. Ask about Steiner while you're at it. According to the doc, his oxygen levels were really low."

The arrangement suited Partio, but he wondered if he should interrogate Larsson about the source of Steiner's gunshot wound. But Partio let it go. They could leave that for the VCU—those guys had to earn their pay somehow.

He holstered his Glock and went to the back door of the cruiser, which couldn't be opened from the inside. Partio pulled the door open to see the mugging victim curled up on the back seat. He looked up at the officer. "What the hell is going on out there?"

"Nothing to worry about. Just had to take care of some urgent police business first, but we'll get you in line for some help soon."

"Who fired?" the man asked as he scrambled to his feet.

"I did. Now get up, and quick."

In three seconds, the man was out of the car. Partio pointed him toward the entrance to the clinic.

The approaching squad car killed its sirens a hundred yards before the hospital. As the cruiser came to a stop under the canopy, the roof lights went out too. Since the roof lights would quickly drain the car's battery, they were used sparingly.

Two big officers stepped out, keeping their hands on the butts of their guns. Nieminen greeted them both, but kept the baton by Larsson's ear.

"Who fired?" asked one of the officers.

"Partio."

"At who?"

Nieminen waved his baton toward the hole in the side of the car. "Just the poor Audi. Unfortunately."

"Aha." The big officer glanced back at the kneeling Larsson and recognized the Skull. "Well, your partner should work on his marksmanship."

CHAPTER 27
TUESDAY, 6:30 A.M.
PASILA POLICE HEADQUARTERS,
HELSINKI

Takamäki sat in his office and smelled the coffee. At this hour, it was either very fresh or it had sat in the pot overnight. Though it was still too hot to drink now, judging by the aroma, it was fresh.

The lieutenant was reading a report on his screen about the early-morning incident at the ER. It matched what he had heard from the night-shift lieutenant in a 5:00 A.M. phone call, though the report described the events in greater detail. Sergeant Partio himself had written it.

"Morning," said Captain Honkala as he took off his overcoat. The NBI captain was wearing the same gray suit as yesterday and his short hair was neatly combed.

After the night-shift lieutenant had awakened him, Takamäki had phoned Honkala, and the two had agreed to meet in Takamäki's office at half-past-six.

"Anything new?"

"Details, mainly," answered Takamäki, and he relayed the main points of the incident at the ER.

"I wonder who shot Steiner, and where the shooter is."

"No longer alive, I suspect. Larsson is in custody, but he hasn't said anything. Steiner is in no shape to talk, yet."

"What about forensics?"

"Just getting started, but they found some soil and sand on Steiner's and Larsson's shoes as well as in the footwell of the Audi, so they'd been somewhere in the woods. No GPS in the car, so it's tough to say exactly where. I bet the shooting happened somewhere in Helsinki, since Larsson drove to the Töölö Hospital and not to one in Vantaa or Espoo."

Joutsamo, dressed in a gray sweater, stepped into the office. "We got the results of the residue analysis. Larsson didn't fire his weapon last night. Actually, the preliminary results show that neither of their weapons have been fired for some time. Steiner's knife has traces of fresh blood, so we sent it to the lab."

"Thanks," said Honkala. "No surprise about the knife, but could it be possible that the bombing was intended for the Skulls after all? Seems like someone is after these two. What if Salmela's behind all this? At least he'd have a motive, and that "rat" note on his dead friend has got me thinking."

Takamäki didn't comment, but turned back to Joutsamo. "Have you gotten a hold of Suhonen?"

"He's not answering his phone."

"Okay. He's probably been working all night and turned off his phone to get a few hours of sleep."

"It's definitely ringing, but nobody's answering," Joutsamo added.

"Well, it could be on vibrate."

Honkala brushed a piece of lint off the shoulder of his suit jacket. "I called Nykänen. He told me they'd been doing the rounds till about midnight before Suhonen dropped him off at the station and went home. Nykänen will get here as soon as he can."

"Well, Suhonen will show up too, once he wakes up."

Honkala was still standing in the middle of the room. "What about Larsson's and Steiner's phone records?"

"We put a rush on them," Joutsamo replied. "The phone companies promised them by noon."

"Okay," said Takamäki. "We have to remember that we have three parallel cases: the bombing in Käpylä, Nurminen's stabbing, and most recently, Steiner's shooting. The car bombing is connected to the Skulls. We have no suspects yet in Steiner's shooting, but in Nurminen's case, we have Larsson and Steiner. That looks like the easiest case of the three."

Joutsamo nodded. "Forensics has been cranking all night, but I haven't heard any results yet."

"They promised them by nine this morning."

"And there's a fourth case here, too," Honkala noted. "The shooting at the Skulls' compound. Of course, the state prosecutor will investigate police conduct in connection with the fatalities. The NBI techies have been scouring the building all night. I haven't heard what they found."

Honkala fell silent for a moment, "This calls for another meeting with the bosses so we can sort out who takes what."

"I agree," said Takamäki.

"Quite a case, but we've got plenty of time. Now that Larsson and Steiner are in custody, we're in no hurry. How about nine o'clock in your conference room?"

"Sounds good," said Takamäki.

"We should think about the press, too. And by that I mean what are we going to make public," Honkala continued. "Yesterday, if memory serves, I promised to have a noon press conference at the NBI headquarters, but it's probably better to have it here."

That was the last thing on Takamäki's mind.

"I could go for some coffee here," said Honkala.

Take a big mug so you wake up, thought the lieutenant. Just as Honkala was leaving the room, Takamäki spoke up, "I'd like to interrogate Larsson personally. Like now."

* * *

Suhonen's mouth was parched and his muscles ached. His stance on the wobbly stool was precarious. The undercover cop's hands, cuffed behind his back, were strapped to his feet with zip-ties. The noose held up his head. Carefully, he attempted to shift his weight to the other knee and shin, but it was difficult. The rigid zip-ties had taken the feeling out of his feet some time ago.

The shed was dark. Only a small window admitted the faint yellow street lights of Beltway One. Suhonen's phone had rung twice and startled the men enough that they had almost fallen over. Suhonen had shouted for help numerous times, but nobody had heard, or at least hadn't come to help.

Salmela hadn't said anything for a while, but despite his talk of suicide, he was still balancing on the stool.

"What's the status?" Suhonen asked quietly.

Salmela took a while to answer. "Terrible. I feel like shit. I'm not gonna last long. How long we been here?"

"Don't know. Couple hours probably."

Salmela was quiet for a couple of minutes. "It was Juha Saarnikangas who ratted on me. I can't prove it, but I know he called Larsson because I had just called Juha to ask for a place to sleep right before the assholes found me."

"Juha's always played with a couple of decks. We'll go pay him a little visit when we get outta here."

"If we get outta here."

"*When* we get outta here."

Silence set in for another few minutes, amplifying the pain in their bodies, but they had to endure.

"Where the hell is Larsson? I almost wish he'd come back, even if he kicks these stools out from under us. I'd take the plunge myself, but I'm afraid I'd knock you over in the process," said Salmela. His voice was nearly at a whisper now.

The men listened closely for a moment. Only the quiet hum of cars on Beltway One reached their ears.

"He'll come. He hates me so much he wouldn't miss this."

"My whole body hurts like hell," Salmela moaned.

Suhonen tried once more to move his hands. If he could only work them free of his feet, his predicament would improve substantially. The noose wouldn't cinch if he could just get his feet on the floor.

"Something must have happened at the hospital," said Suhonen.

"Think he got busted?"

"Possible." Suhonen was quiet for a second. He didn't want to speculate, since Larsson's arrest would mean that nobody would be coming back for them. They had been left to die. They couldn't hold on much longer.

Steiner's blood lay on the cement floor, and had dried into what looked like an ink blot.

"No use crying over spilt blood."

"What?" Salmela blurted.

"No use crying over spilt blood." Suhonen repeated. "I've always thought those old proverbs should be updated."

"Huh?"

"Yeah. With police lingo, you know… A crook in the hand is worth two in the bush."

Salmela chuckled—a good sign, Suhonen thought. At least he was thinking of something else.

"A shooting cop seldom bites," Suhonen went on.

Salmela jumped in too. "A penny stolen is a penny earned."

Now it was Suhonen's turn to laugh. Laughing made the pain seem to recede momentarily. "Don't bite the hand with the billy club."

"I got another," said Salmela. "Snitches can't be choosers."

Suhonen almost lost his balance. "That's good. And this one's for Larsson, "There's more than one way to skin a gangster."

* * *

Tapani Larsson was seated behind a pale brown table in the VCU's dreary interrogation room, wearing orange police-issue coveralls. Takamäki sat opposite him and was accompanied by his side-kick Anna Joutsamo. Behind them was a sheet of one-way glass, through which Honkala and a couple of other officers were observing.

Larsson's arms were crossed defiantly across his chest and he was scowling.

"This is not a formal interview, just a preliminary discussion," said Takamäki, leaning forward and staring into the bald man's eyes.

"I don't have anything to talk about."

Takamäki was pleased—at least he had gotten a response.

"You were arrested as a suspect in yesterday's

murder of Kauko Nurminen, amongst other things," said Takamäki tersely.

"Who is *he*?"

"Was," the lieutenant corrected. Joutsamo, next to him, looked stern.

"Pretty lady cop you got here. You banging her?"

Takamäki ignored the comment. "Larsson, you were released from prison on Wednesday—so exactly five days ago. Right now you're on the fast track back to solitary in Turku Prison. For Nurminen's murder, you'll get life and serve at least fourteen years. Once we unravel this car bombing case that will probably go up to twenty-plus years for the cop killing. By the end of the 2020s, the media will be calling you 'Finland's longest-serving inmate.'"

"Well, if it's so obvious, why are you asking me?" Larsson smiled. "Lock me up and throw away the key. What's the point of this?"

Despite the attitude, Takamäki could see that his words had sunk in. The man's posture had slumped a half inch.

"I'll be enjoying my retirement before you get out."

"Congratulations. But, you look so young!"

"I know you're not stupid. You know the difference between murder and manslaughter, so I don't need to explain that to you. Both the car bombing and the stabbing look like murder, but we'll investigate them objectively. If we determine that the criteria for murder aren't met, they'll be investigated as manslaughters. If you ask me, Kauko Nurminen's death looks like murder. You're gonna have to tell us what actually happened there."

Takamäki doubted a confession would be forthcoming, but according to the blood type results, only Steiner's clothing contained traces of Nurminen's blood. Though most of the blood on his pants was his own, they had found several blood drops on the left leg that were the same blood type as Nurminen's. DNA would confirm it, but he wanted to give Larsson the opportunity to tell his side of the story.

"Is Steiner alive?" asked Larsson.

Takamäki considered lying and saying he was dead, since that was what Larsson was after. The gangster wouldn't cast blame on a brother if he was still alive, but if the man was dead, Larsson could be more truthful.

"He's alive."

"I'm not saying anything. I understand you have to go through the murder versus manslaughter stuff, but I'm not buying it. I do appreciate that you didn't lie to me about Steiner."

"That's not how we operate."

Larsson laughed. "Uhh. Is that so?"

"What do you mean by that?" Takamäki said. Maybe this could lead somewhere.

"Fuck. You guys have the country's biggest bullshitters."

"What are you talking about? The case that landed you in prison last time?"

Larsson laughed. "Including that one. That Suhonen is a goddamn clown. He deserves his fate."

A cold ripple ran down Takamäki's spine. "What fate?"

Larsson laughed, but said nothing more.

"What did you mean by that?"

Had Suhonen shot Steiner only to fall victim to Larsson, he wondered?

"You can try, but you won't be able to beat the Skulls."

Takamäki massaged his jaw. This called for a change in tactics. "What Skulls? Your president is serving a life sentence and ten or so others are in prison too. You and Steiner will get life. Niko Andersson and Osku Rahkonen are dead. Roger Sandström is in jail on suspicion of murder. We have a warrant for Sami Aronen's arrest on the same charge."

Larsson didn't respond, though he was clearly listening to the lieutenant.

Takamäki went on. "And just for your information: Osku shot Andersson, and the police shot Osku. So I was wondering if their names will make it on the headstone you guys got, or do they get asterisks? Is the epitaph going to say that one was shot by his buddy, and for the other one, that he shot his buddy? Your problem is that you don't have anybody to carve the names. Your gang has crumbled. The Skulls don't exist anymore."

Larsson still didn't say anything.

"The police shot Korpela a year ago. I was there myself when Kahma and Jyrkkä were shot in that abandoned parking lot in Hanko… Do you get it, Larsson? You've lost."

"Bullshit," Larsson tried to growl under his breath, but it came out feebly.

"You could put it on the back of your vests—The Skulls: Motorcycle Club for Inmates and the Dead. You're unable to commit crimes anymore. You won't see another gang member for years when you're all spread out in different prisons. And your bodies in different graveyards."

Larsson's face was vacant as he hissed through his teeth, "You're at the top of my hit-list."

"Sure, but who's gonna carry out the hit? We found a cell phone in Osku's pocket with a photo and

GPS coordinates. A GPS unit was also recovered from your offices with coordinates marked for various spots in the woods. Narcotics is digging them up right now. I don't know if it's weapons, drugs or money, but I will soon."

Larsson was furious, but he wore a mocking smile.

"You and all the others are either in prison or dead. Try to understand…your gang is gone. And with the evidence we have, we'll put your wife in prison too."

"She isn't…"

"Cut the bullshit. With the intel we have, we can nail Sara Lehto as an accessory to plenty of your jobs."

"She's not actually… Fuck. Stop the bullshit. If you're gonna go there, then…"

"Then what?" Takamäki asked. "Try to understand. We won."

Takamäki laughed with willful arrogance. "I told you before that I don't lie. Believe me. The Skulls lost. Sorry about that."

A genuine grin spread across Larsson's face. "A Pyrrhic victory then. You'll never find him alive."

"Who?" asked Takamäki, though he knew exactly who Larsson was talking about. Larsson laughed aloud. "You'll have a grand spectacle for TV when that NBI agent and Suhonen get a joint burial. Shit, you can take bids from the news networks. They'll pay big money for it. Yeah…I'll have a good laugh watching it. Fuck!"

Takamäki said nothing.

"But the snitch will be quietly cremated, right?"

Takamäki stood up and walked out. Joutsamo followed close behind.

"What, you get the urge to fuck?" Larsson shouted

after them. "I did!"

Two guards came into the room after Takamäki and Joutsamo were gone.

In the hallway, Honkala stepped out. "Hell, I thought…why are you spelling out the whole case to him? But now I see what you were getting at."

* * *

Salmela was swaying on his stool from one side to the other. Suhonen was coping, though the pain had numbed half of his head.

"Sing along now. *I shot the sheriff…*"

"*…But I didn't shoot no deputy*," said Salmela wearily. "Fuck…I can't go on."

"*I shot the sheriff…*"

Salmela strained his head in Suhonen's direction. "Listen. If you get outta this, scatter my ashes at the Lahti Soccer Stadium. They won't give you permission, but just do it."

Suhonen knew all about Salmela's soccer fever, but he wanted to keep up the conversation. "Why?"

"That's where I stashed my boy's ashes. On the ski jump side, right-hand corner. That way we can watch the up-and-coming stars together. Whoa… Dammit, no."

"Focus!" Suhonen shouted. "Keep your balance, now. This isn't over."

"I… I'm trying…but I…I just can't…anymore."

Salmela pitched away from Suhonen. The stool clattered out from under him and he dangled at the end of the rope.

"Dear God…" Tears welled up in Suhonen's eyes. Salmela wheezed as the rope cinched tight under his weight. A typical hanging would have snapped his neck, killing him immediately, but in this case, he hadn't fallen far enough. The rope was slowly strangling him. A painful end.

Suhonen heard the sound of a car outside.

"Help us! Help! Hurry!" he shouted. "Help! Help!"

The car stopped and Suhonen heard the doors open. It could be Larsson, but he didn't care. He wasn't afraid of showing distress.

"Help! In the shed! Hurry!"

Hurried footsteps approached and the door burst open.

Joutsamo was the first inside. Behind her were Mikko Kulta and Takamäki.

"Salmela!" Suhonen shouted.

"Jesus!" said Kulta. He seized the dangling Salmela in his arms. The rope slackened, and Kulta tried to release tension on the noose with his fingers. Joutsamo pulled a folding knife out of her pocket and cut the rope off of Salmela's neck, accidentally nicking him beneath his left ear. A thin trickle of blood ran down his neck. Takamäki took out his phone and called for an ambulance.

Kulta lowered Salmela onto the concrete floor. Joutsamo cut his hands and feet free of the zip-ties. Kulta felt around for a pulse, but couldn't find it. He plugged the man's nose, tilted his head back and blew a puff of air into his mouth.

Joutsamo came to Suhonen's side. "How long..."

"Nice to see you. My feet are completely numb so I won't be able to stand. In other words, take it easy, alright?"

Takamäki dropped his phone into his pocket and came to Joutsamo's aid. Kulta went from mouth-to-mouth to chest compressions.

"One, two, three..." he counted aloud.

Joutsamo cut the rope around Suhonen's neck first

327

and Takamäki braced him so he wouldn't fall. Joutsamo cut the zip-ties and opened the cuffs with her key.

"Okay. You're free," she said.

Suhonen dropped his hands to his sides and tried to straighten his back, but to no avail. "I'm cramped up real bad," he groaned.

"An ambulance is on the way. They'll have some muscle relaxants," said Takamäki as he knelt at Suhonen's side. He nodded at Joutsamo. There hadn't been a moment to spare.

After Larsson's interrogation, they had called in an emergency request to locate Suhonen's cell phone. The data had led them to the vicinity of the storage building. Suhonen's shouts had reached the car and spurred them on.

Joutsamo shifted Suhonen into Takamäki's arms, and the lieutenant lowered him carefully to the cement floor.

"Larsson?" asked Suhonen.

"We got him," said Takamäki. "Don't worry."

Suhonen tried to get up, but his feet and hands couldn't bear his weight. "Salmela!" he bellowed.

Kulta blew into Salmela's mouth twice and went back to chest compressions.

Joutsamo checked for a pulse in his neck. Nothing.

The sirens of an ambulance approached from afar.

CHAPTER 28
TUESDAY, 12:25 P.M.
PASILA POLICE HEADQUARTERS, HELSINKI

"Thank you," said NBI Captain Honkala before walking away from the podium in the lobby of Pasila Police Headquarters.

Takamäki had been watching the press conference from the sidelines, near the elevator. Honkala had informed the media of the events of the previous evening: the Skulls' compound, the ER, and the tool shed.

The state prosecutor, who always handled investigations into police conduct, had started to look into the S.W.A.T. team's role in the deaths of two Skulls during the raid at the compound.

The prosecutor had read his statement, "Since the victim died as a result of the use of police force, this investigation is of particular concern. Therefore, we'll be undertaking a pre-trial investigation to look into whether the aforementioned shots were fired by a police officer and whether any officers are guilty of any acts, which could be interpreted as criminal. Only through a preliminary investigation can we obtain a comprehensive and objective analysis of the facts. At this time, the matter is being investigated as a justifiable homicide."

The reporters had glanced at each other. Had the matter not been so serious, somebody would surely have cracked a smile at his legalese.

This time, Honkala had answered a few questions. One reporter had asked him to comment on the extraordinariness of the recent crime wave. Honkala had responded that, since five people had died in a short period of time, it had been extraordinarily violent.

Takamäki opened the elevator door and Honkala stepped inside. Takamäki waved his access card past the sensor and pushed the button for the fourth floor.

"Anything new on Salmela?"

"He'll make it," said Takamäki. "Suhonen will be at the hospital till this evening, maybe overnight."

"I'd say he's earned a couple days of sick leave."

"A couple days—no more."

At the 9:00 A.M. meeting, the cases had been divided up so that the NBI would take the car bombing and the incidents at the Skulls' compound, and the Helsinki police would take Ear-Nurminen's murder and the torture at the storage shed. All of the investigations would fall under Honkala's purview.

Their objective was clear: put all living members of the Skulls behind bars. Honkala and Takamäki believed it was possible, though two mid-level members were still unaccounted for.

Salmela's drug offense was a separate case, which would be handled by Narcotics. Honkala felt that if Salmela would agree to testify against the Skulls, he could talk the prosecutor into a suspended sentence. There was no more need to conceal Salmela's informant role, since it had already been revealed.

The elevator stopped at the fourth floor and Takamäki stepped out just ahead of Honkala.

"You in a hurry?" asked Honkala.

"Not especially. Why do you ask?"

"Let's go to Meilahti Hospital. We can visit Aalto.

He's pretty weak, but I'm told he's conscious and might need some cheering up."

The agent had lost his hand and one of his eyes in the explosion. It was possible he might never work again.

"Sure, I'll go. We can drop in on Suhonen too. Joutsamo was there this morning and said he was a little hopped up on pain killers."

* * *

Sanna Römpötti was sitting in the front seat of the camera van. The live broadcast of the press conference was over and one assistant had stayed to pack up the equipment.

"Where to now?"

"First let's shoot some footage of the storage building and then head over to the Skulls' compound. After that, we can go to the site of the murder in Kallio."

"You have the addresses?" said the cameraman as he dug out his GPS.

Römpötti remembered Sami Aronen and took out her phone. His number was in the address book.

It rang several times, but nobody answered. Maybe Aronen was in jail too. She could check with Takamäki later.

The cameraman turned on the ignition and pulled away from the police station.

They were in for a long day, she thought. It would be well into spring before any of these cases went to court.

* * *

A semi truck was roaring along a three-lane rural highway toward St. Petersburg. The Russian M-10 Highway, flanked by tall spruces, was wide and had little traffic. The trucker was a forty-something man with short, bristly hair, sunken cheeks, a sleeveless T-shirt, and tattoo-covered arms. He was listening silently to a CD of mournful Russian numbers. Next to him sat Sami Aronen, who didn't care to chat, since the Russian spoke English poorly. Though the gangster was exhausted, he felt compelled to stay awake.

Yesterday evening, Aronen had picked up Niko Andersson from the harbor, dropped him off at the compound and then continued to his garage to work on his new motorcycle. When stressed, the ex-soldier liked to tinker. Not that he had much else to do anyway.

Mike Gonzales had called at around midnight in a panic to ask what had happened. The news had reported a shooting at the compound. Aronen didn't know anything about the incident, but with Gonzales' help and a few phone calls, the scope of the catastrophe had become apparent.

Aronen had asked Mike to arrange a ride across the Russian border. There, he'd have time to think and plan. Mike had found him a semi with an empty passenger seat, which was slated to leave Helsinki at 5:00 A.M. Passport checks on both the Finnish and Russian sides of the border hadn't been a problem, since the stowaway had been hiding in a secret compartment built into the cab.

The ride wasn't cheap, but Aronen could afford it. He had emptied three caches in the woods near his garage. All together, they contained 80,000 euros in cash and thirteen pounds of amphetamines.

Raiding the gang's stashes would've been a bad

idea. If the cops had raided the compound and found the GPS locators, they probably would have already found the stashes too. His three caches had been his personal insurance policy.

The road was straight and Aronen was exhausted. His eyelids drooped shut. He had tried to come up with another plan, but knew that, at times, retreat was the only real alternative.

Gonzales had wanted his money immediately, so Aronen had driven to the man's house. There, Gonzales had attempted to squeeze more out of him, but Aronen wouldn't pay. That the guy had tried to take advantage of his position had irritated him. Five grand to Gonzales and five grand to the driver—that would have to do.

The semi would take him to St. Petersburg, and from there, he could make his way to Moscow, Kiev or anyplace else where he could disappear. He had swiped an additional thirty thousand from a poorly hidden stash in Gonzales' apartment, so there was no shortage of cash. He was actually in the black.

The tattooed trucker lit up a cigarette and the smell of Russian tobacco filled the cab. Aronen cracked his window. The driver said something Aronen didn't understand, so he just smiled back.

He'd have to get some sleep and hatch a plan. Staying in Finland wasn't an option, since the cops would find him sooner or later. The Scandinavian countries and Europe were also out of the question. But the Wild East—that would work. There, money meant something.

Aronen had his arms folded across his chest and his duffel between his feet. As the semi cruised along steadily, his eyelids sank shut. The next bump would toss his head to the side, and they would open, but soon they would close again.

Aronen didn't know how long he had slept, nor did it matter anymore. In the middle of a dream, he noticed that the semi had come to a stop.

A Bowie knife sank into his throat, and amidst the pain, he could feel the blood filling his windpipe, taste it in his mouth. He opened his eyes to see the tattooed trucker, smiling wistfully. After that, everything went black.

The semi was parked in the back yard of a run-down industrial building. Ten yards away was a wooden outbuilding, and beside that, an old well.

Sergei Zubrov put out his cigarette, reached across to open the passenger side door and pushed Aronen's body out. It fell headfirst in the dirt. He dragged the body by its feet to the well and heaved it in.

Zubrov returned to the truck and glanced at the duffel. It had just been too easy. The tired Finn hadn't even resisted. Zubrov grinned as he turned the ignition.

* * *

The doctor said Aalto was in the OR for another operation, so there would be no visitors until the day after tomorrow. Salmela was sleeping, but Suhonen was awake.

She led Honkala and Takamäki into the room where Suhonen was lying on the bed. He was the only patient in the room.

The officer's eyes were closed, but he opened them when Takamäki and Honkala came in.

"How you feeling?" asked Takamäki.

"Light," said Suhonen. "They gave me a bunch of pills for the pain. Feels like I'm floating over the bed."

The doctor smiled broadly. "No permanent

injuries and no need to amputate."

"Good." Takamäki turned to Suhonen. "The case is in the bag. Every Skull is in custody except for Aronen, who vanished. We'll find him sooner or later."

Honkala nodded at Suhonen. "Well done."

Suhonen said nothing. In truth, with the body count as high as it was, the case hadn't gone all that well.

"Take it easy for a couple days," said Takamäki. "Then back to work, right?"

The doctor was already shooing Takamäki and Honkala out of the room.

"Yeah," Suhonen managed before closing his eyes. He was damned tired. At last, he could sleep in.